RUINED TERRA

BOOK ELEVEN OF THE EMPIRE OF BONES SAGA

TERRY MIXON

YOWLING
CAT PRESS

BOOK ELEVEN OF THE EMPIRE OF BONES SAGA

RUINED TERRA

Sometimes the enemy...

...holds all the cards!

TERRY MIXON

BESTSELLING AUTHOR OF *RACE TO TERRA*

Published by Yowling Cat Press ®

Digital edition date: 8/15/2020

Print ISBN: 978-1947376298

Large Print ISBN: 978-1947376335

Cover art - image copyrights as follows:

DepositPhotos/Taden1 (Denis Tabler)

Luca Oleastri

Donna Mixon

Cover design and composition by Donna Mixon

Print edition design and layout by Terry Mixon

Audio edition performed and produced by Veronica Giguere

Reach her at: v@voicesbyveronica.com

ALSO BY TERRY MIXON

You can always find the most up to date listing of Terry's titles on his Amazon Author Page.

The Empire of Bones Saga

Empire of Bones

Veil of Shadows

Command Decisions

Ghosts of Empire

Paying the Price

Recon in Force

Behind Enemy Lines

The Terra Gambit

Hidden Enemies

Race to Terra

Ruined Terra

Victory on Terra

The Humanity Unlimited Saga

Liberty Station

Freedom Express

Tree of Liberty

Blood of Patriots

The Imperial Marines Saga

Spoils of War

The Fractured Republic Saga

Storm Divers

The Scorched Earth Saga

Scorched Earth

Omnibus Volumes

The Empire of Bones Saga Volume 1

The Empire of Bones Saga Volume 2

The Empire of Bones Saga Volume 3

Humanity Unlimited Publisher's Pack 1

The Vigilante Series with Glynn Stewart

Heart of Vengeance

Oath of Vengeance

Bound By Law

Bound By Honor

Bound By Blood

Want to get updates from Terry about new books and other general nonsense going on in his life? He promises there will be cats. Go to TerryMixon.com/Mailing-List and sign up.

DEDICATION

This book would not be possible without the love and support of my beautiful wife. Donna, I love you more than life itself.

ACKNOWLEDGMENTS

I want to thank the folks that support me on Patreon. You got to read this book as I was writing it and that kept me working. You have my deepest thanks.

In particular, I want to thank those patrons that supported me at the $10 level and above:

Bryan Barnes

Christian A. Michelsen

Dale Thompson

Finally, I want to thank my readers for putting up with me. You guys are great.

1

Princess Kelsey Bandar stared at the bright stars spread across the dark sky over her head like diamond dust on velvet. The brilliant Milky Way showed far more points of light than she'd ever seen from Avalon, with the exception of her stays at the Imperial Retreat. Even in the less populated areas of her birth world, light pollution from the many cities made it impossible to see the dimmest of the stellar masses.

Not so on Terra.

With the total destruction of civilization here, there was no artificial light to dim the stars. The single large moon wasn't in the sky at the moment, and there was nothing between her and the majesty of the universe. It was beautiful, sad, and horrifying all at the same time.

She stood on what looked like a plain of tall, wild grass, though it was hard to make out clearly now that night had fallen, even with her enhanced vision. The chill wind was steady from the northwest and carried the earthy scent of vegetation. Maybe there was a forest off in that direction.

That battled with the scent of scorched electronics and leaking fuel from the crashed pinnaces nearby. Talk about a sour note.

Everyone had walked away from *that* disaster, but it had really left them in a bad spot.

She had left them in a bad spot. If only she'd gotten around to focusing more of her flight training on emergency landings, she could've gotten the disabled pinnace down in one piece. Or at least avoided crashing it into the *other* pinnace, wrecking them both.

Just one more thing that she couldn't fix after the fact.

"It's beautiful isn't it?" Elise Orson asked as she came out of the tent they were using as an ad hoc command center, at least until they figured out what they were going to do next.

Kelsey turned to her friend and forced a smile onto her face. "It is. Even in the depths of misery and destruction, there's still some beauty left around us, and that gives me hope. How's Jared?"

"Lily says that he has a concussion, but she'll have him up by morning, just like your pilot. Those were the only injuries we had in this entire affair, and I find that absolutely amazing."

Kelsey turned again toward where she'd crashed and stared at the wreckage sourly. With her enhanced eyesight, she had no difficulty seeing that they were screwed. The pinnace that she'd brought down had punched a hole through the hull of the other craft and warped its frame. Neither of the small craft would ever fly again.

"They say that any landing you can walk away from is a good one, but I think I'm going to disagree," she said with a grumble. "We have to get to the Imperial Palace to recover the override, and that means we're going to have to travel at least a thousand kilometers on foot. Probably more. Potentially a *lot* more. All of that with our supplies on our back."

"Well, I always did enjoy a good hike," Elise said with a sigh of resignation. "Can't the powered armor the marines brought help carry what we need?"

"No," Kelsey said with a resigned shake of her head. "Their power supplies won't get us more than a few days into the journey. The best we can manage is to get some of what we have to a less exposed position and stash it there for emergencies. Not that I'm sure how it will benefit us once we've left the area. Talbot is working out the details with Major Scala.

"Once we really get going, we'll only have the supplies we can carry with us. A good chunk of that's going to be weaponry and other military hardware. Add to that food, water, and other consumables, and we'll be packed down pretty heavy. We'll have to gather all that and get to marching as soon as we can tomorrow, since this site is in danger of being spotted from orbit.

"The pinnaces have stealth materials woven into their hulls, but we can't take a chance that the AIs will spot them and destroy our extra gear or ourselves. If we can find a place somewhere close that will work as a supply cache, we'll stash everything there and begin the long march."

Kelsey let the silence drag on for a few seconds and then turned to face her friend directly. "Tell me about my doppelgänger. She and I haven't spoken more than a couple of words, and it's hard for me to even believe she's real. A version of me from another universe? I'm having trouble getting my head around that. What's she like?"

"It's odd," Elise confessed. "Sometimes, she's so very much like you, and then she's… not. She's been through so much. I grew up in terror of becoming a Pale One, and she had to live through it, even if only for a short time. That gives me the cold shivers, and my heart goes out to her."

The Pale Ones were the savage descendants of human survivors on the planet Erorsi. A mad computer there had been utilizing Old Empire equipment to forcibly implant them with Marine Raider hardware and then reprogramming their cranial implants so that it could control their actions, even over their resistance.

They'd became vicious killing machines that had attacked Pentagar on primitive ships built by the computer for five centuries. Many Pentagarans in danger of capture would kill themselves to avoid that fate, and Kelsey completely understood their motivations.

If she'd really understood what the computer would do to her, what she'd have become for the rest of her life if Jared and the rest hadn't saved her, she might have taken her own life in the heat of the moment once she'd fallen into their grasp.

The Pale Ones had captured her and her marine escort because she'd been an idiot. She'd let a petty, nose-in-the-air, noble girl tantrum put her into harm's way, and she'd paid the price for that. To her everlasting shame, so had her marines.

That had been the moment that she'd finally grown up. That had been the point in her life where *everything* had changed. Never again would she allow herself to fail her people, or herself. She'd die first.

How much worse had it been for her other self? Talbot and Jared had saved her, but that hadn't happened in the other universe. There, that version of her had become a Pale One, lost control over her own body, and been forced to do brutal, terrible things. Things that horrified Kelsey to even think about.

"One thing we did settle," Kelsey said once she'd set her horror aside, "was that having us be Kelsey One and Kelsey Two like you guys came up with was ridiculous. This universe is my home, so I'm Kelsey. She's decided to use one of our cousin's names and will now be Julia. We both always loved that name.

"If the situation is ever reversed, I'll use that name in her universe. Not that I expect my father to ever allow me over there, mind you. At the very least, it'll make talking about each of us a little less complicated.

"Now, to change the subject, what do you know about the Terrans? Sean said that your people observed some of them through the drone feeds. Can you tell if there are any around us now? Do they know we're here?"

Elise chuckled. "After that landing, *everybody* within a *hundred kilometers* probably knows we're here."

Kelsey felt her face redden. "Yeah, I suppose that's true. And?"

Elise shook her head. "Not that we've seen. Terra is a mixture of dead megacities and land originally meant for growing food. I gather the Terrans don't feel comfortable coming out into the wilds with the AIs looking down from above. We've got at least a little separation from their obvious dwellings."

No one really had any idea how populous Terra was now. Once it had housed many billions of people, but those days had ended when the artificial despot in orbit had started the kinetic bombardment. Only a tiny fraction of the people alive before that event had survived the next year, she was sure.

That said, the ruined megacities might still house a lot of people, relatively speaking, even without power. How they'd grow food, Kelsey had no idea, but they'd seen some humans on the drone feeds, all scattered around the globe. And the AIs wouldn't have tried to exterminate a nonexistent population, which was what they'd thought Jared and his people were here to do, if there wasn't a significant number of people down here.

She still didn't understand why the machines wanted to kill the people of Terra. They had them trapped inside the system and had destroyed their civilization at least a century ago, based on the decay of the megacities and the amount of overgrowth that occurred since.

Humans were good at finding places to live. She'd seen that on Erorsi, and that had been worse than Terra. Whether they were savage or still retained some degree of civilization, Kelsey had no idea. That would come out in time, since she was absolutely certain that they'd meet people along the way to the Imperial Palace.

She just hoped they could avoid fighting them. There was no need for humans to kill one another when they had the sadistic computer over their heads that deserved their full attention.

That made her start worrying about how they'd get off Terra again once they'd succeeded. She wasn't even going to allow for the chance of failure in their mission. It was too important.

Still, once they had the override they'd come for, they had no way to get back into space. With both pinnaces wrecked, the only other ship they even had in the system was going to be unable to retrieve them.

Persephone had six fighters that she carried on her hull in makeshift cradles. Those weren't stealthed, so they'd be spotted if they tried to approach Terra. Even if they *could* make a few successful runs, they'd only get a couple of people off the planet before they were caught.

And say by some miracle that they did get everyone off the planet. There was still no way out of the Terra system. The far flip point that she'd used to get here was a restricted one. *Persephone* had been small enough to make it through, but the trip had been a one-way ride. There *were* other flip points leading out of the system, but the AI had them under heavy guard.

No, they were trapped here, unless Angela Ellis found a multi-flip point that the AI was unaware of. While that *was* still possible, Kelsey wasn't holding her breath.

Kelsey rubbed her face tiredly. Those were problems they'd have to deal with after they got their hands on the override. One major crisis at a time, please.

She was about to say something to that effect when Commodore Sean Meyer stuck his head out of the tent. "We need you inside. There's a problem."

"Of course there is," Kelsey muttered. "How could there *not* be?"

She allowed Elise to precede her inside. The tent held several small tables with portable computers that Jared had brought down from his destroyer before the AI had blown it to bits. They were being monitored by members of his crew.

"What is it?" she asked, already dreading the answer.

"I'll let Carl explain," the Fleet officer said, deferring to their friend.

The young scientist looked up from the computer where he sat at with a grimace. "We were monitoring the drone network that the admiral seeded. The one that the AI thinks distributed the Omega Plague.

"I was using it to look around our general area when everything went dark. I had to go back through the logs to find out what happened, but it seems the AI sent a destruct code into the network. All the drones are gone. We're blind."

Kelsey sighed and pinched the bridge of her nose between her thumb and forefinger. "I thought we had control of the network. How could the AI do that?"

Her young friend shook his head. "We had a hack into the system. One that the admiral's people inserted so that they could monitor and screen out information that they didn't want the AI to see. The AI still had access to the command codes.

"We probably should've planned for this, but no one locked the thing out. That makes sense, I suppose. If they had, the AI would've noticed the moment it sent any command and saw that nothing happened. That would have been... bad.

"As it is, we've lost the network monitoring everything going on around Terra, but the AI still doesn't know we're here. That's a win of sorts. Right?"

"It's just one more thing," Kelsey grumbled. "Why can't we catch a break? There's so much going on around us, and all of it seems to have a downside. Without the drones, we're not going to be able to see what's between us and the Imperial Palace."

Sean gestured for her to take a seat. "We may not have real-time data about what's happening between us and the Imperial Palace, but we did get a pretty good map compiled while the network was up, so it's not a total loss."

Kelsey took the offered seat and used her implants to link up with the computer in front of her. She had to admit there *was* a good bit of data about the terrain between them and the Imperial Palace.

They'd landed northeast of a dead megacity once known as Frankfort. It was still intact, though ruined and decayed. The Imperial Palace was built over a previously existing city once known as Albany.

Legend said that the corruption of the ruling elite in that place before the Imperial Period was so great that the people chose to raze it utterly, leaving no two stones standing together. That was the harsh judgment of history, indeed.

If they were to go in a straight line, the journey would be somewhat more than a thousand kilometers. Unfortunately, there were several abandoned megacities between them and their destination.

Those would be dangerous and time-consuming to deal with, so it would be best if they could simply avoid them. Since they'd be moving on foot, that was going to add at least five hundred kilometers to the trip. Probably more.

"Do we have *any* good news?" Kelsey asked somewhat plaintively. "Is *anything* going our way?"

Elise put her hands on Kelsey's shoulders and started massaging the stiff muscles of her neck. "Relax. This will make it harder, but we'll manage. Just breathe."

"You're usually the optimistic one," Sean said, leaning over the table directly in front of her. "Look at the upside. We're still alive and able to get to where we need to be. Don't let the scale of the march get to you. We've got to set small goals that add up to making it to the Imperial Palace. We've made it hundreds of parsecs. What's a few thousand kilometers more?"

"I suppose you're right," Kelsey said, slumping a little. "We've traveled across the freaking Old Empire to get to Terra, and now we're only fifteen hundred kilometers from the Imperial Palace. That *has* to count for something."

"On the bright side," Carl said, "you've been telling me I need to get more exercise. That's positive, right?"

"You think this sounds like an adventure?" she shot back. "I'll bet that none of us has marched a hundred kilometers, except for the marines. This is going to be really, *really* difficult in ways that we can't possibly begin to imagine. Mark my words."

"You're still not looking at the bright side," Carl said with a smile. "Pretty much everything that could go wrong, has. Everything should be easier going forward, right? What else could happen?"

The tent flap pulled back, and Talbot stuck his head in. "Kelsey, we've got a problem."

Kelsey wanted to scream but settled for shooting Carl a hot glare. "This is *your fault*. How could you have even *said* that?"

Without waiting for a response to her rhetorical question, she sighed, got to her feet, and walked over to her husband. "Show me."

———————

2

Talbot led his wife out of the tent and into the stygian darkness that was night on Terra. His ocular augmentation could help with that, but Terra was *dark* at night, especially when the moon was down.

Major Adrian Scala was standing just a few meters away waiting for them. That officer gestured toward where the pinnaces sat. "The crash had more consequences than we thought, Colonel," Scala said to Kelsey, his lips tight. "The impact point where Pinnace Two struck Pinnace One was right where we had our weapons stored. Frankly, I'm astonished the munitions didn't blow up."

That wasn't good news, but it still made Talbot's lips twitch hearing the other man use Kelsey's marine rank. Anyone less like a field-grade marine officer would be hard to imagine.

His wife didn't see his reaction because she was busy rubbing her face furiously with both hands. "How much of a loss are we talking about here?"

"Just about total," Scala said tiredly. "We planned for the possibility of serious fighting, so we brought along a lot of gear. Most of that is gone. The marines have their sidearms and a few rifles, but only limited ammunition for either. The weapons and munitions for their armor are intact, but it won't do us much good long term. The armor won't have the power to get us very far."

"I already figured that out. How far will we be able to move the armor?"

"I'd expect we've probably got a couple of days of juice, and we might reach a hundred kilometers before they're done," Talbot said. "If we have to transport other gear, that's going to cut the range some."

"That's worse than I'd feared," Kelsey said after staring off into the darkness for a few moments. "We're going to have to carry what supplies we can away from here and stash them somewhere. It's possible the AI will see something down here that it doesn't like and nuke this area from orbit. Well, not using a nuke, but a rod from god is pretty much the same thing when you're on the receiving end."

Talbot had to agree that orbital kinetic bombardment *would* ruin their day.

"We'll salvage what we can," he said. "Frankly, I'm not certain that we're going to need to make more than one trip. We'll have to carry the majority of our supplies with us on our backs to the Imperial Palace, so we'll need to lean heavily toward food and other items that will get us to where we're going.

"One positive is that we'll be able to hunt along the way. This being Terra, almost everything that we run into should be edible. We'll be careful and test, just to be sure, particularly when it comes to plants. The animals should be good to eat, though, and we've got enough small arms to provide for food as we move."

He turned to face Kelsey. "I'm not going to lie. This is going to be hard. We'll be traveling light, and that means only taking what we absolutely have to. If you've never been on a long march—which I'm wagering almost no one outside the regular marines have—you'll have to be exceptionally picky about what you bring. A couple of extra ounces may not seem like a lot, until you have to pack it for fifteen kilometers. Or a hundred and fifty kilometers. Or ten times that."

"I second that," Scala said with a nod. "This is going to be particularly difficult for the scientists. They have no muscle for this, but they're going to have to come with us anyway, bringing whatever equipment they absolutely must have.

"*Everyone* is going to have to pull their share of the load. You're going to get a *lot* of complaints, and there's going to be plenty of cranky people."

"Wonderful," Kelsey said as she stared up into the sky. "Getting to Terra was supposed to *solve* most of our problems, not create a whole new set of them. Why is it that nothing goes as planned? Why can't *something* be easy? Did I offend the gods in some way?"

Talbot chuckled and put his hand on his wife's shoulder, pulling her into a hug. "You're doing everything right, Kelsey. That crash was *not* your fault. Circumstances sometimes conspire to put us in a bad place, but you've proven time and again that you can get us back out.

"This time is just going to be a little more… intense. Accept that the march isn't going to go as planned and that we're going to run into problems along the way. Probably some serious ones. At least we have the ability to scout all the way to the Imperial Palace with the drone network that the admiral seeded. That's a plus."

Kelsey made a show of rubbing her eyes. "Yeah, about that… It turns out that the System Lord sent the destruct signal into the drone network. It's gone. All we have is the data we collected before that. We won't be getting any real-time updates unless we bring drones of our own. Yet one more thing to haul along."

That *was* going to complicate matters, Talbot admitted. Still, his troops were used to carrying their required gear, and now that he was a Marine Raider, he could haul a lot more than he had before. He wasn't sure how that was going to work out over a long march, but this was going to be an interesting experience.

"Cheer up," he finally said. "We've overcome worse, and we'll beat this too. If we run into somebody along the way, we'll have enough weapons to take care of ourselves. Don't let this overwhelm you. Just stand up straight and take care of the problems as they happen. Improvise and overcome."

He checked his internal chronometer. They had roughly six hours until dawn.

"Adrian and I will continue going through the equipment we can salvage and get things sorted out. The marines will be beat by the time we're done, so we're going to have to catch a little sleep before we head out. Plan on us being ready by noon.

"You need to get some sleep, too. Once we start moving, we won't stop for more than eating and sleeping until we reach the Imperial Palace."

No matter how long that took.

* * *

Julia—she was still struggling to remember to use that name for herself—sat in a dark tent next to Olivia West and watched Scott Roche as he slept on the cot the marines had set up for him.

She'd stunned him before all the madness, so that he couldn't take her place on the mission to fool the AI about their escape from orbit down to Terra. He was going to be *supremely* pissed about that when he finally woke up.

"I met your version of me," she said softly to the other woman. "Just for a little bit after we got down on the surface. After we crashed. She's… intimidating."

"You don't need to be frightened of her," Olivia said, shaking her head slightly. "Seriously, she's you. Parts of her story are different, but as a person, she's you."

It didn't feel that way to Julia. Here in a universe that wasn't hers, she felt like an outsider, even after she'd made the jump across dimensions. And now she'd met this universe's version of herself, and she was like one of those damned action vid heroes.

The woman had singlehandedly *crash-landed* a pinnace with *no engines*. There was no way that she could have done the same. No, even if she'd known how to pilot one, she'd have frozen up or screwed up and they'd all have died. What did this woman do? Pull off a damned miracle.

"I know," she finally said. "That still doesn't make it any easier. She's always so confident, so in command of the situation. We'd barely gotten the hatch open and she was shouting orders, getting people doing things that needed to be done.

"It was shocking. She's a *lot* more assertive than I am. I'm a church mouse by comparison. Give me something to research, and I'm happy. Put me in charge of people in a crisis? Not so much. I understand that I'm the crown princess of the New Terran Empire, but that doesn't mean I'm well suited for something like that."

Olivia chuckled and reached out to squeeze her arm. "Don't mistake Kelsey for something she's not, Julia. What you're seeing is a couple of years' worth of hard experience. Under the same stimuli, given the same time to grow into the role, you'd do the same.

"In fact, I think you've already started. Would you have had the courage to stand up to Commander Roche otherwise? I mean, you *did* stun him, after all."

Julia sighed. "He's going to be so mad about that. And you're probably right. Before all of this happened, I'd have deferred to everything he said. But if I'd let him go on this mission, I'm sure that both he and Mertz would be dead now."

She held up a hand to forestall any defensive response. "Don't get me wrong, I'm sure that Mertz is very capable. He just needed a little extra help to make his plan work. I'm just not convinced that Scott would've been able to provide that, no offense to him."

"Provide what?" Scott said as he reached up to rub his face. "Holy hell, my head is killing me." He blinked up at her for a moment, and then his eyes widened. "Did you stun me?"

Julia nodded. "I did, and I'm sorry. Doctor Stone said you're going to be fine."

"With the way my head is pounding, I'm not certain that I agree."

With an obvious effort of will, Scott levered himself up to a seated position and then groaned. "My head feels like it's about to fall off. Why the hell did you do that, Highness?"

She took a deep breath and let it out slowly. "Because you weren't the right person for the mission, and you wouldn't let me do what had to be done. I just short-circuited the argument. It's all over now."

Olivia stood and headed for the tent flap. "On that note, I should probably go check in with Sean. Why don't you two work out your issues in the privacy of your own tent, and I'll catch you later? Good to see you up, Commander Roche."

With that, Julia's new friend strode out of the tent and left them alone.

"I'm sorry, Scott," Julia said softly. "I really hate that I'm responsible for your pain, but it was necessary. If you'd gone, both Mertz and you would be dead right now. I'll give you all the details about what happened later, but his plan went sideways and only my augmentation allowed us to escape."

Her friend took a deep breath and let it out slowly. "Okay. I'll accept that. I'll even do you the personal favor of not pressing charges. After all, it would look really bad for a Fleet officer to bring assault charges against the heir to the Imperial Throne."

She smiled. "That *would* be awkward. Seriously, Scott, I didn't want you to die."

He looked at her face for a few moments and then reached out and took her hand in his. "Highness, it's my *job* to die if it means that you get to live. That's just the way it is. You're more important than I am."

"Bullshit!" she spat out, her anger suddenly blazing hot. "I'm not more important than *anyone*."

"I'm afraid I'll have to politely disagree."

The two of them stared at each other for a few seconds before she looked away, her rage suddenly gone, making her feel empty. "I met the other version of me. She's kind of scary."

"Scary in what way?" Scott asked as he leaned forward. "Did she threaten you?"

Julia smiled at his suddenly aggressive posture. "No. She couldn't have been nicer. In fact, even after crashing the pinnace, I'd say that she was downright chipper."

Scott opened his mouth to say something and then closed it again before narrowing his eyes. "She crashed a pinnace. Would that happen to have been the *same* pinnace that *you* were on?"

"Yeah. Mertz is being treated for a concussion, but he survived. In fact, everybody survived. Well, other than the second pinnace, that is. I'm afraid she crashed hers into the other one and now we're basically going to have to walk to the Imperial Palace."

Scott stared at her for a moment and then laughed.

"It's *not* funny," Julia said with a scowl. "I didn't exactly bring hiking boots."

Her friend laughed even harder. "Oh, Highness, I know that I'm going to pay for this, but I can't wait to see you hiking. How far are we talking about?"

She shrugged slightly. "A thousand kilometers? Maybe more. I don't really know."

That shut him up. He sighed as he put his head back down into his hands.

"I guess I shouldn't be surprised," he said after a minute. "Nothing we do is *ever* easy. Why should this situation be any different?"

Julia stood and held out a hand to him. "Come on. Let's go get Doctor Stone to give you a look. I'll bet she can give you a shot to make that headache go away. Then we can get some food into you, while I explain why you need to call me Julia from now on. After that, we can try to get some sleep. Tomorrow is going to be a *long* day."

3

J ared woke to a light touch on his shoulder and found Lily Stone hovering over him. That brought back the memory of the mad escape from orbit and the destruction of his most recent command, the rechristened Rebel Empire destroyer they'd called *Athena*.

That was two ships with the same name that he'd lost. He certainly hoped they weren't coming out of his pay.

He'd woken sometime after Kelsey had crashed her pinnace and been briefed about their current status, over Lily's grumbling objections, so he wasn't as hyper this time.

Jared sat up, swung his legs over the side of the cot, and rubbed his face. "What time is it?"

"Roughly an hour before dawn," the doctor said, brandishing a small penlight. "I need to do one final check of your eyes, and then I'll cut you loose. This is probably going to hurt a bit."

She flashed the light into one of his eyes and then flicked it away. She did that several times on each side to see how his pupils reacted. The light hurt, but not as much as he'd expected.

"I'd rather be up and about, but I do still have some pain," he said. "Is that going to be a problem?"

"Your head is probably going to ache for a few days. I've taken care of the worst of your symptoms, but without a full regen, you're still going to be dealing with a few aftereffects.

"You're cleared for light duty, including hiking. No heavy loads until I say so. Keep in mind that you're the commanding officer and can *delegate*. I expect you to do so as much as possible."

"Yes, Doctor," he said with a smile. "As if Elise would let me overexert myself."

He looked over at the cot his wife had been using earlier. It was empty. "Where did she get off to?"

"I sent her to get something to eat while I did the final checks. We'll need to do the same, as I understand that we're all going to be busy today. Kelsey issued orders that we're moving out by noon. I suspect we'd be leaving after breakfast if the marines didn't need some rest."

That made sense. If the marines had been recovering what they could from the crashed pinnaces all night, they wouldn't be in shape to march come dawn. He was certain that they could do it, if need be, but noon was good enough.

"I'll step out and let you get dressed," Lily said. "Once you're ready, we can head over and see what they've got for us to eat." At his nod, she rose and walked out of the tent.

Jared found his neatly folded clothes on a nearby stool, and he dressed quickly. All he had was his shipboard uniform and knew that wouldn't hold up over a long march.

The landing site they'd chosen was just a bit more than a thousand kilometers away from the Imperial Palace. That was under the best case. If they had to dodge around anything—like one of the abandoned megacities—that distance would increase.

His shoes were sturdy enough for shipboard wear, but not exactly made for traipsing about the wilds of a planet. Thankfully, they'd brought extra marine uniforms, including boots. If they'd survived Kelsey's epic crash landing, that was.

If Jared thought talking to his sister would make her stop doing that kind of thing, he'd do so in a heartbeat, but that seemed like a fantasy. In any case, this time wasn't her fault. The System Lord orbiting Terra had damaged the pinnace, and the crash had been the end result.

The second pinnace getting caught up in it might have been correctable with more experience, but he wasn't going to quibble. The situation was what it was.

Once he'd dressed, he stepped out of the tent and joined Lily. The night still held sway, but it was starting to grow lighter off to the east. The smells of the wild and the sounds of insects and other creatures were profoundly strange to him.

Together, he and Lily headed off to where the cooks had set up. He could already smell something in the air. A little bit of woodsmoke and perhaps the hint of some kind of food. He wasn't certain. It smelled like bacon, and he felt his stomach grumble. His last meal had been a long time ago.

To his surprise, Jared found most of the major players gathered near the cooks. Elise, Olivia, Sean, both Kelseys—Kelsey and Julia, he corrected himself—Commander Roche, and Carl Owlet were sitting around a lively fire. The only members of his leadership team missing were Talbot and Scala.

Everyone slid over just enough to make room for Lily and himself.

"I'm sure you're all wondering why I've called you here," Jared said with a chuckle as he sat. "Kidding aside, is everyone okay?"

The lack of smiles around the campfire told him that things were probably a little bit worse than he'd imagined. Putting aside his poor attempt at a joke, he looked around the group. "I can tell there's more bad news. Give it to me."

Kelsey filled him in on the loss of the drone network and the fact that the crash had cost them most of the small arms ammunition and rifles. That was bad news, but it could've been worse. No one had been killed, and they could still continue on to their target.

"I understand that this seems like an ugly blow," he said quietly. "But it's no worse than anything else we've faced along the way. In fact, this is far from the nastiest position we've ever been in. It's going to be a hard march, but we've got everything that we need to make it."

"How do we get off Terra once we're done?" Julia asked. "Let's say that everything goes smoothly—which I seriously doubt—and we make it all the way to the Imperial Palace and into the vaults below. Glory of glories, we recover the override. What then? We've still got to get off Terra and past the murderous AI in orbit. How do we do that?"

"We'll figure that out when we get to it," Jared said, keeping his voice calm and level. "The Imperial Palace is intact, so it's entirely possible that there are small craft underneath it. Ones that we could potentially use to get to orbit, if they aren't damaged or decayed beyond repair.

"Also, *Persephone* is hiding out in the system somewhere. Angela and her people will try to get us out if we call. We have the FTL link to them, though I don't want to use it unless we absolutely have to. The details of how we escape really aren't important right now because none of it matters unless we get the override, so let's focus on that."

He looked around the fire, meeting everyone's gaze. "We need to get to the Imperial Palace alive and in one piece. Once we get there, we'll get into the vault. I have the key and the right DNA, so I think that's going to work. Kelsey has all of the Imperial codes that an heir to the Imperial Throne would have, so if we run into anything unusual, she can get us in."

He gestured across the fire toward Julia. "Excuse me, I should have added that Julia does as well. Either of you could probably get us in. You both likely have the same set of authorization codes."

He held his silence until they'd all nodded. "It's going to be dawn soon, so we need to eat and start gathering what we need to take with us. Whatever we can't carry, we'll have to leave here, or transport to a safe location.

"I'm going to assume that the marines have deployed some of our tactical drones and that we have some potential cache points mapped out from the original drone network. Once the sun is up, I'll review all that and make some decisions on the route we'll take. I want to get away from here as quickly as we can manage.

"It's possible that the AI will discover the crash site at some point. If that happens, we can expect to be hunted. That won't be pleasant, so let's hope that the System Lord never learns that we've made it down to the surface alive."

He glanced toward the east. In half an hour or so, the sun would peek over the hills in the distance and their day would begin in earnest. It was the middle of summer where they'd landed, so it wouldn't be cold. On the other hand, he really didn't know how hot it was going to get. Or how muggy.

It really didn't matter. They'd have to march every day, and it was going to be grueling. He and his people would do what they had to. Adapt and overcome, as Talbot would say. They didn't have a choice if they wanted to save humanity from slavery at the hands of the AIs.

* * *

Julia stepped into the tent they'd been using for drone monitoring. The only person inside was Carl Owlet, who was busy tearing down the computers and packing them away. He looked up as she approached.

"Good morning, Highness. What can I do for you?"

She opened her mouth to ask a question but then paused. "I haven't said a single thing, yet you already know that I'm not your Kelsey. The regeneration on my face removed the scarring, and we look *exactly* alike, right down to our hair length. How did you know it was me?"

He smiled. "No one else—other than Talbot and Admiral Mertz —would be able to tell, I'd wager, but I'm the one who installed some of the extra hardware inside our version of you. Well, not personally. Doctor Stone did that, but I designed it. You don't have the same gear, so that means you're not my Princess Kelsey."

She found one of the folding fabric seats and sat slowly. "And you figured that out in just a few moments. Were you worried that I wasn't Kelsey and checked?"

He shook his head. "Not at all. The identification was almost subconscious. I have the same hardware installed inside myself as my princess does. That means my equipment recognizes her equipment on a deep level. It's almost like an electronic handshake. My implants use that to know which one of you I'm speaking with. I set that up when I found out you were visiting, as it seemed prudent."

She found herself smiling slightly. "That's very proactive. I've heard a lot about you, Carl Owlet. I haven't met you in my universe, but I sent a message home to find and recruit you as soon as I heard your story. One doesn't find a genius of your caliber every day."

He grimaced slightly. "I wish people wouldn't take things to that extreme. Yes, I'm smart. Yes, I'm plugged into the Old Empire technology. All that said, plenty of people could've done *exactly* what I did. I was just in the right place, at the right time, with the right know-how, and put everything together."

"Humble, too. That's a plus."

His brows furrowed. "Excuse me?"

Julia's smile widened slightly. "Oh, nothing. I'm just thinking about something that I mean to do when I get back to my universe. Basically, I'm making a mental checklist of how I need to approach my version of you to talk about… an alliance, shall we say."

"If other me is anything like me, he'll jump through hoops to help you."

"I certainly hope so. We could really use his help. I don't know if you've heard anything about the situation in my universe, but we're behind the eight ball. I picked that phrase up from your version of Kelsey, by the way. I'm not really sure where it comes from, but it means we're in a difficult place. A much worse place, really.

"We don't have the ships or technology that you do, and the Rebel Empire is aware of us. The AIs have already taken control of Pentagar, and it's only a matter of time before they come for Avalon. We're going to need every bit of help we can get."

Before he could respond, she waved a hand dismissing everything she'd just said. "Let's just leave that aside for the moment. I know Angela Ellis from my universe. I think with all of the changes that have occurred, she's basically filling the same role for me that your Talbot does for your version of me, minus the romantic aspects. I know her really well, and I have to say that I'd never have expected you to be her type. No offense.

"I understand that there's a lot more to you than meets the eye, not just in how you think and act, but that you've got grit, as Kelsey would say. That's important. Don't dismiss what you've done. It takes a lot of hard work to achieve success."

Carl shook his head. "Angela is a special case. She and I meshed under a weird combination of circumstances and pressure. I never expected anything like that to happen, and in your universe, I'd wager that other me is probably not going to get along with her very well at all. Are you trying to figure out if you can set up other me up with other Angela? Please don't."

She cocked her head slightly to the side and pursed her lips. "I'm not in the habit of playing matchmaker. My own love life is hard enough to figure out. For my part, I don't see me and other Talbot getting along the same way that Kelsey and he do here, for similar reasons. I'm not Kelsey. I don't think like her, even though I have the same implants, mostly."

She gestured around at the packed equipment, ready to change the subject. "Are we taking all this with us? It seems like an awful lot to carry."

He shook his head. "We'll leave most of it inside the crashed pinnaces. I'll probably pack one of the computers to take with us, just in case we need the extra computational power when we get to the Imperial Palace, but honestly, there's not going to be a lot of science on this mission. We'd hoped that we'd be able to examine a bunch of stuff there when we landed, but that's going to have to wait for another visit. If there is one."

With that, he gestured toward the tent flap. "I think we'd best get to where the marines are laying out the equipment. It's time to get some durable clothes and boots that are more suitable for hiking."

She nodded and stood, having made up her mind. This young man *was* worth further attention. He might *just* be who she needed. Of course, convincing other him of that might be a challenge, but she was willing to put out the effort for someone she now thought of as a warrior scholar.

By the time they reached the Imperial Palace, she'd know for sure if he'd make a suitable consort. No one could hide their true natures on a march as difficult as this was going to be. Over the next few months, they'd all find out how tough they really were.

And, just in case, Julia would make certain that other him and her Angela didn't meet before she'd wooed him. No matter what he said, she wasn't going to tempt fate. Her luck had been mostly bad for the last few years, and she'd be damned if she was going to blindly take that kind of risk.

Her Angela would just have to find someone else. Maybe she and other Talbot would make a good pair. Perhaps she'd have to try her hand at matchmaker after all, once the universe wasn't trying to kill her and everyone she knew.

4

———

Talbot watched as Adrian and his marines assisted the Fleet personnel and civilians in adjusting their new clothes to fit properly. Thankfully, they'd done most of the measuring before they'd come down to the surface.

Adrian had known they'd be on Terra for a while and seen the problem of worn-out shoes and clothes coming. The standard marine loadout for deployment included one set of extra boots and a total of four uniforms, and that's what everyone now had.

Even back in the days of the pre-expedition New Terran Empire, Avalon had made some tough boots and clothing for their marines. The Old Empire had them beat, hands down. The footwear would survive the worst Terra could throw at them, and the fatigues were almost as durable.

He and Kelsey had arrived late to the party, but they'd also come prepared. He'd made certain to bring along his normal loadout and had forced her to bring the pack that he'd prepared for her.

Like his pack, hers didn't just contain fatigues and boots, but a complete marine basic kit. She'd moaned and groaned about having pinnaces to get them to where they'd needed to go, but he'd stood firm. Now he could smugly tell her that he'd been right, and she'd be forced to admit it.

He chuckled at his own joke.

This march was going to be hard on the Fleet personnel, but he was confident that they'd make it. The civilians, on the other hand, had him concerned. Scientists, as a group, were a bit on the sedentary side and not used to exercise or privation. There were exceptions, of course, but those folks were definitely rare in that particular population sample.

This march would involve juggling some priorities. The entire group was chained to their slowest person. That meant they'd need to speed up the weakest among them to a level that would get them to the Imperial Palace in a reasonable amount of time, without turning them into casualties.

And you could only push someone so far. He'd just have to accept that they wouldn't get to their target as quickly as he'd like. Of course, his standards on how long the trip should take were different than Admiral Mertz's. The flag officer might not realize how much faster marines as a group could march than the other shipboard personnel.

Adrian stepped over as Carl and Julia came over to the tables they'd set up so they could get their gear. Talbot eyed the woman that looked exactly like his wife. She didn't know him at all, and she certainly didn't care about him in the same way as Kelsey. It was weird and more than a little spooky.

He watched Julia as she headed into the ladies changing tent. Unlike the marines, whose members were used to stripping down and armoring up in a mixed gender environment—not that they were doing so out here in the open—the Fleet personnel and scientists still had body modesty, so they'd arranged for multiple tents for everyone to change in.

Kelsey had lost her body modesty years ago. Julia had not. One more difference.

"She's an odd one," Adrian said quietly. "She looks like our princess, but she's not the same woman. She doesn't think the same way as your wife. She's not as impulsive or outgoing."

Talbot had been shocked when Kelsey had finally told him that her doppelgänger from another universe was with Admiral Mertz. She'd found out over the FTL com but hadn't said anything to him until they'd arrived in the Terra system.

That annoyed him, but he could see how it was something that would get under her skin. They'd have to talk about it, once they had time.

He was going to have to get to know this other woman. She was a potential threat, and one that was close to Admiral Mertz. Adrian had admitted that he was worried about her in the same way.

The admiral had a habit of taking in strays. Of course, so did Kelsey. One of these days, that was going to bite them hard, and he wanted to be ready when it happened.

"Thankfully, we only have her and Commander Roche to keep an eye on," Adrian continued. "They've both behaved well so far, but they probably don't trust us very much, considering how Admiral Mertz in their universe was a traitor. Frankly, I'm amazed that Julia has come around to even considering that he might be different here."

"Are we certain that she *has* changed her mind?" Talbot asked slowly. "If I was among potential enemies and thought one of them was a murderous sonofabitch, I might be inclined to lie about how I felt about him, if it offered me an opportunity to get what I wanted."

Adrian shook his head. "The problem I see with that train of thought is that she went on the mission with the admiral *specifically* to get him down from orbit safely. Admittedly, he's the only one of us that has the Imperial DNA to open the vault, but she went above and beyond. She could've let Commander Roche do the heavy lifting."

Talbot rubbed his face. "It's not exactly like we can do any kind of testing to see if she's a threat or not. That would require direct access to the AI we left on board *Persephone*."

The AI in question was Fiona. She had the same hardware as the System Lords, but with clean code and some additions that Carl Owlet had made. She was loyal to humanity and could use her special connection to an individual's implants—with their consent—to check and see if they were telling the truth.

Well, he'd just have to keep an eye on the woman. She might have the same implants as he and Kelsey did, but she wasn't a Marine

Raider. Even if ambushed, he felt confident that his wife could tie the other woman into a pretzel without much trouble at all. She was, after all, a sensei in the Art.

The Art was a compilation of martial arts styles put together by the Marine Raiders of the Old Terran Empire. It favored his wife's small size, and she'd had the benefit of months of training at the hands of an experienced sensei before anyone else had even started learning it.

Ned Quincy had once been a Marine Raider himself. A fully trained one, and a master of the Art. One of the best in the Old Empire.

Kelsey had inadvertently created an AI version of him when she'd pulled a bunch of memory files into her implants from his body once they'd recovered it from stasis aboard *Persephone* when they'd discovered the ship in the graveyard around Boxer Station.

No one was exactly sure how she'd managed to create an AI inside her implants, but Talbot was glad that Carl had extracted the AI and put him into a holding computer back on the carrier *Audacious* while he figured out how to make an artificial body or computer that could handle the AI.

Having a third party in the bedroom while he made love to his wife was not his thing, even if the AI had sworn that he'd turned off all external sensory feeds.

At least no one had made a crack about him now having two wives, at least not in his hearing. He'd come down hard on an offender if they did. Again, not his thing, and even the thought was weird.

In that respect, he was very relieved that the other woman had no interest in him. Though, from the looks she'd just been giving Carl before they'd gone into their separate tents, he might have a problem there.

Which was also weird. And Angela had the skill and size to tie this other version of Kelsey into knots if she made any moves on the young scientist. If that happened, the fight would be short and brutal, so even though she wasn't here, Talbot would warn Julia to mind her manners.

"We'll just have to keep our eye on her," Talbot said in answer to what Adrian had said. "We don't treat her as an enemy, but we don't mark her as a friend either. As Kelsey says, trust but verify."

He turned and glanced toward the sun. "It looks like we have another couple of hours before we start moving. I want you to make one final pass over your people and make sure they have all of the critical equipment packed and ready to go. I'll do the same with the scientists and Fleet personnel. Once we start moving, we're not coming back for anything."

Adrian looked in the direction that they'd be marching. "What do you think we're going to run into out there? We know there are humans on Terra. Do you think we're going to have to fight them?"

Talbot chuckled darkly. "With our luck, what do you think?"

His friend muttered an expletive and turned to carry out his orders.

Once he was alone, Talbot considered what he'd just said. The chances that they'd have to fight someone on this march were high. He and his people would do it in a heartbeat, if that was necessary, but he'd like to keep the bloodshed to a minimum. The people of Terra had suffered enough.

He sighed. It wasn't as if he were going to be able to stop someone from becoming aggressive. All he could do was hope that they'd either avoid the worst-case scenarios or only have to fight the really bad people.

The best case would be avoiding both, but as he'd told Adrian, he was more than familiar with the kind of luck they had.

* * *

AFTER MARCHING in her armor for the rest of the day, Kelsey was glad that they'd stopped for the evening. The journey thus far hadn't been long—only about five kilometers—but doing it in armor was not something that she'd ever practiced. It chafed in odd places after a while. She'd need to rectify that at some point, but right now she was glad to be getting out of her gear.

Using the data that they'd gathered from the drone network before the AI had destroyed it, Jared had decided to stop at an abandoned building that was isolated from everything around it by kilometers in every direction.

It was low to the ground, somewhat small as a structure, and it didn't look like it had been abandoned for five centuries. That made sense since Terra had been captured intact during the rebellion. The AIs had treated it like the other occupied worlds of the Terran Empire, at least for a time.

If she'd had to guess, based on the decay and damage to the building, the AIs had started their orbital bombardment on Terra about a century ago. In a way, that was promising. It meant that they might still find functioning technology in locations that were well away from the megacities.

Or in the megacities themselves, if they were silly enough to try to go there.

Their best defense against being exposed to the AIs was not being noticed by anyone. To do that, they needed to steer clear of the remaining human population, so that meant it was best to avoid the former cities. They were here to save the people of Terra but needed to do so without their help.

Kelsey forced herself out of her introspective mood and looked back at the building. From the outside, it was impossible to determine what it had been used for. Once she got on the inside—down a wide ramp that led to a subterranean vehicular door that the marines had forced open—its purpose became clear.

It had been a place to store equipment used on what was likely once some great mechanical farming system. There were all types of automated machines in the large basement at the base of the ramp. They'd likely once performed their tasks without human intervention, for the most part. Now they sat alone in the darkness gathering dust.

A lot of dust.

The marines had chosen one corner of the large basement to use for getting out of their armor. It was clear of equipment but held racks of tools and spare parts.

Each marine marched his powered armor to a bare spot on the floor and climbed out before sealing it up again. It took very little time for them to get clear of their armor, since they were very practiced at the maneuver. Then they stripped off their skinsuits and put on regular marine fatigues.

Kelsey watched Julia do the same, though Talbot and Major Scala had to assist her out of her black Raider armor. Then Commander Roche held up a sheet so that the woman could strip off her skinsuit and dress in her marine fatigues.

The other woman obviously hadn't spent enough time around the marines to lose her self-consciousness about the process.

Kelsey got out of her armor as adroitly as the marines. She'd practiced the process long enough to build muscle memory. She turned her back to the Fleet personnel and scientists to avoid shocking them and stripped down to her skin before dressing in the marine fatigues that Talbot had packed for her. They fit perfectly, of course, but the boots and cut of the clothes still felt weird to her.

Once she was done, she faced the main group just as her brother started speaking.

"Everyone grab something to eat and drink," Jared said. "Settle in and rest. We'll be staying here for the night."

His announcement was met by a ragged cheer from the bedraggled scientists and even some of the Fleet personnel.

The scientists had been utterly unprepared for today and were worn out. What they didn't seem to realize was that the marines would be picking up the pace over the coming days and weeks. At today's rate of march, it would take them almost half a year to reach the Imperial Palace. That was completely unacceptable.

Of course, getting there late was better than never arriving at all, but Kelsey wasn't going to dawdle. Everyone—including her—was going to need to toughen up and do so quickly.

With everything that had been going on, Kelsey hadn't had a chance to talk to Julia in any detail. She needed to start the process tonight. She had to know how far she could trust the other woman.

Her other self seemed to feel the same way, because just as soon as she was dressed, Julia walked over to stand in front of her. "We need to talk."

"We do," Kelsey agreed. "Let's find a spot to sit down and eat while we do that. I'm starving and I'll wager you are too, if you're anything at all like me."

"I'm famished," Julia admitted. "I'm not looking forward to survival rations, but I'll take what I can get."

"You'll get used to them after a while," Kelsey said as she gestured toward an area behind the armor that was empty of people at the moment. "Shall we?"

5

———

J ared found a spot on the cold floor near Elise and sat. His wife was already watching Kelsey and Julia as they headed toward the corner of the cavernous room. The Fleet personnel had set up some portable lights, but most areas were still somewhat dark. That particular corner was almost lost in the gloom.

Before he could ask what Elise was thinking, Sean and Olivia joined them. Together, the four of them considered what they could see of the doppelgängers.

"It's really strange seeing them together," Sean said. "It's like double vision, only far more dangerous if they get excited."

Jared laughed. "Isn't that the truth? I don't think they've had a chance to really talk. What I wouldn't give to be a fly on the wall."

Olivia shook her head. "I don't think you would. I suspect some of this conversation is going to be rather raw. Julia has gone through a lot, and she's got some chips on her shoulder that Kelsey is going to have to help her knock off.

"That's not going to happen in a single sitting, but they're going to have to be frank with one another and say things that probably revolve around you. I'll bet those won't be complimentary, coming from your sister from another universe."

That sobered him up quickly. "Yeah, you're probably right."

He started handing out ration bars from a larger box that they'd brought with them. As he was doing so, Talbot joined them. They sat in silence for a bit until Jared forced his mind away from his sister and her double.

"How did we do on the march?" he asked the senior marine.

"The good news is that we didn't lose anybody to an injury," Talbot said. "The bad news is that I think a group of kindergartners would probably have moved faster. We're going to have to pick up the pace if we want to get to the Imperial Palace in a reasonable amount of time."

Jared nodded, but he wasn't really certain what the marine would consider "reasonable." He suspected that it would be far faster than what he'd use the word for.

"It took us roughly four hours to get five kilometers?" Jared asked. "If we stretched that out over the entire march, we're looking at close to five months, right? What pace do you think we should be doing?"

The marine took a bite of his ration bar and chewed with a thoughtful expression on his face. "That's a complicated question. Most of the crew didn't carry what the marines would consider to be a full pack. My people are basically overloaded right now, but they've trained for that. That's also slowing us down, so I'm not blaming the delay solely on the non-marines.

"If it was just the marines with normal loads, I think we could double today's speed. With the scientists in tow and my boys more heavily burdened, I'd be happy if we split the difference, so we could maybe make eighteen kilometers a day, once we get them in shape. That still means almost three months to get to the Imperial Palace, under the best case.

"Now, don't get me wrong. They did okay for the first day, but they're going to feel it in the morning. They'll have a lot of soreness and aching muscles. We don't want to push them hard enough that they injure themselves.

"I think it's best if we keep this pace for the next two or three days. Once they've adjusted to that, we can see about moving a little faster."

Elise rubbed her calf. "I think that I fall into the category of not getting enough exercise. I'm going to feel this tomorrow, just like the scientists. I can't say that I'm happy that I need to get this kind of exercise, but it's going to toughen me up."

Olivia nodded. "It'll be good for Sean too." With that, she poked her husband in the ribs.

He snorted. "I'm in better shape than you are. At least I get out every once in a while. You spend too much time behind your desk."

Her eyes narrowed. "You'd better watch it, mister. It's never a good thing when a husband is critical of his wife."

"Hey! That's what you just did to me."

She smiled innocently at him. "That's a wife's prerogative."

After a moment she smiled in a more genuine manner. "Seriously though, I think we're all going to be hurting in the morning, except for Talbot. He and his marines are going to be jogging circles around us while we slog for the next few days."

"I would never do that," Talbot said virtuously.

"Uh huh," Jared said. "In any case, looking at the map, it seems like we're going to be moving through some rougher terrain soon. There's a lot of forest scattered around in the direction we're heading, but I think this area used to be farmland. Even a century's growth means that the scrub and trees are fairly light. That's going to allow us to keep up a good pace.

"Unfortunately, about the time we'll finally be ready to march faster, we're going to run into what amounts to a real old-growth forest. That's going to slow us down again."

"Maybe not as much as you think," Talbot said. "When you've got larger trees, it cuts down on the light getting through to the undergrowth. That means less trouble moving around. We won't know for sure until we get close enough to put a few drones into the trees and take a look, but I'm hopeful that's the case.

"Honestly, I'm going to feel a lot better once we're under the tree cover anyway. That's going to make it a lot more difficult for anyone to spot us. Someone could use infrared to find us, if they have the technology, but a less advanced set of observers isn't going to be able to tell that we're out there, unless they run into us or our trail."

"And what happens when they do?" Elise asked. "We all know that's going to happen sooner or later, no matter how hard we try to avoid the people here. This *is* their home, and they know it far better than we do. If there are people in that forest, they're almost certainly going to find us before we know they're there."

That was one of Jared's worries. The inevitable confrontation with the locals. He suspected that they hadn't descended to savagery like the people of Erorsi. With any luck, they'd be dealing with people that at least had some of the trappings of civilization.

The Terrans had lived under the heel of the AIs for centuries before the System Lords began smashing their world. They'd only had a hundred years or so of being forced into primitive conditions, if the estimates were right.

As if a century was short.

In any case, he shouldn't minimize what had happened. Terra had once hosted a population in the many tens of billions. The death toll must've been horrific. These people would still carry the scars of their grandfathers and great-grandfathers who'd suffered and fought to survive in the wilderness, cast from the technological Eden that they'd been raised in.

"I don't think that we're going to run into a bunch of kindhearted strangers," Jared finally said. "These people have to be living hand to mouth, and that means fighting over resources. They're going to see other people as competition. We have to be ready for that.

"Everyone needs to get a good night's sleep, because we'll be getting up early. Talbot, set a watch to make sure that nobody gets the drop on us while we're stopped. Use your drones to circle around the area and keep an eye out for anyone sneaking up on us, and also have sentries out. Not that I should be telling you your business, mind you."

Talbot grinned. "No sir, you probably shouldn't. I've already got that all set up. We have drones in the air and scouts keeping an eye on the area. I've got a ready response team already in armor that'll back up the sentries if need be. We can only use powered armor tonight, but why waste the opportunity?

"Trust me when I say that we know our business. You folks can sleep easy knowing that no one is going to be giving us any trouble tonight. Not without a lot of warning."

"Good enough for me, Colonel."

Jared eyed the hard floor. It was made for supporting heavy machinery, so sleeping on it was going to be damned uncomfortable. The small pad that went under his sleeping bag would help a little, but not nearly enough, he was sure.

Well, there wasn't anything to be done about it. He'd best get some sleep and hope the rest of the trip was as uneventful as today.

The last thing he did before settling back and closing his eyes was give Kelsey and Julia another look. He knew that his sister didn't need nearly as much sleep as he did, but he hoped she didn't spend so much time getting to know her doppelgänger that she was overly tired tomorrow.

If things went sideways, they'd need her to be sharp. Her Marine Raider augmentation might just save their lives in a pinch. It had before.

With that thought, he closed his eyes, and sleep quickly overtook his exhausted mind and body.

* * *

JULIA SAT cross-legged on the stone floor, eating her ration bar—her third ration bar—and eyed Kelsey as she did the same. The woman from this universe was doing the exact same thing that she was, assessing her opposite. Only the other woman's expression was a lot more confident than she felt.

"This has to be strange for you," Kelsey said. "We've spoken a little bit over the FTL com, but that's not the same thing as what we're doing right now. We didn't know each other then, but we need to know each other now."

Julia felt her lips twitch up at the corners. "And exactly how do we do that? I feel I should already know everything about you, but I don't. Not really. Neither of us knows exactly who or what the other person is."

"No, we don't." Kelsey balled up the wrapper from the bar she'd been eating and stuck it in her pocket.

That was one thing that these marine fatigues had going for them. They had *lots* of pockets. As both a woman and a princess, Julia loved that aspect of these strange clothes more than anything. There were never enough places to stash things—like ration bars—in a regular uniform.

Or, God forbid, a dress.

"So how do we do this?" she asked the other version of herself. "We have the same goals, but we serve different people. You're here to help your empire, and I'm here to help mine. How do we mesh those two—potentially opposed—goals together?"

"By learning to trust one another," Kelsey said. "I understand that you're here because your people need to defeat the AIs. Believe me, I understand that better than most. I've already told you that we'll do everything within our power to help you, but you're right to worry. You have an entire empire counting on you.

"I've told you a little bit about how circumstances have treated me. I've heard a little about how you've gotten the short end of the stick. I suggest that we start talking about things from when we were kids. That would give us some common ground, and once we have that, we can move forward into talking about the present."

Julia sighed. She didn't want to spend any time discussing the past with herself. In fact, she *really* didn't want to.

"No," she said. "There's no need to discuss everything that's happened since I was a kid all the way through the present. It doesn't matter. What matters is that we're here now and that we have to work together. We've got to set boundaries, and we've got to figure out how we're going to help one another.

"I've already talked this over with Mertz. He said that once everything is done here and you've got the override, he'll send me with the key back to my universe. That's all fine and good, except that it's useless to me. I don't have anyone in my universe that has the right DNA, except for the Bastard. He killed off everyone even remotely related to my father. How do we get around that?"

Kelsey shrugged slightly. "I'm not going to let Jared go back to your universe and help. From everything you've told me, he's like a cartoon villain in your world. They'd string him up the moment they saw him, no matter what you said."

"My version of Mertz *isn't* a cartoon villain," Julia disagreed. "He's *much* worse than that. He's like you described Ethan from your universe, only not so crazy. Maybe he's just rotten to the core. Whatever he is, he'll kill whoever he needs to, and destroy whatever he wants, to achieve dominance over the New Terran Empire.

"Even as we speak, he's out there somewhere in my universe plotting and scheming to overthrow Ethan and take control of the Imperial Throne for himself. You're exactly right that it's not a good place for your Mertz to be, but that still leaves me with my problem."

Kelsey leaned back and looked at her. "Once we've taken care of the Master AI here, we can send the override with you. That way you don't have to make the trip to Terra at all."

"That may be the only real option I have," Julia agreed. "If my universe is anything like yours, I don't dare go to Terra. By now the AIs have delivered the Omega Plague and Terra is a death trap."

Kelsey blinked and opened her mouth to say something but then closed it again. After a few seconds, she nodded. "I hadn't considered that. Without you to stop them, there's nothing to keep the AIs from carrying out their plan, and we have to assume that's *exactly* what they did.

"I suppose that you could drop down onto the Imperial Palace inside a vacuum suit, but that's needlessly risking a horrible death. You'd still have to get past the System Lord and the automated defenses at the flip points, because you can be sure that they won't remove that kind of protection from the Terra system, even after they kill everyone off. Worse, there's no guarantee that they won't start setting up to replicate the massacre everywhere else as soon as they can."

They both sat silently for a few minutes. That was a lot to take in.

"With the Rebel Empire already having taken Pentagar in my universe," Julia said, "I think it's a given that they know about the New Terran Empire now. It's not going to be long at all before they have warships making the trip to Avalon. My version of Elise will try to keep everything quiet, but somebody is going to say something that tips them off.

"By the time we're done here, it might've already happened. Honestly, since I'm cut off from Pentagar, we don't even have a way to find out. We'll be operating in the dark once I get back to my universe, and I pretty much have to assume that the worst-case scenario has already played out."

Kelsey leaned forward and put a hand on Julia's arm. "Even if that's true, we'll still help. We're recovering ships all the time from the graveyard. I'd wager that Omega can get a portal open between the universes. After all, that's what he was created for.

"Since he knows where you're from, when he has enough power saved up, he can open an interdimensional portal and we could take a fleet through."

Julia shook her head. "Why would you do that? You've got your own fight here, and you're going to need every ship you can dig up. There's absolutely nothing that you can send across that's going to make my situation any better.

"I'm going to have to do everything I can to help you succeed here, because I'm going to have to take the override home to even have a chance at this. There's no other way this plays out for my people. Untold millions of them are going to die when the AIs invade the New Terran Empire. I just have to make their sacrifice *mean* something."

The com unit connected to Julia's implants made a tone in her mind to get her attention. It was an alert.

"All marines, this is Talbot," her doppelgänger's husband said. "We've got unknown people in the vicinity of the building. Everyone not already outside, gather up at the ramp. If they decide to come our way, we're going to have a confrontation."

Kelsey smoothly rose to her feet and jogged toward her armor. "The ready response team is already armored up, so let's go help them. At least this time we can have powered armor to curb stomp anyone that really wants to push the issue of our trespassing."

Julia rose and followed the other woman, already humiliated that she was going to have to ask for help getting into her armor. At least if there ended up being a fight, it would be brief and maybe let her release some of the tension that had built up inside her.

She really didn't want to fight anyone. She wasn't a warrior, and she hated the idea of hurting or killing anyone. If she could have, she'd have sat this fight out.

But she couldn't because she had Raider augmentation, and that might make a difference in keeping some of the marines from being hurt or killed. If it came down to the other people or her allies, she'd kill the intruders and suffer for it later.

6

Talbot stepped out onto the ramp and joined the ready response team. Like him, they were in powered armor, minus their helmets. The rest of his on-duty marines were scouts, backing up the drones that watched in every direction.

Corporal Elena Boske, the ready response team leader, turned toward him, her short pink hair looking strange in the dark with his enhanced vision. "The unknowns are about five kilometers south by southwest of our position. Based on the path that they're taking, they'll pass about a kilometer away from our current location."

He nodded. "We can't count on them continuing on that course. If they divert, they can be here pretty quickly."

"Faster than you'd think, sir. They're on horses."

He blinked in surprise, though he wasn't sure why he should be shocked. Terra was the home of horses as well as humans. There were a lot of horses on Avalon. It had been a vacation world in the Old Terran Empire, after all. He wasn't sure how common they were elsewhere.

Personally, he'd never learned to ride. He wasn't sure that he knew anyone that had. Horses were either working animals on farms or the province of the wealthy on Avalon. Maybe Kelsey knew how to ride, but he wasn't sure many others in their party did.

"What speed are they traveling at?" he asked as he checked the feed for himself.

"A slow walk," she said. "While their speed varies, it doesn't look like they're hurrying, and that makes sense as it's dark. I'm surprised they're moving under conditions like this. I'm more than a bit worried that they'd like to use this building to set up a camp until dawn."

"There's no sign of anybody having been inside the building," Talbot argued. "While they could be coming here, I'd think the odds are that they're not. Does it look like they have a destination in mind, based on the maps we currently have?"

"They're headed for the pinnaces," Kelsey said from behind him. "If you expand the map out a little bit, it's obvious that's where they're going. They probably spotted me coming down. It wasn't like I was being subtle or anything."

No, she certainly hadn't been. At the speed they'd come in, the crashing pinnace had probably been a streak of fire across the sky, visible for quite a distance.

A check of the path that the riders were taking confirmed that they were on the way to the crash site, with his implants giving that option better than a seventy percent chance. They'd find everything he and his people had been forced to leave back there, too.

Worse, they'd be able to follow the trail their people had made right back to them.

"They're going to catch up with us," he said grimly. "Even if they spent a few days at the crash site—which we can't count on—those horses can make up the distance in a day."

His wife nodded. "They won't spend a lot of time there. They might leave some of their number to search the wrecks, but they'll come after us. We're probably in their territory, and they'll want to deal with us as quickly as possible.

"On the plus side, that means we can wait for them here and get this over with while we still have the armored marines as backup when I talk to them. We don't know if they'll end up being friends, foes, or just people that want nothing to do with us, but we have to assume that they're not going to be very friendly when they catch up with us.

"These people are survivors. It may have been generations since the AIs blasted them from orbit, but those memories are still going to be very sharp for them. There's plenty of resources on Terra, but if you're being watched and hunted, you don't feel like you can gather them. That means they're going to see us as a potential threat, and they're going to want to deal with us as such."

Julia, who'd come up behind Kelsey, looked uncertain. "Are you sure that you're the right person to talk to them?"

Kelsey shrugged. "I'm the one with the most experience at that sort of thing. I'm also the one best suited to deal with any hostilities, if they break out.

"According to the drones, these people are carrying knives, swords, spears, and bows. That doesn't mean that they don't have access to something more advanced, mind you, but I'd imagine charging something like that would be a screaming bitch.

"On the plus side, I'm not very threatening. I won't be perceived as a serious threat. Unless I want to be."

That made Talbot go back to the drone feed and start counting the riders. There were thirty-three humans and roughly double that number of horses. He couldn't tell whether the spares were meant to be packhorses or remounts to allow the riders to travel longer distances without having to stop.

In any case, the fact that they were traveling at night probably meant something as well. Maybe they were afraid of being observed. Perhaps assuming that these people were the ones who ran this area was a mistake. If these folks were raiders, then his people might be sticking their heads into an inter-clan rivalry of some sort, and that could get ugly.

"A thought just occurred to me," he said before explaining his theory.

Kelsey nodded slowly once he'd finished. "That's something we have to keep in mind. We know absolutely nothing about the situation on the ground. These people could be here to steal whatever they can get their hands on.

"Which doesn't mean that they're bad people. Tribes raided one another on preindustrial Terra all the time, and that didn't necessarily mean they were evil. That's just competition for resources. Raiding isn't quite war, after all."

She then tilted her head back a little, and her eyes went unfocused for a few seconds. "They're not curving toward us, so they'll be at our original camp within two hours. That's going to be slightly before dawn.

"I think I should take a team of people and meet them there. That'll give you time to set this place up in a more defensible manner. If I take marines in suits, we can get there fast. Not as fast as horses, but we'll have plenty of power to fight if we need to."

Talbot didn't approve of her going, but he'd learned the hard way that trying to convince his wife not to carry out any plan that she'd set her mind to was doomed. He might as well see that she was as well protected as he could, since she was going, one way or the other.

"Another thing we have to worry about is that this might not be the only group we'll have to deal with," he said. "A lot of people could've seen the pinnace on its way down. If so, we might have more people showing up tomorrow.

"We can get some drones out to cover part of the area, but the smaller ones don't have the range to cover all avenues of approach. You'll have to be very careful not to get caught up in someone else's fight, Kelsey."

He turned to Boske. "Split the ready response team. Everyone going with the colonel needs to be ready to travel light and perhaps be separated from support for a couple of days. The rest of us will be ready to receive you, if things go sour and you have to come back here in a hurry. I hope that doesn't happen, because that could mean that we're going to have to fight every step of the way to the Imperial Palace."

His wife shook her head. "I think the chances of us going undetected have passed. Hell, they probably never existed at all. We need to find some friends and learn the lay of the land. Knowledge, as they say, is power."

"Be careful, Kelsey," he said quietly as he stepped over to her side.

"If things go badly, we won't be able to get there in time to help you. You'll be fighting with only what you can bring with you."

"I can handle this," she said softly, running her hand across his cheek. The cool metal of her gauntlet wasn't anything like her hand, but it was still gentle. "No matter what happens, I'll do whatever I have to do to get us to the Imperial Palace."

Of that he was certain, even if it put her into deadly peril. He knew there was nothing he could do to change her mind, so he could only hope that she took fewer chances than she usually did this time around.

A hope he was virtually certain was doomed to disappointment.

* * *

KELSEY STARTED GETTING pushback even before they'd set off for the crash site. She'd made the decision that she wouldn't be wearing her armor for this meeting and gotten immediate pushback from her doppelgänger.

Even as she was stripping her Raider armor off and handing it to one of the other marines to carry for her, Julia was telling her just exactly what she thought about that idea.

"This is idiotic," the other woman said, somewhat waspishly. "The odds of them shooting you are really high. Why would you willingly take away your best defense?"

Kelsey didn't answer immediately, settling her weapons belt around her hips and double-checking that all of her guns were fully loaded, well seated, and ready for action. That done, she settled her sword harness securely on her back.

"The mistake you're making is thinking that my armor is my strongest defense," Kelsey said calmly. "It isn't. My strongest defense is not being shot at in the first place. If they see some metallic monster coming at them, they're going to react in a manner that I think we'd all consider extremely hostile. Admittedly, I wouldn't be in any danger from the kind of weapons we've seen thus far, but convincing them to be our allies in this is my primary goal.

"If they decide to shoot first and ask questions later, I can handle that. They're not going to lay in a flight of arrows at me all at once, because one woman is not going to be that threatening, particularly if I walk in with my hands conspicuously empty. Any rational being will want to talk before they engage in violence."

"And what makes you think they're rational?" Julia responded with a scowl. "We don't know them at all. They might be cannibals. There's no telling what they'll consider a reasonable response to this."

"I'll grant you that point. That's why you and the marines are going to be just out of sight, ready to respond if things go badly. I'd much rather settle this cordially, but I'm not going to put myself at undue risk.

"If they want to fight, my Raider augmentation will be more than sufficient to get me clear before they can hit me. Then we can figure out the best way to respond."

She could tell that Julia wanted to argue, but she didn't. The other woman simply raised her hands in a show that she'd given up.

"Fine. It's your life. I can't control what you're going to do, and you probably have a better idea of how this is going to work out than me anyway. That's your call, but we still have to get there over some pretty rough terrain. Are you sure you're up to running through that stuff in the dark without armor?"

Kelsey nodded and smiled slightly. "We've already been over this terrain once. We're just going to go back in the same direction that we came from. I don't remember any unexpected ravines along the way that might trip me up, and my eyesight's pretty good. So's yours.

"If we utilize our Raider augmentation and tune the ocular augmentation so that we're using both infrared and ultraviolet, as well as the normal sight range, that should give us a pretty good idea what we're going to face. It's good practice for what we'll need to do once we don't have our armor with us."

She rested her hand on the other woman's shoulder. "Relax. We'll keep it slow and easy. As long as we get there soon after dawn, I think everything's going to be fine. Coming in during the daylight is probably better in any case. If they can clearly see me, they're less likely to start shooting at shadows."

She checked her internal chrono and made the decision. "We

need to get moving. While they're busy examining the crash site, there'll be less of them ready to respond to my arrival. I'd like to let them notice me on their own, without me making a lot of noise to get their attention. Drama might look good on the vids, but it just makes people react hastily and do things that we'd all regret. Let's do this slow and easy."

Kelsey shared a few words with Jared and Talbot before they headed out. Neither one of them outright told her to take every precaution imaginable, but she knew that they wanted her to be careful. She'd do her very best and see what the circumstances brought.

The trip back to the crash site wasn't too hard. There were a couple of times that she stepped where her footing wasn't that certain, but they arrived near the crash site just before the sun began peeking over the horizon without any injuries. They'd made excellent time. Better than she'd hoped. The marines really could move quickly when they needed to.

Corporal Boske dispatched some short-range drones to take a look and began determining what the locals were up to.

"It looks like they've put all of the horses into a picket together off to the side," the pink-haired woman said after a few minutes. "There are a couple of people keeping an eye on them while everyone else is either moving through the tents or circling around the pinnaces. I count maybe a dozen people keeping watch over the camp as a whole.

"If you approach along the path that we made departing, you're going to encounter two of them. I don't see any concealed sentries, so I'm not worried about an ambush. Whatever their response is going to be, we'll be able to see it coming."

"Sounds good," Kelsey said. "Now remember the plan. I'm going to walk up on them slow and easy, then they'll undoubtedly take me into custody. As long as they're not being overtly violent, just let it happen.

"Once I'm their prisoner, they'll be more inclined to at least talk with me, if only to get me to answer some pointed questions. We need information, and these people are the best source we've found to get it."

With that, Kelsey left the marines to settle into good locations to either act as snipers or to rush in to defend her as she retreated. She really hoped that none of that was necessary, but she wasn't ruling it out. She'd been in situations that she thought would work out one way and seen them go completely wrong. She'd play this by ear and see what happened.

If she got lucky, they might find some allies that would tell them what lay ahead. If she got unlucky, she'd get into a fight.

Well, time to see how her luck turned out this time.

She walked into the area around the pinnaces about ten minutes later. The sun wasn't behind her, but it was near enough that she got damned close before the guards spotted her. Both of them raised bows and covered her with their arrows while shouting for her to stop in recognizable Standard.

She did so in as relaxed a manner as she could and kept her hands out to her sides with her palms exposed.

"I'm not here to fight," she said almost conversationally. "I just want to talk."

Before they could respond, her internal com came alive. *Kelsey, this is Talbot. Our drones just picked up a large group coming from a different direction. It's about three times the size of the group you're looking at, and they look pretty pissed off. They're riding hard and should be at the crash site in about half an hour. Maybe this isn't the best time to initiate contact.*

It's a little late for that, she said dryly. *I'm already talking. Maybe we're going to need some of that backup you were talking about after all. Work with Jared to figure out what the best response is if there's a fight, because it certainly sounds like there's going to be one.*

I don't know which side I should be fighting with, but I'll do my best to figure that out before the others arrive. Try to get me any information you can on them while I deal with the situation here.

Will do. Make friends fast, or they might think you're with the other party. That probably wouldn't be helpful. You might also be able to use the impending attack to get them to see you more as an ally.

I'll see what I can manage, she said as one of the guards approached her warily. *I have to go. Our new friends need my full attention, and I need to pass the word to Corporal Boske so she can prepare. Don't do anything hasty, okay?*

Who? Me? I would never cut into your act.

His quip made her smile, which it probably wouldn't hurt to allow the man coming her way to see. Her humanity and passivity would help speed this along.

She could've let Talbot warn Boske himself, since the armor had the com range to reach him, but this was her fight to coordinate. She needed to do so quickly, because time wasn't on her side and there were so many ways things could still go wrong in the next few minutes.

Boske, she said over the short-ranged com, *we have about ninety incoming horsemen. It sounds like they're not going to be hugging things out with this group or us. Work that into your plans and be ready to give me some cover if things go south. Things just got complicated.*

7

J ared thought about Kelsey's unfolding situation and considered sending the rest of the ready response team after her but rejected the idea. There was no way they could get to the area around the pinnaces in time to make any difference, and they might need them here. If his sister broke away from the first group and avoided the new people completely, she and the marines could make their stand in powered armor and not be in any significant danger.

He'd leave Talbot in charge of the tactical situation while he focused on the strategic. They now had two separate sets of players, and he needed to know as much about them as he could before they started shooting at his people or each other.

"Talbot, what do we know about the second force?" he asked the marine when he stepped out onto the ramp.

The sun was over the horizon, and the scent of the air seemed to be changing in a way he couldn't describe. As a Fleet officer, he'd never been one for camping, so nature was going to take some getting used to. He approved of the cool breeze coming in from the northwest, though. It somehow smelled of water.

The marine officer shared a virtual display with him. It showed a map of the general area, and part of the lower screen was taken up by video from one of their drones. It showed a large force of people on horses, moving quickly over open ground.

They had a determined look about them and were moving very fast. He also noticed that they didn't have extra horses like the first group had come with.

"My guess is that the second group is responding to the intrusion of the first," Talbot said. "You'll notice that they don't have any remounts. They know exactly how far they're going to go, and they don't expect to do a whole lot of riding after that. They're running toward a fight."

That didn't sound promising.

"What kind of scenarios are we looking at?" Jared finally asked. "Should we be getting everyone ready for a forced march?"

"We wouldn't get there in time to make any difference. Kelsey and her people have powered armor, and if they get caught in crossfire, they'll be able to take care of themselves. Even if somebody out there has advanced weaponry, our people are trained and ready to deal with them. They'll be fine.

"Our best plan of action is to position ourselves to deal with the fallout. Let's say the worst-case scenario happens and the two groups start fighting and catch our people in between them without us being able to determine who the good guys are. The marines will be able to put down any direct attacks. What we need to worry about are the political consequences.

"Or I should say, that's what *you* need to worry about. I'm setting my people up to make this building more defensible in case there are *other* groups out there coming to see what all the fuss is about."

Jared didn't like thinking that his sister was outside his ability to help, but she was more than capable of taking care of herself. She wasn't the same woman that had started out with him on the original expedition. She was tough, resourceful, and more than capable of shooting back at someone that wanted to make her a target.

Her doppelgänger could handle herself in a fight too, he

suspected. Julia was tough, even if she didn't think so. What really concerned him was the fact that there might be more than one group making for the crash site. While he hadn't been on the ground when Kelsey crashed the pinnace, Jared was certain that she'd made *quite* a show coming in.

If it had been as visible as he suspected, anyone within a hundred kilometers or more might know about their presence. If that was the case, the wrecked pinnaces might become the center of attention for a large number of potentially hostile groups. That could lead to a brawl that he desperately wanted to avoid becoming part of.

"Is there any way we can minimize the chances that they're going to track us to this building?"

"I'm not sure how," the marine officer said. "We had a lot of people hiking through the tall grass to get here. That's going to leave the kind of trail that *anyone* can follow. Add in the marines in armor, and the arrow pointing directly at us is unmistakable. Since they know where we landed, they won't have any difficulty zeroing in on us."

So, anything they left here was likely going to be taken as loot. Perfect. They might as well have left it all at the pinnaces and tried to make better time.

Worse, even after they left this place, anyone that came across their trail would be able to track them down and attack them at will. He had to figure out if it was even possible for them to evade discovery by the locals. If not, this mission might be over long before they made it to the Imperial Palace.

"What about once we leave?" he asked slowly. "If we abandon everything except the absolute essentials, are we going to be able to get our people off the radar of any pursuers?"

"Possibly." His brother-in-law didn't sound optimistic. "The forest isn't that far away. Once we get there, there'll be a lot of undergrowth and overhead shielding that will help. There are things that we'll be able to do to disguise our tracks and to minimize our trail. Once we've done that, it might be possible to break contact with any pursuers, though I wouldn't count on things being that easy.

"A more likely scenario is that we can have the majority of our people go into the forest while some of us hang a little bit behind in order to dissuade anyone on our six. If we can show them that chasing us is a bad idea, they'll stop.

"Hell, if Kelsey makes a big enough impression on the people back at the pinnaces, they might not pursue us at all. It's going to depend on how things work out there."

"What can we do to support her?" Jared asked. "I doubt she's going to be challenged to the point that she needs to retreat, but that situation could turn into a bloodbath for the locals.

"Just the fact that there are two sets of unknowns coming in means there's almost certainly going to be a fight. If we add in other groups, there's going to be a war over the crashed pinnaces and anything they can salvage from them. How do we deal with that?"

"We're going to have to let Kelsey do what she does," Talbot said simply. "That boat has sailed."

Jared could almost hear the marine's mental shrug. He was right though. The best they could hope for was that Kelsey found them some friends. If they could turn one of the local groups into allies, that would make their mission a lot easier.

If they made nothing but enemies here, that was probably going to be a death sentence for them, the mission, and the human race. He'd just have to hope that Kelsey did all the right things because she was the one on the ground and she'd be making the calls.

He trusted her, but her track record was a bit daunting. She might succeed and *still* give him grey hair. And that was if everything worked out.

If not, well, things would really get ugly really soon.

* * *

JULIA CURSED under her breath as Kelsey passed on the warning about the new group. This was *just* what they hadn't needed. More incoming natives and what certainly looked to be a brewing fight.

With ninety potential hostiles inbound, it was a virtual certainty that they'd be fighting very shortly. The group inside their former camp was going to defend it against this new set of people, and her doppelgänger would be right in the middle of it.

The possibility that someone would shoot her out of hand with one of those arrows or stick a sword through her was *very* high. If they came to the conclusion that Kelsey was somehow connected with the people attacking them—maybe assuming she was a distraction—they'd do their level best to kill her.

Julia wasn't certain how her doppelgänger could talk her way out of that, but she hoped that she could.

Meanwhile, she and the marines had to deal with intercepting the incoming hostiles—if that's what they really were—while still keeping an eye on Kelsey. They didn't have the numbers for that, and they were going to have to improvise. Thankfully Corporal Boske seemed to be very competent.

The pink-haired marine called everyone on the short-ranged com channel and informed them that the situation had just gotten ugly. She passed along the details of the incoming force, which wasn't much. What they *did* know was that with ninety-odd hostiles incoming and thirty inside the camp, they were looking at worse than ten-to-one odds if all of the horsemen turned on them.

Even with powered armor that rendered them invulnerable to primitive weapons, there was going to be a lot happening.

The corporal turned to her. "What's your plan, Highness?"

Julia felt her eyes widen. "I'm not a good judge of military tactics, Corporal. You'd be better off making the decisions on how to deploy your troops than me."

"One learns by doing, Highness. The colonel told me to run anything past you, so that you can improve your education on combat-related matters, time permitting. How would you allocate our people to meet the incoming force and still provide cover for Colonel Bandar?"

Everyone knew that she wasn't a warrior, so why did they keep trying to turn her into one? It was damned irritating.

Rather than argue, Julia accessed the map of the crash site and looked for areas they could use to provide extra cover and concealment. There were some low hills scattered around the area, but most of them weren't close enough to provide effective covering fire for her doppelgänger.

The marine weapons could hit someone at quite a distance, but precision when you had someone you wanted to keep safe mixed with potentially hostile individuals was a more complicated matter.

She accessed the data that her doppelgänger had sent and saw which direction the new forces were approaching from. There were a couple of hills off in that direction that were fairly close to the camp. Those could provide concealment for a few marines without difficulty.

Also near that side of the encampment, there was a single rise that was close enough to allow for a sniper or two to keep the people inside the compound under observation and still be of use against the incoming force.

The beginnings of an idea started percolating, so she sent the map to the corporal with updates.

"These two hills can hold a couple of marines each, ready to respond once the larger force gets past them and closer to the camp. The smaller rise right here can hold some snipers that can keep an eye on Kelsey or the others as the situation requires.

"If the incoming troops pass between the hills like it seems they're going to, they'll be trapped between them and the camp if we decide to fight. With our superior armor and weapons, we should be able to use that constrained space to cause a lot of damage in a short amount of time."

The corporal nodded. "That's a solid plan, Highness, though I'd move the snipers out of the pinch zone. Also, those hills are close enough to the camp that the first group might send a lookout or two of their own, after they process that they might have more than the colonel for company. What do we do if individuals from inside the camp attack her?"

"Kelsey has to be our primary responsibility. If she's in any danger, then we need to neutralize those threats. She'll be able to communicate with us, so she can tell us what's happening inside the compound.

"If she thinks she's safe enough, then we can hold off unless there's an overtly hostile action to respond to. If someone looks like they're going to shoot a bow at her or stick a sword in her back, the snipers can take those individuals out. Otherwise, we need to leave what happens in the camp in her hands.

"The biggest unknown is going to be how the first group reacts when a force three times their size comes racing in on them. Once the second group arrives, we can be pretty sure that the fighting will start.

"These folks don't seem like they're going to be old friends. I hope that I'm wrong, but the second group isn't moving like they're expecting to join somebody for lunch."

Boske chuckled. "I think you've read that just right, Highness. Your basic plan is sound enough. What about our mobile units? We're going to have to get mixed up in the fighting to bring a conclusive end to the engagement. We've got nine people in armor, counting yourself.

"If we put four on the hills to be our backstop against this new force, put two on this rise to act as snipers, that leaves three of us: you, me, and one of the other marines.

"We're going to have to be the hammer that hits the anvil. Just shooting into a group of hostiles isn't going to be enough. You've got to be able to fight hand-to-hand and break their will, or you're not going to be as effective in stopping them as you'd like to be."

The corporal turned and stared out over the grasslands. "I know you don't like fighting, Highness, so I'm going to leave the choice up to you. Where in all of this mess do you want to be?

"Personally, I don't think you're the right person to be part of the blocking force on the two larger hills. You could act as one of the snipers on the closer hill, but I'm still not really sure that's what you're cut out for. Do you have the type of precise fire capability a sniper would need? Can you hit someone next to the colonel without hitting her? Could you even do that kind of thing? Killing at long range is a cold-blooded business."

Julia considered that and thought she could probably do it, but it would require her to allow her implants to control her actions while firing, something she was loath to do. And the corporal was right to doubt she had the mental fortitude to do something like that. Could she kill someone like that, without being in danger herself? She just didn't know.

After a few moments, she shook her head. "I think somebody else would be better suited to that task."

The corporal nodded. "Then you, me, and the remaining marine are going to be the mobile force. If the fighting kicks off like I expect, we're going to drive a wedge into the larger force to keep it back from the camp.

"We don't really know who the bad guys are, so we're going to lead this off using stunners. We may need to resort to heavier weaponry, but there's no need to lead off with indiscriminate killing. The snipers won't fire unless lethal force is called for.

"We've got the tools to take the second force down. If we set the stunners on wide aperture, even with mobile enemies on horses, we should be able to take out at least half their force before they get their act together. Then we have to go to tighter beams and hit targets that are farther away. Targets that are probably going to be trying to retreat.

"Horses are faster than we are, even in armor, though I'm not so sure when it comes to Raider armor. If somebody breaks free, do you think you could chase them down and stop them?"

"I'm pretty sure that I can catch up with a few of them when the horses start tiring," Julia said. "They can't keep up that kind of speed for very long, whereas I can do so in the armor without too much trouble.

"The problem is going to come in when they split off in multiple directions. When they do that—which they will—there's no way that I can catch up with everybody."

The corporal nodded. "We can only do what we can, Highness. Stick close and be ready to start stunning people when I give the order. And by the way, that was a pretty good battle plan. I think you're better at this than you give yourself credit for."

Julia watched the corporal marshaling her forces and dispatching them to the positions she wanted. She disagreed with the other woman's assessment of her, but it was hard to miss the fact that she'd worked out a plan that would effectively deal with this large a force.

She was going to have to think things over again. She'd never be a

Marine Raider, but maybe she could play one on TV, as her doppelgänger said. Whatever that meant.

Meanwhile, they needed to be ready to fight. Kelsey's life depended on them. She wished the other woman luck in convincing the smaller group that she was friendly in the roughly twenty minutes that she had before all hell broke loose.

8

The two men held Kelsey at arrow point while they summoned others to search her for weapons. Which, of course, they found in plenty.

They seemed to know what the pistols were and treated them with due care, so that told her that these people were aware of how dangerous those kinds of things could be. Not a primitive people, just like she'd suspected.

There turned out to be unexpected danger when they took her swords. One of them drew a blade and was about to flick a finger across the edge when she held up her hand and drew a tense response from the people with the bows.

"I wouldn't do that if I were you," she said. "It's a *lot* sharper than it looks, and you could severely cut yourself without trying."

The sword blades had an almost monomolecular edge and could cut through just about anything, if used with enough force. If somebody applied too much pressure, they'd cut themselves to the bone or perhaps even lop off the tip of a finger entirely.

Since that wouldn't be productive for anyone, Kelsey preferred to keep her captors from maiming themselves on her weapons and developing a grudge or starting some kind of blood feud based on them not knowing how to treat her weapons.

The man she'd spoken to eyed her for a moment and then pulled his hand back from the weapon. He slid the sword back into the sheath and placed the harness with her other weapons. None of them had said anything to her, other than the calls for her to stop moving. They were obviously waiting for someone to come and take charge.

That someone else turned out to be an exceptionally tall, well-built woman with an extremely dark complexion. She'd have towered over even Angela, who at two meters, was very well-built herself. This woman was at least a head taller than *Persephone*'s commanding officer, and that meant that she towered over Kelsey by an obnoxious degree.

Like Angela, the new woman appeared to be a warrior. She wore armor, carried weapons, and her bare arms were roped with muscle. Her skin had some scars that certainly looked like they'd come from combat as well.

The armor that she wore was interesting, too. It was formed mostly of leather which looked as if it had been boiled and waxed to make it harder, but there were strips of metal woven into critical areas to provide extra protection while keeping the overall weight down. Based on some of the historical and entertainment vids that Kelsey had seen, she half expected to see chain mail used as part of the armor, but there didn't seem to be any.

The woman's helmet, which she had in the crook of her arm, was made wholly of boiled leather, though it might have had some type of metal insert that Kelsey couldn't see. The woman's belt held what certainly looked like a sheathed longsword. Based on the well-worn leather-wrapped hilt, the woman used it regularly.

The woman's night-dark face showed no expression, and there was no humor in her dark eyes. Her tight, close-cropped, curly black hair seemed well suited to fit inside her helmet. Physically, she was almost exactly the opposite of the short, blonde, long-haired princess with her pale skin.

"Who are you, and how many people have you brought with you?" the woman asked in a slightly accented version of Standard, her voice low and flat.

"My name is Kelsey Bandar," Kelsey said with what she hoped was an easy smile. "I'm not alone, you're right about that. I've brought some friends along just to make sure that this meeting doesn't go badly before we've had a chance to get to know one another. They're out there watching us, but they're not going to interfere unless they think that I'm in danger.

"Before you start thinking that they have to get within bow range, let me caution you that they have high-tech weapons like my pistols and that they'll use them if they feel that I'm in danger. I don't want to see any of your people hurt, and I'd rather not get into a fight with you either. I just want to know the same sorts of things you do. Who are you, and what are you doing here?"

The corners of the other woman's lips twitched upward slightly. "My name is Clarice Beauchamp, and I command this company. As one might gather from looking around us," she said, making a wide gesture with her free arm, "we are here to see what came from the sky yesterday. Are those ships yours?"

Kelsey considered lying but decided that that wouldn't suit their overall plans for very long. Honesty might get them more than deception.

"They are. We had an unfortunate series of accidents, and you also may have seen a large explosion up in orbit. That was the System Lord destroying our main ship before we came down in the pinnaces. Needless to say, I would've preferred a gentler landing, but circumstances being what they were, I suppose that I should be happy that no one was killed."

The woman's gaze went hard and cold. "You are Fleet, then. We have known your kind before. You are the scourge that carries out the will of the System Lords. Give me one reason why I shouldn't cut you down right now as a traitor to the human race?"

Kelsey felt herself tensing but forced her expression to stay calm and open. "Perhaps you missed the part about where the System Lord was trying to kill us. We're not here as its allies. We came from far away, hoping to free the people of Terra.

"Well, to be clear, freeing your people is a secondary goal. We came to retrieve something to fight the System Lords and bring down their rule. We want to free all of humanity."

The woman considered what she'd said but didn't seem convinced. "Pretty words, but they mean nothing. You have two choices, Kelsey Bandar. You may summon your people so that I may take them into custody, or you may send them away. I give you my word that I shall cut you down first if your people attack mine."

Kelsey shook her head. "Not going to happen. My people will never leave me in your custody, and they're not going to surrender. Unlike you, they possess plenty of firepower to make certain that I stay safe, so let me give you the same type of warning.

"I can either speak with you peacefully or you can allow me to walk away unharmed. Any other choice risks forcing them to use lethal force. I don't want to see you killed. Hell, I don't want to see any fighting at all.

"In fact, I'm here looking to make friends, and I can trade valuable information with you to make certain that you understand what that can mean."

The other woman's cold smile widened. "And what kind of information is that?"

"There's a force on horseback coming from that direction." Kelsey raised a hand just enough to point a finger in the direction that the attacking force was coming from. "They have about ninety people and no remounts. They're riding hard, and they should be here in about fifteen minutes or so. If you're planning on defending yourself against a force three times your size, perhaps now would be the time to forget about me and worry about them.

"Or better yet, convince me that I have the possibility of becoming friends with you, and my people will help defend your group. Otherwise they're going to stay neutral and let what happens happen. I'd rather not see your groups kill each other, but I don't know you and I don't know them. This is the one brief window of time that you have to convince me that I should help you.

"If I were you, I'd start talking."

* * *

Talbot, Admiral Mertz, and Commander Roche stood around a tabletop simulation of the battlefield that was projected through their implants via their ocular augmentation. It was as if he were standing around a *real* table, only there was no hardware outside of what was in their heads.

It was strange, but it was damn convenient.

With the feed from the tactical drones, the display had representation for every single individual on the battlefield. Blue for friendlies and yellow for unknown. When the new group arrived, they'd be labeled in red, simply because the odds of them being ultimately hostile were much higher and Talbot had to differentiate between the two groups in some way.

It worried him that Kelsey was still mixed in with the yellow dots. If she didn't get clear soon, she was going to be entangled in the fighting. The worst-case scenario would be that both groups were hostile and she'd be fighting against one hundred and twenty enemies with just a handful of marines as backup.

Since she wasn't in armor—not even unpowered armor—she'd be vulnerable to attacks that the marines in powered armor could shrug off. It was also conceivable that those people had modern weaponry stashed in their gear and no one would know about it until they brought something into play. The same was true of the group that was approaching.

He hoped his marines could stand up to what they were about to face, but it was always possible things could spin out of control and all of his people—including Kelsey—could die in the next twenty minutes.

"What can we do to help?" Commander Roche asked, his voice a mixture of worry and frustration. "There's got to be something we can do."

"I sent the other half of the ready response team," Talbot said. "They're going to get there faster than the rest of my people could, but they're still going to arrive late to the party. If things go pear-shaped, Corporal Boske knows to regroup her people and retreat toward the incoming support.

"Once our people leave the area around the camp—if they can

break contact and move at full speed—they'll join up with our other people in maybe half an hour, but I don't expect that to happen.

"If they get forced out, they're going to be in contact with the enemy, and breaking away is going to be impossible. Horses are faster than armored marines. They'll have to set up a defensible position and wait for relief. That could take as much as an hour. If the enemy actually has modern antiarmor weapons, this could be brutal."

Roche turned and stared at him, his eyes cold. "If something happens to Princess Kelsey—my Princess Kelsey—then we're going to have a real problem."

"If something happens to *Julia*, you can rest assured that the same is going to happen to *Kelsey* as well because she's not going to abandon her," the admiral said grimly. "She's not going to abandon *anyone*.

"And before you forget about it, both of them have Marine Raider augmentation. If things really go bad, as much as she'd hate to do it, Julia will give her combat controller the green light and it will clean house for her.

"She's in Raider armor, with Raider weapons, and has Raider augmentation. If anyone can survive this situation, it's her. The rest of the marines face worse odds. Kelsey, unarmored as she is, probably has the worst downside if things go bad, particularly since she'll be in the thick of things no matter how dangerous it is."

Roche rubbed his face tiredly. "Sorry. We've only been on Terra a single day. How can they have found us so fast?"

"We do the best we can, but we always seem to catch the bad breaks and have to fight our way through," Talbot said grimly. "Let's look on the bright side. The odds that both groups are going to be actively hostile to the marines are small.

"The most likely scenario is that the approaching group isn't going to open fire without talking first. There's going to be some kind of dialogue before there's shooting. Maybe the smaller group will surrender. We just don't know yet.

"The most likely situation is that the smaller group is made up of people that Kelsey can convince to be friendly. She has that way about her. Then our forces and theirs are going to be playing defense against the larger group.

"Unless somebody has antiarmor weapons, the only one of our people in any real danger is Kelsey. I know that Corporal Boske is going to do everything possible to shield her from all threats, even if that means sacrificing every marine in her unit. That's what she's trained to do, and that's what's going to happen if she has to make that choice. Let's hope it doesn't come to that."

"Does the drone system have audio capability?" Admiral Mertz asked. "Are we going to be able to hear what these people are shouting back and forth?"

Talbot shook his head. "They have audio, but it's not going to be good enough to pick up regular conversation, particularly in the middle of a battle. If somebody is shouting something that's meant to be heard at a distance, odds are good that the drones will pick it up. If they have to get close enough to hear something said in a normal tone, they're going to be in the open and the hostiles are going to see them.

"I'm assuming at this point that we want to keep the drones up in the air and not down where they can be detected. They're not armed, and we don't have an infinite supply of them."

After what felt like forever but was probably only a couple of minutes, the yellow dots around Kelsey began moving into what looked like a defensive perimeter from above. Kelsey stayed inside the group, near one specific dot. A couple of others were stationed nearby, obviously watching her from behind.

"Can we have one of the drones provide a visual of Kelsey and the people she's with?" the admiral asked. "It would be helpful if we could see who we're dealing with and pay attention to their body language. That's going to tell us a lot about how this situation is playing out."

Talbot singled out one of the drones flying over the camp and commandeered it with his command overrides. He focused the visual down on Kelsey and zoomed in closely enough to see her standing next to a tall black woman in primitive armor.

The pair of them were staring off in the direction that the hostiles would be coming from, and based on how they were standing, they weren't being actively hostile to one another. Though there were two guards stationed behind Kelsey with bows. If something went wrong, they could easily shoot his wife in the back.

Well, *easily* might not be the right word. They could certainly *try* to shoot her in the back, but he knew that Kelsey was plugged into the same drone network that he was and was undoubtedly watching carefully to see what the people around her were doing. If someone tried to ambush her from behind, she'd be all over them.

If she resorted to her full-powered augmentation to fight and escape, Talbot had no doubt that she had a very good chance of managing it. She was incredibly fast, well trained in hand-to-hand combat, and stronger than a dozen normal men. If push came to shove, his wife *would* escape.

But to do that, she'd have to *choose* to escape.

Knowing her, she was more likely to stand and fight beside people she saw as potential allies than run. That, more than anything, was likely to get her killed or severely wounded.

Commander Roche frowned. "What's she doing? If she's managed to convince these people to be friendly, shouldn't she be heading back out to join the marines and get into her armor?"

Jared shook his head. "That's not how Kelsey's mind works, Commander. Now that she's made up her mind that she's going to fight, she's going to stay beside their leader and fight. She's not going to take the time to retrieve her armor and make herself safer.

"You'll notice that she's not wearing her weapons, so they haven't decided to treat her as an ally at this point. Mark my words, once the fighting starts, she's going to retrieve those weapons from whoever's holding them—whether they're ready to hand them over or not—and be in the fighting before you can blink."

Roche shook his head. "She's insane. Worse, I think she's influencing *my* Kelsey. Or Julia, if you *insist*. She's been doing things recently that I think are unhinged. I just don't know what to believe anymore."

Talbot gave the man a wide grin. "When we have women like them in our lives, we have either the choice of accepting them as they are or having them forced down our throats. Gentlemen, I recommend that we just accept what's going to happen. Kelsey is smart and tough. She'll come through this intact. So will Julia."

Brave words aside, Talbot really hoped that his wife knew what she was doing this time. If she got into a fight with people capable of taking out marines in powered armor, one unlucky hit could obliterate her, and that would kill him too.

9

J ulia watched her doppelgänger through the drone feed and growled. The woman was just standing there like an *idiot*. Didn't she realize that the potentially hostile force was going to be on them in just a few minutes?

"What the hell is she doing?" she demanded of Corporal Boske over the command channel.

"It looks like she's making friends," the corporal said dryly. "Doesn't she just pick the damnedest times to do that?"

"I think using the term *friends* is perhaps a little early," Julia muttered. "It certainly seems like they're not going to give her weapons back, so maybe they're checking to see if she's telling them the truth about the incoming force. How far out are they?"

The corporal made a show of checking her implants by putting her fingers to the side of her head, no doubt implying that Julia could've done exactly the same thing herself.

That was annoying. Why couldn't people just answer her damned questions?

"It looks like they're about five minutes out at their current pace. I doubt that's going to hold, to be honest. If I were them, I'd send out scouts to make sure that the camp is clear, or to at least figure out where all of their potential targets are located.

"I'd also slow the main body down and spread them out a little bit. Those two hills they're coming up on would make for a great ambush site, as you well know, since you suggested using them for exactly that earlier."

Julia pinched the bridge of her nose and counted slowly to five. "Are you saying that they're going to send people up to make sure that the hills are clear? Did I just put a bunch of our people into danger?"

The corporal turned to face her. "Highness, when you're in command of a military action, *everything* you do puts *someone* in danger. Do I think that they're going to send people up on those hills? Yes, I do. Is that going to put our people in danger? Yes, it is.

"Now, the key is that they can't completely search those hillsides. As long as our people have found good hiding places, that's not going to be a serious problem. In fact, it's going to put them in a good position to ambush the enemy scouts, if that's what we decide to do.

"If worse comes to worst, their scouts are going to find our troops and the fighting starts right then. Our people won't be in any danger from people carrying primitive weapons. As Colonel Talbot told me privately, the real worry is that they may have advanced weapons capable of damaging our powered armor.

"If they've ever fought the Rebel Empire version of Imperial Marines before, then they'll have dealt with the type of armor that we have. It may have been a long time since they've had to face that kind of thing, so perhaps I'm worrying about nothing, but I'm not going to be taking unnecessary chances. If they engage, we come down on them like a hammer."

Julia split her attention between her doppelgänger and the approaching force. The people inside their old camp had spread out and formed a defensive perimeter, seemingly watching for danger.

A minute later, she grunted when the approaching forces sent riders toward the hills that she'd selected for the marines. Corporal Boske had been right, and now things were getting a lot more dangerous. It looked like a total of three riders were headed toward one of the hills, so she supposed it wasn't as bad as it could've been.

In fact, the larger force was slowing down and curving off to the left so that it would pass around both hills. That was probably to limit their exposure. It meant that the oncoming forces would circumvent both hills and come on the camp a little bit to the side of their previous path.

Coincidentally, the forces inside the camp had dispatched one of their number to go to the same hill. That was going to put forces from all three groups in the same place at about the same time. It would be interesting to see if everyone could avoid contact with everyone else.

Corporal Boske made an announcement over the general marine frequency. "It looks like we're about to make contact with the larger group. Everyone on the hills, keep your heads down and avoid being spotted for as long as you can. If we can hold out until the main force rounds the hill and engages the group at the camp, we might be able to keep ourselves hidden.

"Snipers, be ready to cover the colonel. If it looks like she's in danger of being attacked by the people around her, those two guards behind her are your primary responsibility. If the woman she's standing next to decides to make a move, I have no doubt the colonel can handle herself. Your job is to make sure that no one sticks a sword through the boss when she's not looking. Weapons free at your discretion."

With that, Boske closed the channel and turned to Julia. "This is where we get down to brass tacks, Highness. Once that larger force engages—which I have no doubt at this point that they're going to do—it's going to be our job to take them down a notch or two. Once we go rushing into their center, our people on the hills will pin them against the camp. That should leave only one direction for the larger force to escape.

"You're pretty fast with that Raider armor, so when we start moving, I want you to dash around the hills and be ready on their other flank. It's going to be your job to plug that last exit point. If they try to run, that's going to be the direction they go.

"Stun anybody that comes your way, no matter which side they're supposedly on. Under circumstances like these, it's best we figure out who's a friend and who's not when the shooting is over. Any questions?"

Even though her stomach was roiling, Julia nodded, slapped her helmet into place, and locked it down. "I'm ready."

And ready or not, she'd be acting in just a few minutes because there was no backing out now. It was showtime.

* * *

JARED WAS CONSIDERING the impending fight at the crash site when a soft beep through his implants preceded a change on the virtual display. Actually, *changed* was the wrong word. It had expanded its perspective and now showed him a much larger area, including another set of scarlet dots that were crossing the map.

These were beyond the outer edge of the drone's range, which momentarily confused him. A closer inspection revealed that it wasn't the drones at the original campsite at all. These readings were coming from the drones accompanying the second half of the ready response team.

A swarm of additional red dots had entered the map behind the marines, who were sprinting toward Kelsey's position. He watched as the new arrivals seemingly turned in place and began racing away from the marines, heading directly toward the building where Jared and his people were hiding.

Cursing under his breath, Jared opened a link to Talbot and Roche. "We've got trouble. It looks like another force has found our trail and is trying to backtrack us. Based on how fast they're moving, I think they're probably on horses, which means that the ready response team isn't going to be able to help us."

Even before Talbot responded, Commander Roche raced up to the virtual table and stared down at it, his expression worried. "It looks like this force is almost as large as the one that's attacking the camp. How do these people have so many troops ready to fight?"

"Whatever the answer is to that, it won't be good," Jared assured him.

Talbot came on the channel. "I'm taking a look through the

drones now. They're on horseback, and they look a lot like the other big group. While I'm only guessing, I think that the two sets are probably part of the same organization, based on the style and details of their armor.

"The ready response team can back us up, but they're going to arrive after these people have a chance to attack. Even moving at full speed, I think it's going to probably take them twenty or thirty minutes past the arrival of the new people to get back, if we order them to turn around right now. They're almost directly between the camp and us. Bad luck, that, though if they'd been a little faster, we wouldn't even have any warning that these guys were coming."

"Princess Kelsey and the others have half the ready team already," Roche said. "We should bring the second half back to help us."

"I think you're right, Commander," Talbot said. "If the force they have isn't enough to stop the group at the camp, then we're not going to stand a chance if a group of similar size attacks us. We're short on rifles, even though most of the marines have pistols. We're also short on ammunition. We could really use the extra support."

Jared thought furiously, comparing the benefits of sending the marines on to help his sister versus bringing them back to protect the Fleet crewmen, scientists, and other marines.

It wasn't really a hard choice, though it made his stomach churn a little bit when he realized that there was only one viable option. He was going to have to bring them back because his force wasn't nearly as able to defend itself as Kelsey's.

"Have them turn around," he ordered. "We'll have to hope that we can take care of our problem before the ready response team arrives, but they should be able to settle things if we haven't."

"Order sent. Should I notify Kelsey that her reinforcements aren't coming? Or should I just tell Corporal Boske and have her keep that information to herself for now?"

That was a no-brainer as well. "She's focused on the negotiations. She doesn't need to be distracted by what we're doing. It's probably better if she doesn't know that we're under attack, so that she can focus on her own issues.

"Tell Boske to make sure that the information gets to her as soon as the fighting there is settled. It shouldn't take her and her marines long to repulse the initial attack and have some breathing room where she can pass on what's happening here."

Jared looked around the basement. There were two stairwells leading up to the main level, such as it was. Other than those and the ramp, there were no other ways in or out of the large basement.

"How are we going to handle this, Talbot?" he asked. "Are we going to keep our people inside the building, or are we going to move them outside and form a perimeter?"

Talbot chuckled darkly. "Kelsey made me watch a bunch of prespaceflight vids that involved mounted forces attacking stationary groups of people. They'll have a level of mobility that we can't match. If we put our people outside, they're going to hit us from every side.

"As things sit, the building is secure. I've got marines stationed at ground level, and they can shoot through the windows at the people racing around the building. The only access they're going to have directly to where we're hiding is through the ramp. I have marines there to hold the line and keep them out.

"If all the enemy has is primitive weapons, our unpowered armor is probably going to be enough. We'll likely take some casualties, but we'll win. If they have any hidden surprises, things could get ugly fast.

"Our best option is to hold them off as best we can until the ready response team gets back. I can handle the tactical details, but you're going to have to figure out what strategy you'd like me to implement. I'd recommend talking first and shooting second."

It wasn't as if Jared had a lot of options to choose from. "Set up the defensive perimeter like you said. I'll try to talk to them. If they start shooting, we're going to shoot back. I don't want to start a fight, but if they do, we'll end it."

"No dice," the marine officer said. "If they shoot the messenger, we can't afford to lose you, Admiral. I'll do the talking."

Jared's initial impulse was to argue, but he knew that Talbot was right. The marine officer could talk if the strangers were willing to negotiate. If all they wanted to do was fight, Talbot could handle that, too.

He really hoped they could deal with the people coming at them because he didn't want to distract Kelsey at this critical moment. She had enough on her plate as it was. She didn't need to be worrying about the rest of them. That, after all, was his job.

Well, if everything went to hell, at least he'd keep these new people from racing in to attack his sister while she was already engaged. Even the marines in powered armor she had with her might not be enough to save her if that happened.

Now he had to hope that he could pull this off without losing any of his people to the Terrans he'd hoped to save.

10

_____

Kelsey stood beside the warrior woman, trying not to let her impatience show. Beauchamp was waiting for word from the scout she'd sent out. As soon as the man arrived on the target hill, he was going to discover that the large force had circled around and was coming in from their left.

The larger force was also sending scouts onto the hills, so it was entirely possible that the man wouldn't report back at all. She didn't think the marines who were on the hill would allow that to happen, but it really depended on the situation. They'd keep to their concealment, but if the scout groups came face-to-face, she suspected that they'd stun everybody and wait to sort it out later.

And that was as it should be. The fewer deaths they had in this confrontation, the better the chances she could play friendly with both groups. Just because they were at odds with one another didn't necessarily mean that her people needed to be taking sides. If that didn't work out, she still hoped to have enough time to make an informed decision about who her allies would be.

A few minutes later, even as the main group was just about to come into view of the camp, the scout on the hill signaled. He was using a mirror to reflect the sunlight and reporting in via some kind of code.

It wasn't Morse, but Kelsey thought it was very similar. Maybe some type of encrypted form of code that could pass information in a similar manner. If each set of flashes represented a very limited set of words, then it was likely that they could pass messages quickly.

She vaguely remembered that the wet navies of prespaceflight Terra had done something similar. Ships would use lights to signal one another when radio transmissions wouldn't be advisable. They had short code groups that could transmit specific meanings from a limited playbook of options. Perhaps that's what this was.

She recorded everything and would study it when the space and time to do so presented itself. If nothing else, it would give Carl and the scientists something to argue about while they marched.

The larger force was roughly sixty seconds away from being visible at the camp when Beauchamp got confirmation of everything Kelsey had said. She could tell that's what had happened because the other woman began cursing in a low monotone.

She turned to Kelsey and glared at her as if this was somehow her fault. "It seems that you weren't lying after all. My scout has confirmed the rough numbers you gave and said that they are coming in from our left.

"As you indicated, they outnumber us three to one. With them this close, it's unlikely that we're going to be able to escape an engagement. While our horses are rested, they're right on top of us."

The woman smacked a fist against her armored thigh. "Dammit. I'd hoped to avoid meeting them at all. My warriors are good, but they're not good enough to win a fight at these odds."

"If I was convinced that we could be allies, I'd be willing to lend you a hand," Kelsey said quietly. "My people can tilt the balance in your favor. I just need you to be honest with me. Who are you people, and what are you doing here?"

The other woman chuckled sourly. "We don't exactly have time for that sort of thing, but I've already told you my name. We came to salvage what technology we could. We gather what we can from the ruined megacities, but the residents there always force us back out. We thought we could pick up something useful without having to fight for it this time.

"One of our enemies controls this area. We call them the horde. They're vehement foes of my people. They blame us for what happened to Terra, and I suppose when it comes right down to it, they're not exactly wrong."

Kelsey considered that. "Since we don't have much time left, what exactly did your people do to piss them off? How could you possibly be responsible for what happened on Terra so long ago?"

The other woman smiled grimly. "My ancestors were part of the general resistance against the System Lords here on Terra. Over the years, decades, and centuries, they increased the level of guerrilla warfare to the point to where the System Lords eventually had enough. They bombarded many of the cities and killed this world in everything except name about a century ago.

"The horde and other groups like them loathe and fear us because they consider us responsible for the deaths of so many people. I don't believe they cared for the System Lords any more than we did back then, but they chose to live as pampered prisoners rather than fight for their freedom. Now we're all the same, living in conditions that would have likely horrified our ancestors."

The woman made a gesture toward the pinnaces and the tents. "Our goals have not changed. We still hope to defeat the AIs, and we had hoped to recover useful military equipment, but that's not going to happen now."

Kelsey allowed her smile to widen. "I think that's something we can work with. At this point, we need to have a chance to sit down and talk this through. That's not going to happen with the horde trying to kill all of us."

The woman gave her a grim look. "You need to be warned. The horde has access to advanced weaponry. They won't tolerate an intrusion by what they consider forces of the AIs. They'll see you and your people as that, in case I wasn't clear enough.

"There have been incursions in the past, including people in incredibly powerful armor. The horde has weapons capable of killing them. I don't know whether they brought any of those with them or not, but if you're counting on technology protecting you from them, I suggest you disabuse yourself of that notion."

Momentarily horrified, Kelsey sent a quick message to Boske. *Corporal, the locals say the attacking group may have access to antiarmor weapons. I don't know what kind, or if they have any with them, but if they do, your people are in danger.*

Don't take any chances. Put them down as fast and hard as you possibly can and stay under cover if you can't. Do what you have to do to protect your people, and I'll see what I can do to get our potential allies clear of the firing zone.

Copy that, Boske said. *The enemy is just about to you. Good luck, Colonel.*

At that moment, a wide line of men on horseback crossed over a low rise and looked down on the camp. There were an awful lot of them. Ninety didn't sound like a large number, but seeing them arrayed like this made her heart quiver.

She'd expected them to talk, but one man in the middle of the line raised his spear and shouted something unintelligible. The rest of the men raised their own spears and shouted in return, then all of them charged forward, their spears lowered as they thundered toward the camp.

The attack was on.

* * *

TALBOT ALREADY HAD his people scattered around upstairs and on the ramp leading down to the basement, so it took no time at all to have them ready to defend the building. He watched the forces headed their way over the feed from the drones around the ready response team. The riders vanished briefly as they left the area under observation and then reappeared on the drone network surrounding the building a short while later.

Like the first group, the video feed showed that these were warriors mounted on horses. Men and women in armor, with primitive weapons, riding single mounts. No remounts with them at all, so they seemed to have only one task in mind: to fight.

It took a few minutes to have the drones zoom in as much as possible without revealing themselves, and he examined the riders carefully. All of them wore leather armor with strips of metal attached to critical locations. They had hard faces, determined expressions, and their weapons looked well used. These were people that knew how to fight and considered it their business.

At the speed they were traveling, it only took them fifteen minutes to arrive in the vicinity of the building. They circled around it and passed on the other side, staying outside of easy bow shot, he would imagine. From their expressions, they were looking to see if the trail continued past the building.

They stopped perhaps five hundred meters away from the building and had a brief consultation before the group split into four parts. Each went around the building to cover a different cardinal compass point.

A minute later, one of the men wrapped a white cloth around the end of his spear, raised it high, and rode toward the building. He halted perhaps seventy-five meters away from the ramp. From his expression, he was content to wait there for someone to come to him.

Talbot walked up the ramp and started out toward the man on the horse. He was in his armor, of course, but had his helmet nestled in the crook of his arm.

His appearance caused the man to react. He must've pulled back slightly on his reins, because his horse danced a little bit.

The man's expression, which Talbot could clearly see with his ocular augmentation, went from passive to grim. He eyed Talbot for one long moment and then, without saying a single word, turned and rode back toward the group that he'd come from.

That wasn't good.

Talbot watched the man remove the cloth from his spear and put it into one of his saddlebags as he was having words with others in the group. There was lots of gesticulating and some elevated voices that were *almost* loud enough for him to understand.

After a few seconds of that, the group turned to stare at Talbot. Their expressions were just as grim as the man's had been. Since they didn't know him, it almost had to be the powered armor. He wasn't sure how that could make such a stark difference in their reaction, but these people had been suppressed by the System Lords.

Perhaps Rebel Empire marines had landed on Terra at some point. Perhaps even recently. Maybe they'd been involved in the fighting and these people had a long memory. If so, Talbot and his people were in for a fight, because these people didn't look like they were in a mood to negotiate anymore.

A single rider left the group and raced around the building. He stopped at each of the other groups and spoke for just a few moments before racing on to the next. A couple of minutes later, he'd returned to his original group, which then began spreading out in what was obviously an attack formation. They were going to make a run at the building.

Talbot didn't know how well the windows of the building would stand up to arrows, but they'd resisted the elements thus far. Only a few of them had shattered. His people would break as many as was required to defend themselves, but the people on the horses were going to be moving fast.

If he was any judge of how the battle would play out, they'd race in circles around the building, using their mobility to stay at a distance while they fired arrows toward his people inside the building. Since they knew the ramp was the most likely entrance, that would undoubtedly be their main target for breaching the defenses.

Talbot backed up to the ramp, clapped his helmet on, and opened a general channel. "All marines, be prepared to repel an assault. They're going to force an entry above ground, if they can't get in through the ramp. We have to hold them off until the ready response team gets back. Stick with stunners if they get close enough. Remember that horses are larger targets than people."

Kelsey wouldn't like that he'd targeted the animals, but she'd understand the tactical logic. She'd *still* tear a strip off him, but he had lives to protect.

He checked the drone feeds and decided that they had to keep the attackers occupied for between fifteen and twenty minutes to allow for the armored marines to return. This was going to be ugly, no doubt about that.

Talbot wished he could've talked the others out of an outright attack, but they hadn't to try. They'd chosen to fight, so the bleeding was on their heads.

He only hoped he and his marines could get this situation under control quickly, and that his wife was having a better time of it than he was.

_____

11

J ulia had only just made it behind the hills and was racing toward the other side of the pair when the larger group attacked. She could hear shouting as the invaders charged toward the camp.

That spurred her to run faster, which in turn caused her to trip over something and skid onto her face, before rolling over and stumbling back to her feet. She'd never practiced this kind of thing in armor, and she wasn't very graceful in the heavy suit, even with her artificial musculature. One more weakness.

The tenor of the budding battle changed almost immediately, and she knew that Corporal Boske and the others had revealed their presence and opened fire with their stunners. She couldn't see any of the blue bolts from where she was, but she wasn't sure that she would have anyway. At their wider aperture, the stunners didn't really fire bolts at all. More like fans of energy that only went a short distance before petering out into nothing.

As she was moving between the two hills, though still far away from the battle itself, she was able to jump up into the air and see over the rise enough to glimpse the mounted forces milling around in

chaos, firing their bows at the marines. If that was the best they could
do, the battle would be over fast.

She put on as much speed as she could and made it to the other
side of the second hill just in time to have two men on horseback race
over the rise directly for her. She pulled her stunner, raised it, and
fired at them. The blue beam was still set to narrow aperture and only
struck one of them a glancing blow. Or perhaps it missed him by a
very small margin. She couldn't tell.

Seemingly, whatever it was wasn't enough to knock him out. He
wavered in his saddle, but his trained reflexes seemed to pull him
down, where he held onto his horse while his compatriot raised his
spear and charged directly at her, screaming at the top of his lungs.

She tried to sweep the spear away before the man could strike her,
but the surprising speed of his horse threw off her timing. The spear
shattered against her armor, causing her no harm, but the horse
running into her with its shoulder sent her flying. She landed in a
heap, and the rider raced past her.

With a grunt, she rolled onto her stomach and fired her stunner at
the retreating horseman, striking him squarely in the back. He
spasmed and tumbled from the saddle.

She started to roll over onto her back and engage the remaining
rider, but he'd been a lot quicker closing the distance than she'd
thought possible and brought his horse's front hooves down directly
on her back before she could move.

The impact was blunted by her armor, but not stopped
completely. The incredible force of the blow drove the air from her
lungs, and she gasped. Apparently being pinned between a huge
animal and the ground was not the kind of place that even a Marine
Raider in powered armor wanted to be.

With an effort of will, she rolled away from the animal and raised
her hand to fire again, only to discover that she'd somehow lost her
stunner. She jumped to her feet and scanned around for it, but it was
lost somewhere in the tall grass. Just perfect.

The rider turned and tried to use his horse to ram her as he drew
his sword and struck at her. She thought the sword was less of a threat
than the horse, so she dodged to the side and exposed herself to the

strike. Her raised arm deflected the blade, snapping the length of steel in two when he struck.

That seemed very disconcerting to the rider, and he stared at his broken weapon in shock for a few seconds that he didn't really have to waste.

She took advantage of his lack of focus and dragged him out of the saddle. Once he hit the ground, she carefully metered her strength to strike him with the lightest worthwhile blow she could manage. It was sufficient to knock the air out of his lungs and made her confident enough to strike him in the face. That knocked him out. And broke his nose, which she hadn't intended to do.

Off to her left about seventy-five meters away, three more horsemen raced out of the fighting and headed toward the wider grasslands. A loud explosion on the other side of the hill announced that her doppelgänger's warning had been spot-on. Some of these bastards had heavy weapons.

She turned her enhanced ocular implants up to maximum and looked around until she spotted her stunner lying in the grass by the output of its power pack in the ultraviolet range. It wasn't very bright, but it was distinctive at this short distance.

Julia snatched it up and considered how best to chase after these people. She could run faster than a normal person, but they were on horses. She wasn't that fast.

With a sigh she decided she was going to have to do this the hard way. She raced over to the horse standing near its fallen rider and vaulted up into his saddle—it was *definitely* a male—with more grace than she'd actually expected to have. Perhaps all of those riding lessons were finally paying off.

She'd never have been able to do such a thing without her augmentation, but she'd always been comfortable around horses. Such gentle creatures that always seemed to be such a pleasure to ride.

That experience was not replicated when she landed on *this* horse. She was able to quickly grab the saddle horn and stuff her feet into the stirrups, but the horse immediately spun in place and tried to bite her leg. Of course, her armored thigh was invulnerable to his teeth, but he didn't seem to care as he kept trying.

Julia grabbed the reins and pulled his head around. "Calm down, boy. I'm your rider now."

She wasn't certain whether or not he was going to pay attention to what she'd said. He was a trained warhorse, and he was probably bound in some way to the rider she'd taken out, so it was entirely possible that she was wasting her time.

To her shock and pleasure, he responded to the reins, and she quickly had him off in hot pursuit of the fleeing riders. Her armor was heavy, but she wasn't a large woman. She figured that even with her Raider armor, she probably weighed less than the man who'd been on the horse before.

With more assertiveness than she actually felt, she put her heels to the beast, and he responded by surging forward. Her experience with riding horses had been limited to a more sedate pace, and over even terrain. Here, she was racing at breakneck speed over grasslands that could conceal holes or irregularities that might send the horse and herself tumbling.

She'd probably survive that kind of thing, but the horse would be gravely injured or killed. She really didn't want that to happen, but she *had* to catch up with those warriors. If they spread the alarm, everyone might be screwed.

The warriors ahead of her were aware that she was coming. At least one of them had glanced over his shoulder and spotted her, shouting a warning to his fellows as she closed. She hoped they'd turn and fight, because that would've made her job a lot easier. As it was, they really couldn't hurt her, whereas, if she could get them into range, she'd stop them.

Unfortunately, it seemed that they were onto that particular trick and kept racing away as fast as they could. To her benefit, they didn't split up.

After a minute of hot pursuit, she was finally getting into the range where she might actually be able to start picking them off with her stunner. They stayed glued to their horses, obviously trying to keep her from getting a decent shot.

She could shoot the horses, but the idea nauseated her. She had no desire to injure an innocent animal. If she could do this *any* other way, she'd avoid shooting them.

The riders ahead of her crested a small rise and disappeared momentarily from view. When she raced over the top of it herself, she found that they'd set a trap for her.

Two of the riders were still racing away at full speed, but one of them had dismounted and pulled some kind of object from his saddlebags. She didn't really know much about weapons, but it was obviously a high-tech weapon, even if it looked cobbled together.

She was sure that her implants could tell her more about it, but she had no time to check them. The man was already kneeling on the ground, with his horse lying in front of him. The bastard was using it for cover as he fired at her.

There was a flash of light as something raced out of the tube and directly toward her. It was as bright as a star.

Julia did the only thing she could. She urged her horse to swerve as she launched herself into the air, using her legs to push off the horse and hoping she managed to pull her feet out of the stirrups.

She prayed that that would give her enough distance to avoid being struck by whatever that was, because the person who'd fired it seemed pretty confident that it would kill her.

The force of her jump was just enough to get her to clear the warhead. Even as her body arched, she saw it fly under her, missing her legs by no more than a handful of centimeters. Thankfully, it missed her horse, too. A detonation at this range might have killed her along with the beast.

It struck the rise that she'd just come over and exploded. The shockwave grabbed her out of the air and slammed her into the ground with more force than she dreamed possible in a nonlethal event.

For such a small device, it made a *huge* crater. If it had struck her, the weapon would've blown her armor apart and killed her instantly.

Julia figured all that out as she was tumbling to a stop. She'd lost her stunner again, but no longer cared. That son of a bitch had tried to kill her, so she was going to kill him back. She leapt to her feet.

Or rather, she *tried* to leap to her feet. What happened instead was that she staggered drunkenly upright, her sense of balance totally ruined by what had just happened.

The man who'd tried to kill her was busy reloading, and she realized that she had to stop him before he finished, or she'd be dead. With her body not functioning correctly, that really left her with only one choice. She hated having to do it. Hated, hated, *hated* it. But she did it anyway.

She activated the combat controller built into her implants and ceded her body to the machine in her head. It was like a switch had been thrown because her own personal balance issues no longer seemed to matter as the computer compensated for them and made things happen. Things she no longer had any control over.

Unfortunately for the warrior, the merciless computer in her head had no overriding desire to take him alive. Her hand darted down to where her flechette pistol was holstered, drew it cleanly, and fired a short burst right through the center of his chest.

His reinforced leather armor was worse than useless against this kind of attack. Not only did the flechettes penetrate the boiled hide, they blew chunks off of the protective metal, which then also plunged into his vulnerable flesh. He fell back, dropping the weapon he'd been trying to reload, dead before he hit the ground.

The computer turned her now merciless eyes toward the fleeing horsemen and immediately determined that she wasn't going to be able to catch up with them. They were outside her weapon's range, and by the time she gathered her horse and pursued, they'd be able to elude her. They had gotten away.

That wasn't what she'd wanted, but it wasn't exactly like she'd had a choice. They'd ambushed her with a weapon she really hadn't expected, even after hearing the explosion back at the main fight.

She deactivated the combat controller and shuddered in relief as she regained control of her body. Trembling, she found her horse, mounted him, and raced back toward the camp. She had to get there as quickly as possible. Every second counted now.

12

J ared made his way up one of the stairs and stood watching as the marines looked out through the windows on the ground level. He knew that he probably shouldn't be there, but as soon as Talbot had gone outside, he'd been unable to resist the urge to see what was happening for himself.

He probably should've worn his powered armor, even though he couldn't use it very well, but doing so would've put the people below into an even worse state of terror. If a commander showed fear—even though armoring up wasn't based on fear in the middle of a battle—then they'd be a lot more inclined to panic. He had to exude confidence.

The above-ground part of the building wasn't all that large when compared to the underground area that held all the farming machinery. Based on the debris left behind on this level—the remains of dividers between small cubicles, desks, and ruined computer equipment—he suspected that this had been the office area overseeing the vast agricultural network the machines below had once served.

The marines had moved everything they could over to the exterior walls, figuring that almost anything would be useful in stopping arrows. They'd strategically broken out some of the windows, or used some that had already been broken, based on the staining on the floors. The glass had to be pretty tough to have survived this long, so he wondered what they'd broken the panes with.

The marines had chosen to split their forces into four equal groups and cover each of the outside walls. The center of the building contained offices that were closed off from the rest of the large room, probably for management. Not a very good way to provide leadership, but they hadn't consulted him.

The marines didn't have enough people to cover every angle the enemy would come from, so they'd supplemented their numbers with any Fleet personnel that had training in the use of firearms. Even so, he wasn't certain they had enough weapons to go around.

Since some of the marines had had both rifles and pistols, they'd probably passed the pistols to the Fleet personnel, possibly their stunners, too. Ammunition and powerpacks were going to be a problem very soon. Based on what Talbot had told him, they really didn't have enough to be shooting indiscriminately.

They'd win this fight, of that he had no doubt, but this was only the first five kilometers of a fifteen-hundred-kilometer journey, during which they'd undoubtedly meet additional enemies.

They had to live as if the supplies they had now were all they were going to get. If they could salvage something along the way, that would be wonderful. If they couldn't, then pretty soon they'd be fighting with rocks.

He made his way over to Senior Lieutenant Chloe Laird. "Give me an update."

Laird turned to face him, her red hair damp with sweat. With no environmental controls, the building was already warming as the sun rose outside. It was also terribly humid inside the abandoned structure.

"It's not looking good, sir," she said. "They probably outnumber us three to one, if we're only counting fighting personnel. On the plus side, they're going to have to come at us through a fairly limited number of entrances. We should be able to use our rifles and pistols to good effect.

"If they come too close or lump up, we've got a few plasma

grenades that will ruin somebody's day. We've also got a number of stunners we passed out to the Fleet personnel backing us up. They're going to start shooting first and hopefully take down a number of the attackers as they are closing in. We'll only resort to lethal force if we have no choice.

"Senior Sergeant Coulter has the other side of the building covered, and I'm keeping an eye on this side. Between the two of us, we've got a handle on things. You should go back down before the shooing starts, sir."

He ignored her pointed advice. "How easily are the arrows going to be able to penetrate the glass?"

The marine officer shrugged slightly. "The glass is tough, but a sharp strike from an arrow will probably crack a pane. A few hits like that and they'll come down. They're made to be strong against the elements, not against direct physical assault.

"I'd say that after a couple of minutes, we won't have glass in any of these frames. We've piled up a bunch of office furniture to use as cover, and that should work well enough against what they can throw at us.

"The problem is going to be when they get inside the building. They've got swords, and all we'll have are our marine knives. Admittedly, what we've got is a *lot* sharper, but they've got reach on us. Unpowered armor might save lives in some cases, but they've got to be well trained to work around armor with their weapons. If they get inside our guard, they're going to kill a whole bunch of people."

Her tone indicated the toll might include headstrong flag officers, but she politely left that as an implication rather than stating it out loud.

"Then we'll just have to make sure they don't get inside," he said grimly.

A loud series of shouts went up outside, and Jared turned his attention to look at what was going on in the early light. There were a lot of people racing around the building on horses at this point, so it looked as if the attack was underway.

"You'd best get back downstairs, sir," Laird said firmly. "The party is about to start."

Jared opened his mouth to decline, but a massive explosion on the other side of the building tossed him into Laird, sending both of them tumbling into the makeshift barricade beside them. The blast was powerful, so it took him a moment to blink himself back into focus and roll off the marine officer who was even then surging back to her feet.

"All marines, open fire," Coulter shouted from the other side of the building. "Aim for people with heavy weapons if you can spot them."

Jared could see at least half a dozen marines down near the blast site, though some were moving. The Fleet personnel that had been backing them up were in much worse shape. They hadn't been in body armor, and the blast had torn through them. He knew there had to be fatalities.

"Reinforce the area they just hit, Lieutenant," Jared said over his ringing ears. "If they try to push through there, they'll be able to get into the building."

"Don't teach your grandmother to suck eggs, sir," she said as she moved to direct her marines. "I'm already on it."

Marines from the other positions rushed to the area that had been struck and began firing out the windows at the riders. Jared didn't think it was going to do them any good because at the speed the horsemen were moving, the person with the heavy weapon was probably long gone. In fact, he was almost certainly going to strike from a different side of the building next.

Even though it was a stupid idea—and he knew it—Jared edged his way up to the glass and stared outside, looking for anyone carrying one of those weapons. Several arrows struck the glass in front of him, splintering the clear material until it fell away in a shower of small fragments. He shielded his face and eyes as the shards fell, but still managed to get some cuts that were going to sting later.

Once he could see again, he refocused his attention outside. All he saw was a bunch of screaming and shouting horsemen with bows. Then he saw one that had something that was different. A tube of some kind that he was aiming toward the building somewhere off to Jared's right.

"Incoming!" he shouted as he covered his ears with his hands.

An unbearably bright spark of light shot from the weapon and lanced into the building, hitting the corner off to Jared's right in another massive explosion. This not only killed or wounded more of his people, but it damaged the structural integrity of the building itself, and the roof came down in that corner.

Coughing from the dust that had washed over him, Jared crawled to the person nearest him. It was an enlisted Fleet crewman. A length of metal had gone all the way through her chest. She gasped twice, her hand twitching toward the debris that had impaled her, and then lay unmoving, her eyes focused on infinity.

Burning with anger, Jared crawled past her and found a marine with a similar shard of metal through his shoulder. It had pinned him to the barricade that they'd been using, and he was struggling to pull free.

"Stay still until someone can help you," Jared said calmly. "If you pull the metal out, you might bleed to death. Just leave it right where it is."

Jared reached down and grabbed the man's rifle. He then shrugged apologetically as he took the reloads from the man's belt. He looked for a place that he could shoot from while still being out of view of the attackers.

Once he was in place, he lined up on the first horseman that he saw and pulled the trigger. The flechette missed the man, flying somewhere behind him, Jared imagined. He was going to have to figure out how much to lead them.

He jinked the rifle to the left and fired again, this time achieving some success as the man wobbled sideways in his saddle but kept going.

Jared started looking for anyone with those strange weapons. They had to be his primary target. A few more hits like the last two would bring the entire building down on their heads, and that would be the death of them.

* * *

WITH EVERYONE'S attention focused on the charging horde, Kelsey stepped back to the man holding her weapons. "I think I'd best take those," she said, holding her hand out.

The man seemed to consider her words for a long moment before handing her weapons belt back to her.

She quickly strapped her pistols on before reaching for her sword harness. That was also quickly returned.

Now fully armed, Kelsey turned her attention to the battlefield and saw a wild melee. The force of horsemen had charged toward the camp where the defenders had drawn up to receive them, but halfway there, several armored marines had come out of hiding almost in the middle of them and began using stunners to take down riders and animals alike.

Set to wide beam, a stunner's range was short, but it could take out a number of targets for long enough to be quite useful in a battle like this. Unfortunately, at the speed the horsemen were traveling, there were going to be serious injuries and fatalities when they fell.

Just as the charge was breaking around the marines, an additional four marines charged down from the hills at the rear of the horde. It would be a minute before they'd be in range to use their stunners, but just the sight of them charging roiled the attacking forces, giving the local defenders an opportunity to push forward and engage on a more equal basis.

With a good portion of the enemy focusing on the marines, Beauchamp and her forces were able to decisively engage the troops directly to their front, and the melee was on. The people on horseback had spears and what amounted to cavalry sabers to strike down from their height at the people on the ground.

Kelsey had seen that sort of thing in a number of old Terran vids. The people on the ground had similar weapons and the reach to strike up as well. What surprised Kelsey the most was the fact that they seemed disinclined to strike at the horses.

Someone off to the side was taking single shots with a stunner on tight beam. It must've been one of the snipers that Corporal Boske had set out. With the way the marines were arranged, there was only one viable route to retreat, and Kelsey wondered how long it would be before the horde took it.

Or would they just choose to fight? If they had some of those antiarmor weapons, they might decide to push on. That was Kelsey's main concern and one of the reasons that she'd wanted to take the enemy down as quickly as possible.

With that in mind, she drew her stunner and one of her swords before racing into the fray. She picked a direction full of enemies and triggered her weapon on wide beam. Half a dozen men and horses dropped where they were.

Almost immediately, one of the horsemen tried to shoulder her aside with his horse as he sliced down with his saber. Kelsey raised her blade to deflect his, knocking it to the side and also severing the enemy blade completely. She fired the stunner and took him and his horse out before seeing what else the field had to offer her.

This was what they'd once called a "target rich environment." There were enemies *everywhere*. Thankfully, they were more worried about the armored marines than they were about Kelsey or the people in the camp, which was going to cost them.

While that might be safer for her, she quickly discovered that it wasn't safe for the marines. Out of the corner of her eye, she caught someone wielding a weapon that she wasn't familiar with.

One of the horsemen had pulled some kind of tube out of his saddlebags and was aiming it off the left. A glance indicated one of the armored marines was the target.

Kelsey immediately raced toward the man, knowing what was coming and doing everything she could to get to him before he fired. *Incoming heavy weapon!* She sent over her internal com, praying that the marine would dodge.

Even as she gave the warning, Kelsey flipped the focus on her stunner to narrow beam and fired, but the man's horse moved at the wrong moment, moving the warrior just enough for her to miss him.

A bright spark flew from the tube and struck the marine, who was already dodging. A massive explosion marked the spot, and pieces of armor and flesh rained down in a wide circle.

Anguish filled Kelsey for just a moment, before rage pushed it out.

The rider turned just in time to see Kelsey as she launched herself into the air at him at a dead run, her sword slashing down at his head.

He raised his tubed weapon to deflect her blow, but the edge of her blade sliced through it and him, sending his body tumbling from the saddle in pieces.

All marines, they have antiarmor weapons, she said into her implant com. As if they didn't already know. *You are cleared and encouraged to use lethal force.*

Look out behind you, Highness! Boske shouted back.

Rather than look, Kelsey used her powerful leg muscles to spring to the side and spin in the air. A bright spark from another one of the antiarmor weapons flashed through the spot where she'd been just a moment before and struck one of the horsemen to her side right where his body met the animal he rode.

The massive explosion killed them both instantly and sent blood and bits of flesh over everyone close to the blast, including her. The blast smashed her out of the air, but she tagged her combat controller to get her back on her feet and attacking the riders closest to her. They'd all be blown out of their saddles and couldn't defend themselves. Too bad for them.

Once her body seemed to have shaken off the effects of the blast, she resumed direct control and waded back into the fight. She'd lost her stunner but didn't care. With blades in both hands, she became death incarnate, making even the hardened warriors she was fighting recoil from her.

Not that that would save them. Playtime was over.

13

Once the fighting had kicked off, Talbot hunkered down on the ramp with his marines and waited for the assault that he knew was coming. He suspected that he knew the enemy's plan, and he intended on giving them an ugly surprise when they tried it.

He expected them to try to distract him, and then have someone with one of the antiarmor weapons pop up over the lip of the ramp and fire down into the group of marines below. The door behind him was fairly heavy, but it wouldn't stand up to a significant explosion. If they breached the door, they'd be among the noncombatants before he could stop them.

That meant he had to be ready to act instantly. They couldn't have many of the damned things, and if he could take out the people wielding them, he'd be able to stop the attack cold.

The next few seconds proved his expectations dramatically wrong.

An above-ground explosion shook the building and sent clods of dirt raining down on him.

"Report," he said over the command channel, tensing and preparing for the attack he was sure was coming down the ramp.

"We just took a hit on one corner of the building," Chloe Laird said. "Unknown number of casualties. Coulter is handling that side."

"Find those bastards," Talbot said through clenched teeth. "Shoot any son of a bitch that looks like he has anything bigger than a bow and arrow. Hell, just start shooting all of them. At this point, they've initiated hostilities and we should just go ahead and clean house. The gloves are off. Weapons free and cleared for lethal force."

"Copy that."

Another explosion rocked the building, and Talbot cursed. At this rate, he wasn't going to be able to wait for the enemy. He was going to have to go out to them.

He almost started up the ramp but paused. Maybe that was part of their plan.

They'd seen him in armor and knew where he'd gone. They had to know how dangerous powered armor was, or they wouldn't be carrying weapons like that. What if the explosions were meant to draw him out?

Coming at the problem from that angle, the answer seemed obvious. They'd have somebody making a ruckus upstairs to bring him back up the ramp. That had to mean that there was someone out there waiting for him with one of those weapons. He'd probably just stopped himself from walking into an ambush.

So, if he wanted to get up top while keeping his skin intact, he needed to make certain that whoever was waiting for him wasn't going to be in a position to hurt him. To do that, he needed more intelligence about the layout of the enemy.

He tapped into the drone network and watched the enemy running around the building. There were a lot of them, and even though folks from upstairs had taken some down, their main force appeared to be intact.

The building itself was in worse shape. It looked like the two explosions had struck different corners of the building, and one of those had collapsed. That had to be bad for the marines and Fleet personnel inside. They'd come out of this with dead and injured friendlies, there was no getting around that.

He refocused his attention on the enemy. All of them were in motion except for one. That solitary dot was positioned inside the rough ring that marked where the enemy riders were circling.

The man had hidden himself behind a small rise in the ground—probably less than a third of a meter tall. He had a tube that just screamed antiarmor weapon aimed right toward the ramp. There was no sign of his horse.

With his newfound knowledge, Talbot had the drones scan the other riders, looking for any other antiarmor weapons. He found two more with the tubes. One was in the process of reloading his weapon with something from his saddlebags, while the other one was taking aim at the building as he rode around it.

His companions had moved clear of the area behind and in front of him to give him a clear shot. Moments later, a bright spark of light fired out of the tube and slammed into the building in an area that hadn't been struck by an explosive yet. More of the roof came down after the blast ripped the wall out.

The enemy riders hooted their approval and shook their bows in the air. That pissed Talbot off, and he decided it was time to end this farce once and for all.

He plucked one of the few plasma grenades they'd been able to recover from the pinnaces from his belt and pulled the pin. With the drones flying overhead, he knew *exactly* how far away the man in front of the ramp was. With a plasma grenade, all he needed to do was get close, and that little rise in the dirt wouldn't make any difference at all.

"Fire in the hole," he said over the general channel. "Duck and cover."

He cocked his arm back and engaged his combat computer. It double-checked his calculations, adjusted the angle of his throw and the strength he was going to use, and then lobbed the grenade out over the ramp for him. Through the drones, Talbot watched it arc cleanly through the air and land directly in front of the man, rolling to a stop almost underneath him.

The target attempted to scramble back. He might not have known what the grenade was, but he obviously thought it was bad news.

He was right.

The grenade went off in an unbearable burst of light that put dots into Talbot's vision, even down on the ramp with a helmet on. The shockwave struck the building, probably blowing out every window on this side of the structure. He hoped everyone had taken his warning seriously.

Another check of the drones revealed a fairly deep crater and no sign of the enemy or his weapon. They'd been atomized, along with a number of horsemen that were too close to the blast.

Even more were down, injured and screaming in pain. The wounded horses sounded like hurt kids, and that tore at his heart. The sound was going to torment his dreams for a while, but he hadn't had a choice.

"Chloe," Talbot said over the command channel. "The drones show two more bad guys with antiarmor weapons. I'll take out the first one as he comes around. I'm marking him as target A. Target B is your responsibility."

"Copy that."

Since he had complete drone coverage, Talbot wasn't worried that he'd lose the location and identity of the next man on his hit list. The building itself had shielded the horseman from the blast, and he was still coming around on his previous course, if a little more cautiously.

When the man cleared the building and raced into the area closest the ramp, Talbot ran up the incline and tore straight for him. The guy saw him coming and swung the antiarmor weapon around, but he was far too slow.

Before he'd even closed a portion of the distance, Talbot raised his rifle and fired a burst, cutting the man in half. He'd targeted well enough to miss the horse, so Kelsey would be pleased about that. That only left one threat to them now.

"Got him," Chloe said moments later. "He's down on the other side of the building, and our people have him covered. If anybody tries to go for the weapon, we'll take them out. If there are no more high-tech weapons, we should be able to turn this fight around."

Talbot sure as hell hoped so, because the butcher's bill was already going to be too high. Now that he'd seen these weapons in action, he was deathly afraid for his wife. He prayed to the gods that they'd watch over his impulsive woman and keep her from the fate that so many of his people here had just suffered.

* * *

KELSEY LAID into the attackers all around her, leaping as needed to come up to their level. After a few engagements, no one wanted to duel her. She was death on two feet.

The enemy forces didn't have any more of the antiarmor weapons. Without them, they had zero chance against her marines. In less than two minutes, they'd broken the will of the attacking force and sent them scattering.

With the marines using their stunners or lethal weaponry, not very many of the enemy had gotten away, but that didn't mean that everyone fighting them had been captured. The drones were able to tally each of the fleeing riders, so they knew that twenty-six of them had escaped.

When Julia arrived back at the camp, she'd passed word of the ones she'd taken out. Corporal Boske sent a couple of marines to retrieve them and tasked others with helping Beauchamp's forces gather the horses. They'd accumulated quite a few, which might be useful in the upcoming journey.

If, of course, the other woman didn't just take them. Kelsey and Beauchamp still had some things to figure out.

Most of the prisoners were unconscious and laid out in a long row. Others had been taken awake but wounded in one way or another. Those were shackled and seated in a rough circle, with armed guards around them. The last group were the dead, who were also laid out in a line.

Only the one marine had died in the fighting. His name had been Thomas Reed. Kelsey knew virtually nothing about the man, as he hadn't been part of *Athena*'s original complement.

As for the defenders, they'd had half a dozen killed and maybe twice that many wounded. Their leader still moved among them, assessing the damage and preparing her people to move.

While Kelsey watched the woman, Corporal Boske stepped up to her side, her helmet off and resting in the crook of her arm.

"There was nothing you could've done, Colonel," she said softly. "Even if we'd attacked them before they'd arrived at the camp, they'd have still pressed forward. These weren't the kind of people that just broke and ran."

Kelsey didn't know about that, but she wasn't going to argue with the woman. If there was one hard lesson that she'd learned over the last few years, it was that second-guessing yourself was a path that led to misery. You did the best you could with the information that you had at the time and dealt with the consequences. Which was what she needed to do now.

"We need to bury him," Kelsey said tiredly. "We're not going to be able to take him with us."

The other woman delicately cleared her throat. "Colonel, he was struck by high explosives that utterly destroyed him. It would take a long time to find all of the pieces, and that would be one of the grisliest jobs I could imagine. I found part of one boot with his big toe. That might be the largest part of him left in one piece.

"Perhaps that's sacrilegious of me, but I have no desire to dig through the dirt and find bits and pieces of a friend. Let him lie here where he died."

Kelsey grunted and nodded. "You're probably right. Have you kept Jared informed about what's happened?"

The other woman nodded. "Yes, but I haven't kept *you* informed of what was happening *there*. They're engaged with a similar size group right now. Our reinforcements turned around and are almost back to the building."

Kelsey spun on the corporal. "Why didn't you tell me as soon as we'd finished fighting? Get everyone gathered up. We move out in three minutes."

"Colonel, take a breath. By the time we get there, the fighting will be over. Your husband is *more* than capable of defending that building, and from what I've heard, he's taken steps to eliminate the antiarmor weapons. They took some casualties, but the fight has already swung in their favor.

"You have a job here that you need to finish. If we don't find allies, we're all going to die. We've offended this horde, and now we need to know what they're going to do about it. We need to find out if we're even going to be able to start the journey toward the Imperial Palace, or if we're going to be digging in somewhere for a last stand.

"Friends would help us a lot right about now, and we can't let this opportunity pass. You've made a connection with this woman. It's time for you to do what you do best: make friends."

Kelsey felt the corner of her mouth twitch up. "Is that what I do best? I thought it was breaking things and killing bad guys. They certainly seem to think so."

She gestured toward the prisoners, many of whom were staring at her with expressions of terror on their faces. She'd made a strong impression, it seemed.

The other woman seemed to consider her for a moment and then shrugged. "I've always considered that more of a hobby for you. Right now, your ability to make a connection with these people is what's going to get us out of the trap we're in.

"If there's a way to get to the Imperial Palace, to know what threats are between here and there, and come up with a plan to help us to dodge them, she and her people might be our best source of information about them."

Kelsey considered that for a long moment before nodding. She took a deep breath and looked over at where the others were gathering. The marines were still patrolling, but Julia had stepped over to, and was talking with, Clarice Beauchamp.

Interesting. Kelsey hadn't considered that possibility, and she wondered what the other woman was going to tell the warrior. Was Julia a better diplomat than she was? Now might be the time to find out.

"You're right, Corporal. Gather as many of the loose horses as you can. Since we did most of the heavy fighting, I'm going to press our claim to them. If Talbot can capture those around the building, we might have enough for everyone. That would cut our travel time down significantly.

"Meanwhile, I should probably head over and see what my doppelgänger is telling our new friends. We wouldn't want her to give away the farm, would we?"

14

J ared kept firing until the enemy finally broke and raced off in numerous directions, undoubtedly to regroup at a safe distance. He had no idea how many of the horsemen they'd killed or stunned, but he thought they might have gotten more than half.

They stayed on guard in case the enemy returned for another run at them, but after about ten minutes, Talbot told everyone to stand down.

Jared stood and shook the debris and dust off of himself. They hadn't had any more ceiling collapses, but a lot of the material had drifted down onto the combatants during the fighting.

He wanted to assist in pulling survivors from the rubble, or treating the moaning and screaming wounded, but he knew that he had to pay attention to the overall picture first. He'd find out what the butcher's bill was soon enough.

Commander Roche was waiting when he got downstairs. He'd been in charge of the non-combatants, even though he wasn't technically in their version of Fleet at all. Jared had made an exception for the grave circumstances they'd found themselves in.

He'd had Sean Meyer heading the armed Fleet personnel to defend the room if the enemy breached it.

"What's going on?" Roche asked quietly once he'd come down the stairs. "I can see from the drone network that the enemy has broken off, but did we win?"

"We survived," Jared replied as he found a brush on one of the walls and started getting the worst of the debris off of his marine fatigues. He'd just finished when Talbot came down the ramp with his helmet off.

The larger man headed directly over to him. "We've driven them off, Admiral, and the building is secure. Chloe is still working on rescuing the trapped personnel and tallying our casualties. We've got a number of injured that are going to start coming down fairly quickly. Commodore Stone is waiting to be receiving them."

The other man's eyes narrowed. "Is that dust all over you, sir? Were you upstairs?"

"Of course I was. I wasn't about to let them fight without me. I'm my sister's brother."

Talbot chuckled. "I suppose that I shouldn't have expected anything else. In any case, the fighting is wrapped up at the landing camp as well. We lost one marine there to one of the antiarmor weapons.

"I'll have Chloe gather our dead so that we can bury them. There are a lot of enemy bodies as well, so we'll create a separate grave for them. We've got a few prisoners, but not as many as you'd think. Apparently falling off of a horse racing at full speed doesn't do well for your chances of ultimate survival.

"What we do have is plenty of armor and weapons suitable for use under primitive conditions. A lot of bows and arrows, a lot of swords, some spears, and some leather armor that we can probably use for a number of our people.

"The marines have their unpowered armor, so they won't need that, but the Fleet personnel and scientists could probably do with a little bit of extra protection, when push comes to shove again."

"Are we going to interrogate the prisoners?" Roche asked. "Maybe they can tell us what we're up against. Maybe they can tell us why those people felt the need to kill us."

Jared nodded. That kind of information would be good to know. If they were going to have to fight people like this all the way to the Imperial Palace, they needed to have a better idea of what they'd done to offend them. Had it just been their presence? Or had it been something murkier?

"What about the horses?" Jared asked. "How many did we capture? Do any of us know how to ride them?"

The marine's eyes unfocused for a moment as he checked something through his implants. "It looks like we've captured roughly forty. We'll probably pick up a few more as we finish sweeping the area, but I'll bet we get no more than fifty. Kelsey's group also captured a number of horses, though it's uncertain whether they'll get to keep them or not. The other group might object.

"I'm hopeful that she can make a deal with them. At some point, the enemy is going to come looking for payback. They don't know exactly who we are, but they know where to find us. I'd imagine it's going to be a significant force with as many heavy weapons as they can gather. Since we won't have powered armor when they come back, we need to be gone without leaving an easy trail for them to follow."

"How do we do that?" Roche asked, throwing up his hands. "No matter what we do, we're going to leave a trail a kilometer wide. Even if we figure out how to ride the horses and take off for the forest, they'll still be able to follow our tracks right to us. Nothing we do is going to get us clear of their response."

Jared nodded. "There's something to what you're saying. We'd best hope that Kelsey can make friends with these new people. If they're already involved in a war with our new enemies, throwing in a few more people behind their protective walls isn't going to hurt them. We can probably trade equipment for our safety, if we can trust them."

He scratched his chin and looked up at the ceiling. "I want everybody ready to travel within the hour. Have Doctor Stone consult with me about who's too injured to move and what we can do to move them anyway. We can't leave anyone behind, so she's going to have to figure out how to make this work.

"Let's hope that Kelsey makes us some new friends. We really need a few right about now."

* * *

JULIA FOUND herself amused as Clarice Beauchamp studied her closely. The other woman was undoubtedly confused at how the woman she'd been speaking with earlier had suddenly gotten into armor. Or perhaps even why she'd bothered to do so after the fighting was already over.

"I'm not the woman you think I am," she said with a bland smile. "That's my twin sister."

While that wasn't *technically* true, giving the woman the impression that she and her doppelgänger were twins by birth rather than variants of one another from different dimensions was *a lot* easier than trying to explain the whole story to someone that she imagined either wouldn't believe her or didn't need to know the truth.

"Sisters?" the other woman said slowly. "I see. What's your name?"

"I'm Julia. Now that the fight is over, what are you going to do next?"

"We'll gather what equipment we can quickly salvage and then depart. We thank you for your intervention, but the horde will not allow this invasion to pass. If we're still within their reach by dusk tomorrow, they'll do their absolute best to kill every single one of us. They don't take intrusions to their territory lightly."

Julia gestured toward the tents. "Everything that we couldn't carry with us is in those. Take whatever you like. It's not something that we're going to be able to carry with us."

Though that was possibly inaccurate, if they got their hands on some horses. Other supplies were inside the pinnaces, so they could play this by ear if they got their hands on enough mounts.

She looked out at where the other group's people were busy capturing the loose horses. "As we shared in the fighting, I believe it's also customary that we share in the spoils. While we don't want any of the equipment, we would find it useful to have extra mounts. Do you have any objection to us taking the horses that were orphaned in the battle?"

The other woman seemed to consider that for a moment and then slowly nodded. "Horses are easy enough to come by. They roam free, and we can capture and train those we need or raise them in our own corrals. These are *warhorses*, however, and they may be somewhat dangerous for your people, particularly new riders. If I were you, I'd definitely wear at least leg armor before trying to ride them."

The other woman was undoubtedly referring to the more primitive armor that was being salvaged from the dead. Those that had been shot with modern weapons had most of their armor chewed up, but perhaps the leggings could be salvaged. Or it would be a case of mixing and matching to find what worked. In any case, that grisly task belonged to someone else.

She did some quick calculations. Based on the number of people they had back at the building, minus the casualties, and the number of horses that Colonel Talbot said that he'd recovered, added to what she was getting here, they still didn't have enough to give everyone a mount of their own. They did have enough to put two people per horse, with some left over for the experienced riders. That would have to do.

At that moment, Kelsey stepped up and joined the conversation. "Julia."

"Kelsey," she responded with a wry smile. "I've been talking with our new friend and arranging for us to take possession of whatever horses can be captured. We'll also take all the armor that we can salvage. In exchange, they can have everything in the tents."

"That sounds like a good deal," Kelsey agreed. "I'll also open up the pinnaces so that they can look inside and determine if there's anything they'd like to take with them. Though, we have some supplies there that we could carry on horses, so we get first pick of that.

"The horde will eventually manage to breach them. If there's anything that you feel worthy of salvage, Miss Beauchamp, it's yours. We'll never be using these craft again."

The other woman smiled slightly. "That's quite generous of you. I believe there are likely several things that we would like to salvage. We can carry them on our remounts as we retreat. And my rank is captain. These men and women are my company: Beauchamp's Bastards."

That was... quite the name.

Beauchamp then stared at the two women. "I find myself quite curious as to the story behind your arrival here. It saddens me that I'm not going to hear the end of it. Perhaps there is further business we can conduct."

Julia hadn't ever heard a better opening than that. The other woman obviously wanted to make a deal that might involve getting them to safety, and at this point, they certainly needed a place to go.

"As it happens, we're not going to be able to get away from the horde unless we have some local assistance. I suggest that we accompany you to a location that is convenient and safe."

"We've got other people about five kilometers from here," Kelsey interjected. "They'll be moving within the next hour. At least the ones that have horses.

"They were attacked as well and recovered about fifty horses. With the ones we have here, that should be enough for almost everyone to ride doubled up, but they won't know how to do so very well.

"Let me be clear. They won't know how to ride *at all*. Is it going to be possible for us to still get out of the horde's territory in time to keep them from catching us?"

Beauchamp nodded. "My people have an outpost a day's ride from here. My company was dispatched from there to salvage what we could from the crash. If your people are prepared to travel, and aren't too slow, we should be able to reach the walls of the outpost by dusk tomorrow. If it was just my people, we'd be able to make it much sooner, but that should be enough time for your people. Barely.

"The horde will know roughly where we're headed, but right now they don't know that we've thrashed their forces. They'll find out about the battles just before dark. They'll respond with every warrior they have close at hand. For such a large force, they're not going to want to travel while it's dark.

"They'll set out first thing in the morning, bringing remounts to pursue us with all the speed they can manage. It's going to be close, but I believe that we can make it to our outpost before they do. Once we get behind its walls, you'll be under our protection while we negotiate further agreements."

"And the horde isn't going to try to burn your city to the ground?" Julia asked.

"They're welcome to try," the other woman said grimly. "It has fixed emplacements of advanced weapons capable of killing any who come too close. If they could've destroyed that outpost before now, they would've already done so.

"This incident is going to anger them greatly, but I don't believe it will change the balance of power all that much. In fact, the loss of the warriors they've had today will blunt them to a degree. They'll still hate us, they'll still want to kill us, but they won't be able to do anything serious about it for now."

Kelsey raised an eyebrow and gave her a slight nod. "I can provide whatever you want quickly, but in exchange, I'd like some of your remounts. That trade-off will allow us to make better time and still let my people all ride. The building where they're at is almost directly back in the direction you came from, so we won't lose much time going for them."

Beauchamp considered that before slowly nodding. "I have some things that would make that agreement worthwhile. Let's gather everything we want and get ready to move out. We will await your riders and then return for the rest of your people. Let's not waste daylight."

15

Kelsey watched Julia as she gave lessons to the marines about how to ride horses. She shook her head at the sight of the otherwise competent marines falling off horses and tried not to smirk.

Her amusement temporarily satisfied, she turned her attention back to where Captain Beauchamp's people were quickly sorting through the equipment in the tents and deciding what they could take and what they'd have to leave behind for the horde.

They obviously wanted to take *everything*, but circumstances weren't going to allow that. The horde would be here sometime tomorrow. If they wanted something other than what they'd asked Kelsey to find for them from the pinnaces or the camp, they'd need to take it with them today.

She'd consulted with Talbot and Jared as soon as she'd been able to, and some of them were on their way to the camp even now. Once they arrived, they'd pack what they could and then head back for the rest.

With the horses, it would be possible to take their powered armor with them, though it would have to be packed away. That would be *extremely* helpful. Still, with all of the antiarmor weapons that the horde seemed to have, they were far from a panacea.

They'd have to be extremely careful about how they fought the locals because they didn't have that many marines and they were all her friends. She didn't want to lose a single one of them. They'd gotten lucky in their first fight. Damned lucky.

With their improved ability to carry supplies, she'd selected a lot of extra food from inside the pinnaces. The extra rations would drastically improve their ability to move quickly, at least for now. If they had to stop and hunt, enemies might catch them.

With horses, that equation changed. If they could parlay the other gear into more horses and some assistance, they might be able to get to the Imperial Palace in a couple of months rather than half a year.

Captain Beauchamp interrupted her introspection when she stepped up beside her. "My people have selected what we're going to take from the tents. We should be loaded in the next twenty minutes. Are you going to be ready?"

Kelsey nodded. "We've already gathered some extra food. We don't have those oversized cargo bags that you do, so we're doing the best we can to get it all loaded. It's nice to have more supplies, but it's a little unwieldy right now."

The other woman pursed her lips and nodded. "Traveling long distances can be challenging. It's all a balance between taking everything you need while not carrying too much. Larger saddlebags and using dedicated pack animals would improve your speed. Looking at your people, I'm not certain that you're going to notice much of a difference right now. Forgive me for saying so, but they are terrible riders."

Kelsey was forced to agree. "Thankfully, they're getting a good bit of education from my sister, and they'll manage to figure it out. None of them are stupid. They're going to be slow in the beginning, especially doubled up, but I believe that we can get them moving at a decent pace.

"If we can get your people to assist us in poking them to change behaviors that they shouldn't be doing, I think that will speed us up even more. Riding along and telling someone don't do that, do this, and showing them an example. Like I said, they're bright. They'll figure it out."

"Having spoken to both your sister and you, I have to say that you're an odd pair," the other woman said. "I've met twins before, and they often have relatively different personalities. I suppose it comes from wanting to make one's self different from someone that looks just like themselves.

"The two of you seem inseparably close. You use a lot of the same turns of phrase, your opinions on things are often very similar, and it's eerie how difficult it is to tell the difference between the two of you. Even with twins, one can usually tell which is which with a little time.

"With you two, I'm never certain. Each of you has peculiar quirks that I'm starting to pick up on, but you also have some that are identical. That's unusual."

Kelsey grinned. "Let's just say that we spent a lot of time together when we were younger, and our experiences only really diverged when we were adults. You'll find that Julia and I can be reliably the same in a lot of ways, and then you'll run into a landmine where our opinions are completely different."

"A landmine? As in bombs planted in the ground? Thankfully, I've never run into any of those, though I have read about some in the texts put together by our ancestors during the guerrilla wars."

Kelsey really wanted to ask more about that. That history hadn't been in any of the data banks, either for the Old Empire or even the Rebel Empire. The AIs had perpetuated the myth that Terra was still a civilized world, never allowing word that they'd bombed it a century or more ago to get out.

Learning how they'd fought the AIs and been successful enough that the computers had written them off would be fascinating. There were probably hundreds of tales of derring-do that she could use to distract the people making those idiotic vids about her on Pentagar. If she could get them interested in the siege of Terra, then she could have her life back.

"I'd really like to learn more about that," she said. "It sounds fascinating. Maybe once I have us ready to move out, we can talk more. With our people about to arrive, I need to get the last of the food packed so that it won't take too long to get everyone out of here."

"I'll leave you to it, then," the other woman said, shooting her an oddly casual salute with two fingers to her forehead before rejoining her people.

Kelsey took the next several minutes to make sure that the marines knew that they needed to wrap things up. She didn't want to delay their departure any longer than necessary. By the time they reached the outpost, every minute might count.

She'd heard about the aftermath of Jared's battle. The horde had managed to damage the building where they'd been hiding, killed six people, and wounded fourteen others. Thankfully, the wounds were within Lily Stone's capabilities, and everyone could still ride.

Talbot hadn't directly said so, but she suspected that Jared had been involved in the fighting, and part of her approved. Her brother was a little too restrained when it came to personal combat. Put him on the bridge of a warship and the man would fight like nobody's business, but slap a gun in his hands and he became reticent. A good commander needed to learn how to fight on the ground, in the air, and in space.

She didn't consider herself a leader in that mold, but she was working on it. He, on the other hand, was a genius when it came to fighting spaceships. If she could expand his capabilities with ground fighting, he'd be one of those people that could do anything up to and including commanding marines in action.

Her thoughts were interrupted when Corporal Boske stepped up. "We're done, Colonel. We've bagged everything we can, and the marines have stripped off their armor. Everything is packed away, and our people are ready to travel.

"Captain Beauchamp's people will help us guide the extra horses, since even once the rest of our people get here, we don't have the skills to make it work. They should be here in ten minutes, and we can move out.

"Do we have any idea how we're going to handle this on the way back to the building? Watching my people attempt to ride horses is a comedy of errors. I can only imagine what the Fleet personnel and scientists are going to look like. Can you imagine Carl Owlet trying to ride?"

Kelsey could, and the vision made her laugh. "We'll figure it out. Mount up. Let's join Beauchamp's Bastards and get the hell out of here as soon as Jared and the others get here."

16

Talbot struggled to stay in the saddle while simultaneously glaring at Carl, who rode easily beside him, moving as if he'd been riding horses for years. "How the hell do you know how to ride a horse? Better yet, how did you make friends with that mean bastard you're on?"

Carl gave him an insulted glance. "Buttercup isn't mean, he's just misunderstood."

"Buttercup?" Talbot asked incredulously, feeling his eyebrows rise toward his hairline. "I'm pretty sure that horse is a dude. And a major hardcase, based on the marine he almost stomped after he threw him. The bastard is vindictive."

"The name is kind of an inside joke," Carl said with a grin. "I'll wager Kelsey gets it right off. My mother sent me to a camp when I was a kid because I had difficulty socializing. It was a nice break from all of the tutoring and studying, so I didn't mind too much, even if it meant I had to deal with other people. The instructors said I had a real talent for riding, they taught me all the tricks they knew, and I soaked it up. Up until we went on the expedition, I still rode every chance that I got.

"As for Buttercup, he and I have come to an agreement. I'm not sure what kind of relationship he had with his previous rider, but I showed him who's boss. The trick is making sure that you're the master of the situation and that the horse can't smell your fear. Frankly, it's better not to be afraid at all."

He raised an eyebrow Talbot. "You're not afraid, are you, Talbot? You look kind of nervous to me."

Talbot scowled at the insult. The fact that it was somewhat true was just an added irritant. The big beast he was riding seemed determined to test him at every opportunity and had already tossed him off twice.

These horses had to be trained to obey commands, but only a few of them knew what did what. Worse, everyone was ham-handed with the reins, and that just seemed to make the beasts cranky. There was nothing like having a horse take off into a gallop when you least expected it, leaving you hanging on for dear life.

At least Carl had been able to help them. He'd gone from person to person, giving them what instruction he could to help them at least stay in the saddle. If they were going to make it back to the camp and then move out with the experienced riders, they were going to have to know at least a little about how to keep up.

Having most of them doubled up wasn't helping. Nothing to be done about it though. They only had so many horses, and they couldn't leave anyone behind.

From what Kelsey had said, the woman leading the force at the camp was going to task some of her people to help teach them what they needed to know, so that they could get to the outpost before the horde caught up with them.

Based on what he could see of their performance so far, his people were going to need all the help they could get.

No matter how this worked out, it was terrifying to think that they had to count on these unruly creatures to make it to safety. He wasn't sure that any amount of instruction was going to do them any good over the short term. They were lucky that no one had been injured falling off the horses. Yet.

He glanced over at where Doctor Stone was overseeing the wounded. All of them could ride, though none of them was one hundred percent. Grisham, the worst of the wounded, had his left arm bound tightly to his chest.

They'd selected what seemed to be the most pliable of the warhorses for the wounded and put someone solid behind them. That seemed to be working out so far, as the animals looked as if they were sensing their riders' injuries and going a little easy.

And, Carl had a few extra people to help show them the ropes. Elise and Olivia knew how to ride, though the warhorses were more than a bit challenging for even them.

Kelsey and Julia also knew how to ride, so technically they had five experienced riders, but that wasn't nearly enough for over a hundred people. He'd gratefully accepted the strangers' help getting them to the outpost because he didn't want to see any more of his people die.

Just having to bury the six that had already fallen burned his soul. Kelsey hadn't been able to do anything with the marine that had been killed at the camp. Some tasks were just too hard to do under these conditions.

If they survived, Talbot had sworn to see them properly interred at the Spire on Avalon. If any of them made it off this cursed world.

Even as he was thinking that, they came over a low rise and he saw the camp spread out below them. There was a beehive of activity still taking place, and he also noted the lines of dead and the captured prisoners still huddled together under guard.

None of the prisoners at the building had seemed inclined to speak, so they'd cut them loose, on foot, and with no weapons or armor. They'd undoubtedly rejoin their friends within a couple of days and that would mean they'd fight them again, but they couldn't exactly take the captives with them.

Kelsey must've noted their approach because she rode out to meet them. As she got closer, she angled over toward Talbot and soon matched his slow pace, grinning at him.

"So, how do you enjoying riding?" she asked cheerfully.

"Don't you start with me," he warned. "My ass is already hurting like a bitch."

"Don't worry about it," Carl said smugly. "By nightfall, it'll be completely numb. And tomorrow? Oh, you are going to be in such pain."

Talbot narrowed his eyes at his friend and considered spooking his horse, but the little bastard would probably maintain control of the beast and then smirk at him.

How that scientist boy could smirk. It was so unfair.

He forced his attention back to his wife. "How are things here? Are you ready to go?"

Kelsey nodded. "Everything's packed. We've loaded up every horse we could catch and have all the food we could gather already loaded. We should be ready to go inside fifteen minutes, and then we'll head back for the rest.

"The stunned horses should be awake by the time we get there. The ones here are already up. It must be because they have more mass than a person. Take a break while we get the last details right. You're going to need more of those than we can give you by the time this ride is over."

Her smile had faded as she'd spoken, and he knew she was speaking nothing but the truth. The next few days were going to be hell.

* * *

JULIA RODE between Scott and Mertz. Unlike the two of them, she had experience in the saddle and sat easily. Since none of the marines, Fleet personnel, or scientists, except Carl Owlet, had any experience on horseback, she'd chosen one of the more recalcitrant beasts. She had the strength to control him and the skill to not need it.

Her doppelgänger had chosen a relatively docile beast—or as close to it as a warhorse got—for Mertz. Even so, his mount had already tried to bite his leg several times and had successfully thrown him once. Scott's horse had done even worse, having thrown him and then tried to stomp him.

She turned her head and looked back over the trail of horses scattered out behind them. They'd made their way back to the building and picked up the horses that had been stunned and the last of their people. Most people were doubled up, but they all had rides. Now they just had to get to the outpost alive.

Clarice Beauchamp's people were spread out along the line of riders, trying to keep anyone from being injured or run over by the horses they were forced to ride. Olivia West, Elise Orison, Carl Owlet, and her doppelgänger were helping, but the group was a sad, straggly sight.

The local riders were also responsible for maintaining the security of the march as they tried to keep the group's speed up. They'd been on the trail for a couple of hours now and had taken more breaks than she was comfortable with. If they were going to beat the horde to the outpost, they were going to have to pick up the pace.

"My ass is killing me," Scott complained. "Please tell me this gets easier."

She nodded, but her smile was anything but reassuring. "It gets easier, but not until it gets a *lot* worse. You're going to be really sore tonight, and tomorrow is going to be agony."

"It doesn't matter how bad we feel, we're going to have to do better," Mertz said.

Jared, she mentally corrected herself. He was not the Bastard, and she needed to get out of the behavior of referring to him by his last name. Either she needed to attach a title to it, to increase the respect that she was presenting—even in her head—or use his first name.

If she'd housed any remaining doubts over what kind of person he was, the stories of how he'd fought with his people to protect the building against the horde had put that notion firmly to rest.

The Mertz from her universe was not selfless. He'd have stayed downstairs and let others do the fighting for him. He wouldn't have risked his skin to save those under his command.

"Let me tell you how it's going to go," she said. "Right now, you're feeling sore. It's because you're not sitting properly. That means that every time the horse moves, rather than moving with him, you're slamming into the saddle. You're also abusing muscles that you've never had to use like this before. If you want to have a smoother ride, you need to learn the right seat and use it for an extended period.

"That's not going to happen today, and it's not going to happen tomorrow, but it *is* going to happen, if we live long enough. Focus on not fighting the horse. If we have to ride all the way to the Imperial Palace, you're going to be accomplished horsemen by the time we get there. You just need to live that long."

Scott grimaced but nodded. "Living in pain is better than dying. We'll manage. Do you think we're going to get to the outpost ahead of the horde?"

She shrugged. "I have no idea. We don't really know how far away it is, and we don't know where the horde is going to come from. Or if they'll come after us at all. They may stop at the camp and decide that we're just not worth the trouble."

Jared laughed cynically at that. "Oh, I think they'll come after us. We've used advanced weaponry, and we came down on ships from the sky. They've got a bug up their butts about that, it seems.

"The prisoners we captured wouldn't talk very much, but just the presence of Talbot in armor was enough for them to try to kill everybody in the building. They associate us with the System Lords, and they tried to kill every last one of us. Seeing the pinnaces is going to provoke an extremely hostile response from them.

"They'll use whatever force they can scrape together to bog us down until an even larger force arrives with more heavy weapons, I'll wager. If they bring enough heavy weapons, they'll feel comfortable dealing with us. As Kelsey is so fond of saying, 'ten men with clubs can beat a man with a flechette pistol, if they're prepared to bleed.'

"It's going to be a race. If we can get to the outpost before they can catch up with us, we're probably going to survive for a little while longer. If we don't, we're going to be making a last stand tomorrow."

Julia turned in her saddle to look back down the line of riders again. Based on her experience, they'd pick up some basic skills in the next couple of hours. Not enough to be comfortable and not enough to avoid pain, but enough to increase the pace. With lives at stake, people were going to grit their teeth and ride through whatever troubles they came across.

One of the riders caught her eye. Carl Owlet was moving up the line of scientists, giving them advice. The way that he sat his horse spoke of years of experience in the saddle. She was surprised to see that and pleased. He was a man of many talents and surprising depths. The more she found out about him, the more interested in him she became.

Again, she wasn't going to encroach on Angela Ellis's territory. The man was her husband, and he was safe from any interest that she might have. But that wasn't going to stop her from spending a good amount of time with him and learning what she could about him.

In her universe, his doppelgänger would be very similar, though less experienced. Just like the Kelsey in this universe, the man she was looking at had been put through the fire. He'd come out the other side forged in a different way than her doppelgänger or herself, but he was still a warrior scholar.

The man back in her universe would probably be a bookish nerd —a word she'd picked up from Carl, ironically—who wouldn't realize what he was capable of. That was fine by her because she didn't necessarily need a warrior at her side, but she still knew that he'd react well under pressure and that he had a backbone.

That was *really* important. All too many people in the nobility ended up being self-centered, spineless jerks. Seeing that this young man was none of the above made him an excellent candidate for her consort.

While she wouldn't know for certain until she got back home, she thought Ethan would like him. Eventually. He'd be shocked at her choice, of course, but he always had been. Not that she'd ever had an active dating life, but Ethan wouldn't guess a mousy scientist would interest her.

She didn't know what was going to happen in her universe, but the odds were high that the AIs were going to arrive at Avalon before she returned home. When they did, they'd force the New Terran Empire to surrender.

Her job, when she returned—if she couldn't stop the AIs with the override—would be to work behind the scenes with whatever forces she could pull together to free them. If she could get people like Carl Owlet to help her, to understand all the technology that they were being given, then the Empire might have a chance.

Right now, he was just a student. He wouldn't stand out on

anybody's scanners as a threat. That meant he wouldn't be locked away—or killed—like Ethan would. Like she would. He'd still be free and approachable.

Much like the people of Terra had formed a guerrilla movement, that was what she was probably going to have to do when she returned home. If she could bring enough information and technology with her, Carl Owlet would be a very potent ally in a fight like that.

She turned and looked ahead of them. "If you gentlemen are ready, I think it's time we picked up the pace a notch. We need to get to a good camping ground by dark, and I'd like to make it as far away from the first camp as possible."

With that, she used her heels and a flick of her reins to move her horse into a canter. Groans sounded behind her as the two Fleet officers followed suit.

17

B y the time they'd stopped riding for the day, Jared's legs and thighs were solid bands of pain, while his rear felt like lead. He'd needed help getting down from the saddle and could barely walk. It only took a single glance around their campsite to see that everyone else without training on horse riding was in just as bad a shape. Or worse.

"Everyone listen up," Kelsey said, waving her arms in the growing dusk. "You need to walk it off. I understand that everything hurts, and I have bad news. It's going to get worse if you don't move around. Walk the campsite, do some stretching exercises, and work those muscles as much as you can. We'll get something together for dinner, and then you're going to have to get as much sleep as you can, because we'll be up before dawn and doing this all over again."

Her announcement was greeted with loud groans, and Jared felt like adding his own to the chorus, but long training as a Fleet officer had taught him that that wasn't wise.

"You heard Her Highness," he said in his best command voice. "We're going to have a long ride tomorrow, and we'll have people that want to kill us right on our tails. I suggest you loosen up as much as you can, because there's not going to be nearly as many breaks tomorrow. Colonel Talbot and Commodore Meyer, take charge of everyone."

His people, with the exception of the scientists, knew better than to groan back at their commanding officer. Kelsey, though, was more like everybody's little sister, even though everyone knew what a badass she was. They'd give her a little back talk, but not him.

The place they'd stopped at looked like every other piece of the grassland that he'd seen this far, except perhaps just a little bit higher in elevation than the surrounding terrain. Beauchamp had had her people gather the horses into a picket off to the side of the camping area.

She had some of her people digging fire pits. Not just places to keep the flames from catching anything on fire, but deep holes so that the light wouldn't go out to the sides. No riders in the distance would see them. Thankfully, there were enough scrawny trees scattered around to provide firewood.

Based on what he'd seen last night, it wouldn't be getting very cold tonight. They were in the middle of the summer season, so the temperatures would be moderate. That had meant that riding during the day had been a hot, sweaty affair though. Jared desperately needed a shower that he knew he wasn't getting anytime soon. The marine fatigues had materials built into them that kept the smell down, but there were limits to what even that could do.

While he was trying to work the worst of the pain out of his legs and back, Elise stepped up beside him, looking as if she'd just had a refreshing and enjoyable day out riding. He tried not to glare at her, but from her expression of amusement, he'd failed.

"I think I hate you," he said matter-of-factly.

She laughed and pulled him into a hug. Then, after a moment, she pushed him back, her nose crinkling in distaste. "You stink."

"Thanks for that," he said dryly. "You're no spring shower either. You don't just smell like sweat. You smell like horse. Then again, I suspect I do, as well. Neither one of us is going to be able to fix that for a while, so you're just going to have to get used to it."

She grinned at him, showing that she wasn't hurt by his commentary. "After a day on the trail, everyone needs a shower. On this planet, I suspect our noses are going to go numb as to how bad we smell after a while, which will be a blessing."

His wife stepped close to him again, tilted his head down, and kissed him. "We'll just have to get used to it. Call it your warrior smell or something."

Their moment of closeness was interrupted when someone softly cleared their throat beside them. He turned his head and found a smiling Kelsey standing beside him, with Beauchamp at her side.

"I'm sorry to interrupt your moment, but we've got some things to discuss," his sister said. "It's time for us to get to know one another. We can't ride in the dark and, even though we need to get some rest, we need to take the time to introduce ourselves.

"Captain Clarice Beauchamp, this is Admiral Jared Mertz of the New Terran Empire Fleet and his wife Crown Princess Elise Orison of the Kingdom of Pentagar. Jared is my brother, though the family tree is somewhat... convoluted. The man who raised me was his father."

Jared repressed a smile. The part his sister was leaving out was that Emperor Karl Bandar hadn't actually been Kelsey's biological father, though he was Jared's. Kelsey's mother had been somewhat... free with her favors.

He extended his hand to Beauchamp. When she took it, her grip was firm and professional.

"It's a pleasure to meet you, Captain. Thank you very much for helping us get out from under the heels of the horde."

The woman smiled slightly. "I'm not exactly certain what an admiral is, but your sister has explained to me that you don't belong to the same organization that works for the artificial intelligences. If you're fighting them, then it serves the interests of my people to help you.

"What we're going to do now is make certain that's true. You could've lied in order to get my assistance. And if you cannot convince me of your honesty, then I believe the officials of my government are going to have some very ugly questions for you."

The woman turned and gestured toward one of the fires. "My

people are preparing enough food for everyone. It's not the best tasting, but trail rations rarely are. We'll eat and then we'll talk."

Jared considered putting the discussion off until Sean and Talbot were done but decided that this needed to be settled as soon as possible. He and Kelsey would be the best choices to state their case. The others would probably arrive before the story was done.

He rubbed his backside. "That sounds good, though if you'll forgive me, I think I'll stand for a bit. I've done a little bit too much sitting today."

* * *

KELSEY STAYED CLOSE to the two as they walked over to the fire. She wasn't surprised when they arrived and found her doppelgänger already seated on the ground and sipping something out of a metal cup. The other woman made an expression that said she didn't particularly care for what she was drinking, but she didn't stop consuming it.

"Julia, how are you feeling?" Kelsey asked. "And what have you got there? Something good?"

The other woman waved her cup around slightly. "It's been a while since I've ridden, but it came back to me just fine. This coffee, on the other hand, I don't think I'd use the word 'good' in reference to it. It's hot, has caffeine, and is hitting the spot, but it's *far* from good."

Even as her doppelgänger was saying that, Elise walked out of the growing darkness with a cup of her own. "Oh, it's not that bad. If all you're used to is something from the palace, then it's pretty rough. If compared to army coffee, it's better than average."

Kelsey raised an eyebrow. "What would you know about army coffee, and how do I get some?"

The Pentagaran noblewoman grinned at her. "I just took a small detour to the next fire over, where I could smell it brewing. I'm surprised that you didn't figure out where it was before you got here with that enhanced nose of yours.

"As for getting around, part of my father's legacy revolves around that kind of thing. As you know, he believes in getting out among the people and did so when he was younger. I took full advantage of that when I was growing up, and I've been to all sorts of places and sat down with a number of people that a woman of my social status probably shouldn't have been associated with, strictly speaking. It's all been very illuminating."

That made Kelsey a little bit jealous because she'd been somewhat closeted as a child. It wasn't that her father had blocked her from going places, it was that her position insulated her from the same kind of people that Elise had been able to visit.

Before she could say anything further, Olivia came out of the darkness with two cups of coffee and handed one of them to Kelsey. "Here you go. Like your sister-in-law said, it's not awful."

Kelsey accepted the hot metal cup from the other woman and took a sip. The coffee was black, unsweetened, and *exceptionally* strong. The bitter flavor threatened to overwhelm her for a moment until the wash of caffeine smoothed things out.

After a few moments, Kelsey nodded slowly. "This works. Olivia, would you do me the favor of getting Jared a cup? I'd imagine that he could use one right about now."

The other woman nodded and headed back toward the other fire.

Kelsey settled down near Jared and listened as her brother explained their people's history. He was starting back at the beginning, where Lucian fled Terra for Avalon while Emperor Marcus led the final fight against the AIs. Or the rebels, as they'd called them back then, simply because the Old Empire had had no idea what they were really facing.

By the time he'd finished his story and gotten to the point where they were fighting against the AIs in the modern age, all of the other leaders of their group had arrived. Each of them had found the coffee and sat. One of Beauchamp's people had brought food around, and they'd eaten while Jared continued telling the story.

Beauchamp might've only expected a brief introduction, but she didn't stop the story. Telling it took a couple of hours, even without questions. By the time her brother had finished, full night had fallen long ago, and the glory of the stars dominated the sky above them.

To Kelsey's shock, the wildlife around them was deafening. The insects, which had been loud during the day, *really* opened up at night. There were also other animal calls in the darkness, but she couldn't put any names to them. She had no experience with anything like that. It was amazing.

Beauchamp sat silent for a long while after Jared had finished speaking. She asked no questions, and she didn't act as if she either believed him or doubted his words. When she finally did speak, her tone held no hint of judgment.

"If it were up to me, I'd be inclined to believe you," she said quietly while staring into the fire. "I'll warn you that others will not be as accepting as I. When we arrive at the outpost, you'll have an opportunity to tell your story. The leaders there will have many questions.

"I also have things that I want to know, but it's not the right time for me to inquire. Tomorrow is going to be a brutal day of riding for all of you, as well as difficult for myself and my people, eking out every single bit of speed that you can give. We will be brutal taskmasters.

"Honestly, I think that we'll make it to the outpost before the horde catches up with us, but they could surprise me. We're going to have to be ready to fight if they try to block us from reaching safety.

"To do that, everyone is going to need all the rest they can get. I suggest you retire for the evening and be ready to rise in just a few hours. We'll ride as soon as we can make out the ground around us. Focus on your survival and worry about the political implications of your arrival once you're safe, relatively speaking."

The woman smiled grimly. "After all, there'll always be time to hang you later if we don't like what you have to say. Tomorrow could be a day of great danger for you, but don't believe for one moment that you're any safer at the outpost, unless you can convince our leaders there of your honesty. If you work for the artificial intelligences, they'll find out and they *will* kill you.

"And if it's true, I'll help them do it."

With that, the woman rose and walked off into the darkness, leaving them alone near the fire, which had burned down to coals over the hours.

Rather than wait for someone to say something, Kelsey stood and extended her hand to Talbot. Together, they walked off toward where they would sleep.

The other woman was right. Their survival depended on convincing their potential allies that they shared their goals. She had a few ideas about how that might best be done, but it was a toss of the dice. They had to be convincing, because if they failed to win friends and allies, they'd all die.

Worse, everyone on Terra would eventually die as well. And if the AIs were willing to do that to Terra, how long before they decided that humanity in general needed to perish?

Convincing them to help her would be the most important task that Kelsey had ever faced. One her Raider augmentation couldn't help her with. One where it might be a strong negative influence on the discussions, in fact. Beauchamp had seen her fight without armor. That *would* come up, and she'd have to explain how she could do what she did.

That was a lot of pressure, but she'd make it work. She had to.

18

The next morning, Talbot woke feeling a lot better than he'd expected to. His medical nanites had done yeoman's work while he'd slept. The pain and soreness that he'd been feeling was mostly gone.

Kelsey was up and seemed to have no ill effects at all, which annoyed him all over again. She made up for it by hunting him down some coffee. He needed it.

He wasn't looking forward to another day in the saddle, much less the more difficult ride he expected them to make today, but at least he wasn't suffering debilitating pain.

A quick check revealed that he was doing better than the regular marines because his Raider nanites were doing a much better job of caring for him. The artificial muscles woven throughout his real ones were also taking off quite a bit of the stress.

The regular marines, Fleet personnel, and scientists also had nanites, but theirs weren't as capable as his. Each of them had been hit harder than him, his wife, and her doppelgänger.

That said, they were doing better than Beauchamp's people had expected them to. He could tell by the natives' expressions and

whispered conversations that they expected everyone to be almost
bedridden. Instead, they were up and doing what they needed to.

Beauchamp cut off their discussion with a loud whistle, and everyone
settled down to eat some rations and get ready for a day of hard riding.

Talbot tried the local version of pre-prepared food and wasn't
surprised to see that it was just as unappetizing as the marine version.
Well, that hardly mattered. They need the calories. He ate his share
and then ate some more.

Watching Kelsey eat everything in sight had always amused him,
but now that he was also a Marine Raider, his appetite dwarfed hers.
Now it was her turn to be bemused by how much food he could put
away. Luckily, he'd packed a *lot* of ration bars for just this situation.

That didn't stop him from devouring everything Beauchamp's
people had to offer. Never look a gift horse in the mouth. That new
saying was completely appropriate for this situation, he decided,
having seen the beasts up close and personal.

By the time they'd finished eating, the sun was coloring the
horizon. It would've been helpful if the moon was showing more light,
but it would've also put them in danger since someone could see them
at longer distances. On balance, it was probably better that only a
sliver of its silvery gray surface was lit.

Talbot wished his marines could help, but their "assistance" would
undoubtedly be more of a hindrance than a help, so they stood by,
stroking their horses' necks, talking to them, and trying to get them
used to their presence.

The Fleet personnel and scientists put on the captured armor,
while his people put on the marine unpowered armor. They also had
the primitive weapons that they'd captured, but they weren't worrying
about that right now. No one had the time to even learn how to safely
handle the swords. When the call came to mount up, they did so, and
the column moved out.

The next four hours were brutal. As much work as their nanites
had done, their bodies weren't ready for the stress of riding as hard as
they did. Unlike the first day, this time they only stopped twice during
the morning, and those only briefly. Not even really enough time to

recover any feeling in their legs and butts before they were in the saddle again and on the move.

He spent his time conferring with Scala, Chloe, and Boske about the overall layout of their troops and the terrain that they were coming up on. With the drones overhead, they had a good view out to about five kilometers. He might've been able to push that a little bit, but he didn't want to lose any of the devices. They were irreplaceable at this point.

That didn't mean that he wasn't willing to risk the occasional one by sending it out on a recon mission out to ten kilometers. He mainly did that going forward, but he also sent out recon missions to the sides and to their rear.

Over the morning, they hadn't seen anything worthy of note. Nothing but animals and long dormant desolation. This borderland between whoever Beauchamp served and the horde wasn't well traveled. There were no roads and very few trails.

They broke for lunch, if it could be called that, and ate quickly. They didn't bother with a fire because speed was more important.

It was late afternoon when he spotted the outpost coming up in the visual from one of his drones. The device was about at the limit of its ten-kilometer range when it spotted the structure growing out of the ground ahead of them.

When Beauchamp had used the word outpost, he'd thought of something fairly small and fortified. That was not exactly what he was seeing now. The structure ahead of them was a walled city. Maybe a small one, but definitely a population center that had thousands of people living in it. Perhaps tens of thousands.

The construction was a mixture of wood and stone, natural elements rather than plascrete. Based on the height of the walls, and the vigilant guards observing land around them, the locals weren't taking their safety for granted.

There were also reinforced positions on the walls that spoke to him of heavy weapons emplacements. He was willing to wager that something high-tech and powerful lurked inside those well-protected locations, though he wouldn't know for sure unless he had a chance to look at them more closely once they were inside the outpost, should their hosts prove willing to show them to him.

He was about to pass that information on to the admiral when one of their drones reported an anomaly. Off to the left-hand side of their column, it had spotted another band of riders. This group was about twice their size and looked all too familiar. It was a horde war band.

He used his implants to do some calculations based on their direction of travel and speed, comparing it with their own. The horde would probably intercept them just short of the outpost. If that happened, this wasn't going to end well.

"Heads up," he said over the command channel and passed along the readings from the drones so that everyone would know the situation. That earned curses as his friends realized they weren't going to get out of this unscathed.

While the higher-ups considered the situation, he called for Corporal Boske to join him. When she had done so, he spoke with her in a low tone.

"You're going to command the ready response team. If we can keep that group off the main column until the admiral and Kelsey can reach the outpost, I'll call that a win."

The pink-haired noncom nodded. "You can count on us, sir. We'll keep them off your necks."

"I know you will. Good luck."

What he actually knew is that he just ordered his subordinate to lead what could all too easily turn into a suicide mission. If they got bogged down in the fighting, even with their technological superiority, they'd be exterminated to the last man and woman.

Of course, since he was going to be personally leading the rear guard, he might find trouble of his own that would keep him from getting to the outpost.

He wasn't going to tell Kelsey that. She'd try to come up with a different plan when they really didn't have any other options.

While Boske was gathering her people, he called Chloe over a private com channel. "Chloe, I'm going to do what we can to keep the horde off your back. I need you to keep Kelsey and the admiral safe while we do it. Work with Howard to make sure. Adrian will be with me."

His officer didn't have to be told what that meant. "You got it, Colonel. Nobody's getting through me or my people."

"Excellent. We're leaving in a couple of minutes. Good luck."

He'd already marked the spots on the map where he'd make his stand, if he had to. Right now, he'd settle for grouping most of his marines on that side of the column. The drones told him the other side was clear out to the ten-kilometer mark. Depending on how well Boske did, he'd make the decision on whether or not to set up a blocking force.

Talbot let his eyes wander up to the front of the column where Kelsey was riding beside the admiral. They were discussing the information he'd sent them, and she wasn't looking back toward him. She was a warrior, but she wasn't as experienced as he was yet. She hadn't realized at a glance what the situation was going to require. When she did, she was going to be pissed.

Well, he'd hope that things were well underway before she caught on. If someone was going to die today, it would be him and his people, not his wife or the admiral. He didn't want that to happen, but if that's the way things fell, he'd rather she live. If those two died, humanity likely died with them.

JULIA WAS STILL TIED into the marine net and heard Talbot's instructions to Corporal Boske. A glance at her doppelgänger showed that the other woman was not aware of what her husband was doing. After a moment's consideration, she decided that was probably for the best.

The hazy outlines of Talbot's plan were already beginning to take shape in the mental battle space that the marines were constructing. She could see exactly how they planned to split off the ready reaction team to meet the incoming hostiles. The remaining marines would defend the column from somewhere closer, making a blocking force if required.

If her doppelgänger realized that her husband was preparing to put himself in harm's way so that she could escape, she had no doubt that the woman would lose her mind.

Oh, she was much more of a warrior than Julia was, but she wasn't going to let her husband sacrifice himself for her. Oh no. She'd make certain that she stood beside him until the bloody end. She wouldn't leave him behind to die when she would live.

Her eyes slid over to Scott Roche. While they weren't in the least romantically entangled, he'd have the same type of reaction if it were her in danger. That was going to be awkward because she'd already decided that her assistance might make the difference between the ready response team being able to break away from the incoming horsemen and being bogged down in a fatal encounter.

They already knew that the horde had heavy weaponry that was capable of taking out powered armor. If they were going to stop the horsemen, they needed a way to do that where they didn't expose themselves or get bogged down, allowing the horde to cut them off from escape.

With her mind made up, she nudged her horse over closer to Scott. "I want you to coordinate with Admiral Mertz and Kelsey. You've been doing a good job of keeping an eye on the scientists, and I want to see that continue. We can't afford to lose any of them on the final rush to the outpost."

He nodded. "I'm on it, Highness." With that, he rode forward to join that part of the column.

With her friend distracted, Julia took the opportunity to edge farther away from the main column so that she was trailing behind Corporal Boske and her subordinates tasked with stopping the horde from cutting them off from safety.

The marines never glanced back at her. They were focused on the task ahead of them, and they had their implant maps to tag everyone who was going. Julia took the opportunity to utilize the overrides that she had built into her implants to add herself to the ready response team listing as a member.

Her ability to do that would probably shock Jared Mertz. After all, he'd recommended to the emperor and the senate in this universe that she be declared unfit to be heir as a way to make certain that someone they didn't trust didn't have authority she wasn't supposed to have.

The problem with that was that now that they were reunited with her doppelgänger, they'd had to find a way to have their cake and eat it too. A turn of phrase she heartily approved of, since she loved cake.

They'd secretly re-enabled Princess Kelsey's authority without telling Julia. She'd already been checking for that because she'd expected that's what they'd do. They'd added some code that Carl Owlet had created to make a perfunctory effort at keeping her out, but it was easily subverted.

At least that's what Austin Darrah had told her when she'd asked him to bypass it. He hadn't even needed to get someone more skilled than himself at programming to make it happen. The system just wasn't designed to keep someone with the right access codes out.

As her codes were exactly as valid as her doppelgänger's, the kludge was never going to work. She'd just needed someone to subvert their hack without letting them know that they'd done so.

She had no intention of abusing her authority as heir to the throne, but when push came to shove, she'd do what she needed to do to be certain that this mission succeeded. It only took a little earnest conversation to convince Austin of that, and now she was able to do what needed to be done.

Someone had to get out of here with the override. Only victory in this universe would see the device get back to hers. If her participation in this fight made it more likely that Scott would eventually return to her universe with the key to victory, then it would be worth it, even if she didn't make it.

She'd taken an opportunity last night to go through the heavy weapons that the marines had brought along for their armor. The last fight hadn't involved the use of them because the marines hadn't expected to run into anything dangerous to them. This time they were carrying weapons capable of knocking pinnaces out of the sky or destroying entrenched positions. *Modern* entrenched positions.

While she was no expert at the use of something like that, she'd taken the opportunity to pilfer one of the spare weapon systems, packing it away with her armor. Now she'd be able to assist in this battle in a way that she hadn't before.

There'd be no stunners this time. They'd hit the enemy as fast and hard as they could. Their only real hope of doing so and getting away was to catch them before they knew they were in danger and exterminate them. And that's what she intended to do.

19

J ared tried his best to split his attention between the interface accessing the drone feeds and riding his horse. As an inexperienced rider, that wasn't exactly easy. In fact, every time he thought he had the hang of it, a change in his horse's gait distracted him.

The marines in the ready response team were moving off to intercept the incoming riders while Talbot sent Major Scala and more of the marines on a course that put them between the column and the hostiles. They'd only dismount if the ready response team wasn't able to delay the horde forces.

The distance between the column and the outpost was shrinking as they rode toward it, but it was a race to see if they reached the walls before the horde caught up with them. A race that he wasn't certain they were going to win.

Out of habit, he performed a check of where his senior people were and what they were up to. A good leader trusted his subordinates to take care of the mission at hand, but as he was ultimately responsible for what happened, it paid to make sure that everything was actually getting done the way it needed to be.

Talbot had the majority of his marines in hand, Scott Roche was taking care of the scientists, Sean Meyer was overseeing the Fleet personnel, Olivia and Elise were safely tucked away in the middle of the column, and Kelsey was furiously studying whatever she was looking at through her implants as she rode next to him.

The one person he didn't immediately spot was Julia. Kelsey's doppelgänger was nowhere in sight.

He double-checked what he could see of the personnel through his implants. Marine officers and sergeants had the ability to track of all their personnel, their condition, and other salient facts about them at a glance. He normally didn't access that type of information, but he did know it existed.

It took him longer than it would've taken Talbot to scan down the list of people in the column, but he reached the end without finding Julia. That wasn't good.

He expanded the view and finally found her tagging along behind the ready response team.

He cursed under his breath. He could order her to return to the column, but he knew that was useless. Just like his sister, the woman never changed her mind when she made it up. If she thought something needed doing, she'd do it and damn the consequences.

"What's wrong?" Kelsey asked, sparing him a glance.

"Your double attached herself to the ready response team. It looks like she's on her way out to fight the horde."

Kelsey said something distinctly unladylike. She'd obviously been hanging around Talbot and the marines for far too long.

"It's too late to stop her now," she growled. "She's got Raider implants and her armor, so she'll be as safe as anyone. Her presence might actually help them accomplish their mission, which I'm sure is exactly what she had in mind. I can't say she's wrong, even if I do want to strangle her."

"Pot, meet kettle."

His sister barked out a short laugh. "I suppose that's true enough. The question is, would slamming these bastards hard enough make our lives easier? Instead of just sending the ready response team to ambush them, maybe we should divert most of the marines to hit them head-on and crush them."

"They've probably got a lot more of those antiarmor weapons," he argued. "They didn't come all this way looking to just fight. They intend to catch us and kill us before we reach the outpost."

"Then they're going about it all wrong," she said bluntly. "Even though they've got more warriors, they've got to know that we're going to punch their lights out. There is literally no chance that that force is going to catch up with the main column."

"I realize that it looks that way, but if we delay them any amount of time at all, the column will make it to the outpost. They're screwed when it comes to keeping us from getting there if that's their plan."

Jared frowned. He wasn't experienced with fighting on the ground, but if he put this into the same frame of reference as a space battle, he could see what she was saying.

Thinking about it that way brought another, uglier thought to mind. If this was a fight he was orchestrating, that attacking force wouldn't be the only one on the board. There'd be others waiting for that obvious group to drive them into an ambush. Ships with their drives down, hiding in plain sight, and waiting for his ships to waltz right into the kill zone.

"Then they're a distraction," he said grimly. "They're herding us into an ambush. There's another force somewhere in front of us waiting to spring a trap. Maybe that's being paranoid, but we have to plan for the worst and hope we're wrong."

Kelsey's eyes widened as she understood what he was saying. "I've got to tell Beauchamp. Get Talbot to get his people on the move. I want them in front of the column right now. We need to have the drones looking more closely at the ground we're going to be traveling over. Damn but that's clever."

With that, his sister raced off in the direction of Captain Beauchamp.

Jared opened a channel to Talbot and passed word of what he suspected to the marine officer. The other man cursed, oddly enough using the *exact* turn of phrase that his wife had used earlier. Maybe that wasn't so odd, now that he thought about it.

"We've sent all the armor to meet the incoming force," Talbot said. "Do you think that's what they wanted?"

"I'd count on it. They have to know that we have the means to see them even when others on this world don't. We've proven it to them in ambushing them at the camp. A canny leader will deduce that.

"Now they've put a large force out there so that we'd respond, so of course we're going to use the strongest force we have available. They probably have other weapons at their disposal that will be just as surprising as the antiarmor weapons. We're not going to know what until we engage them. We also won't know anything about the group I suspect is ahead of us until we find them."

With the tall grass that covered much of the area between them and the outpost, Jared suspected that the intruders were concealing themselves somewhere in relatively plain sight.

The marine drones had the capability of detecting things infrared and ultraviolet, so it shouldn't be difficult to switch them over and locate any hidden groups. They wouldn't have had time to dig a deep enough hole to conceal their presence. In this fallen world, they probably didn't have much need to do that either.

Even though he knew Talbot was undoubtedly thinking along those lines, he added his suspicions.

"I've been thinking about that too," Talbot said. "I've got a couple of drones running through the area ahead of us looking for locations they could be using. Once I find them, if they're there, I'll start putting together a tactical response.

"I've already searched the area closest to us, and it looks clean. I'd imagine they're another two or three kilometers in front of us, if they're out there at all. They have to allow space and time for us to be spooked by their diversionary force.

"In fact, they may not be directly in front of us. They may expect us to change course based on contact with their diversionary force. We don't have enough drones to search all around us for a great distance, but we should be able to provide enough coverage to locate where our problem is going to be before we run over them."

"Keep me informed," Jared said. "If you need to act without direct orders, consider the word given. Do what you think best to defend us. Kelsey is talking with Captain Beauchamp right now, so her people will be in the loop. I'll join her right now to pass along any information you get because I doubt Kelsey will stay in the column when the fighting is imminent."

The other man laughed. "I suppose not. Well, we'll do what we need to do. You'll make it to the outpost."

"Good luck, Colonel. Mertz out."

Jared killed the channel. The unspoken part of what Talbot had just said was that the people in the column might make it to the outpost, but the marines engaging the enemy would take losses. Losses they could ill afford.

Jared considered donning his powered armor but decided he already had enough problems riding. Besides, if the horde did ambush them, the men and woman in the armor would be their primary targets during the initial attack. Best not to paint a bull's-eye on his back when he couldn't react like Kelsey. Her augmentation might give her a chance to survive something like that, but he had no such edge.

He put his negative thoughts out of his mind. There was nothing he could do to minimize what was coming, other than trust the marines to do their jobs. Now he needed to focus on doing his.

* * *

Kelsey laid out the situation for Captain Beauchamp. The other woman wasted no time asking how she knew, instead ordering her people into action. Some of her men went out to bolster the scouting forces ahead of them with orders to spread farther out in front of the column.

Unfortunately, the only way that those scouts would likely get information back is when they were ambushed and some of the number killed. Those were brave men and women, Kelsey knew. Very much like the marines.

Almost as soon as Beauchamp finished doing that, Jared rode awkwardly up and told them what he'd told Talbot to do. The news wasn't pleasing to Kelsey, because she could read between the lines. Talbot was going to put himself and his people between them and whatever danger was out there waiting. She wasn't going to let him do it alone.

Jared could apparently sense where her thoughts were going, because he gave her a stern look and shook his head without her saying a word. "You're critical to this mission, Kelsey. Talbot and the marines can handle the fighting. You need to stay here with the rest of us. We've already got Julia off helping them."

She immediately balked with a firm shake of her head. "I can do more if I make sure we don't get ambushed at all. It's all fine and good that Julia is doing her part, but I need to do mine. The farther away from the column we can keep the fighting, the less chance that any of the civilians get hurt."

"You're looking at this all wrong," he said. "We have the marines to do the fighting for us, just as they should. This is one of those times where you have to stand back and direct what's going on. Talbot is controlling them in the field, and we need you to be our leader."

"You're our leader."

"No, I'm not. I'm the military commander of this mission. You represent the Imperial Throne. Neither of us can afford to die. We need those codes in your head once we get to the palace."

She scowled. "That's playing dirty. Julia has the same codes. She's obviously found a way to make them work, so you should be happy you have a spare."

He shot a look toward Beauchamp, who was focused on directing her subordinates. When he spoke again, he pitched his voice low.

"Even though she's been with me for months, I don't trust her to the same degree that I trust you. She has her own agenda, and I'm smart enough to realize that. Right now, it aligns with what we're doing. What happens when her people would benefit more from working against us?

"Even leaving that aside, you're my sister. I'm not going to lose you fighting out there when it isn't critical to our survival. I'm the senior military officer, and it's my job to declare who does fighting and where. This is one of those times where you have to obey orders, Colonel."

Her scowl deepened, and she felt her teeth clenching. Dammit. As much as she wanted to argue, she knew that she had to support the separation of civilian power from the military. If they were fighting, it really *was* his call, and she had to acknowledge that. She could overrule him when it came to policy, but not strategy and tactics.

This was one of the flaws of being both an ambassador plenipotentiary and the senior officer in the marines. Sometimes she had to follow orders, and other times she had to give them. Sadly, this wasn't one of the latter.

She pulled her horse around to his other side with an easy tug of the reins. Pitching her voice low, she gave in to the inevitable.

"Fine, but I'm going to get into my armor. If those bastards get anywhere close to us, I'm going to smash them into little bitty pieces."

He smiled a little and shook his head. "I'm not ever going to change who you are. All I can do is remind you of what we need to save, the human race. I understand that you want to go out and fight, but your survival is just as critical as mine. We're both going to have to make some sacrifices."

While she didn't disagree, she worried that the sacrifices would be paid for in blood. If the horde came close to the column, she wouldn't hesitate to do her absolute best to pound them into the ground like a tent stake, but she had to bow to reality. He was right, as much as it galled her.

It looked as if it was going to be up to her husband and her doppelgänger to settle this unpleasantness. She hoped they were up to the task, because they'd only get one shot at it. If they failed to stop the horde and reach the outpost, this mission was over and so were they.

20

T he ready response team was more than halfway to the oncoming enemy force by the time Corporal Boske figured out that Julia was tagging along. To say that she was less than pleased would've been something of an understatement.

The woman slowed and made her way directly toward the off-center path that Julia had been following, making no effort to conceal her intentions. She planted herself directly in Julia's path, planted her fists on her hips, and glared at the princess.

At least that's what Julia assumed the other woman was doing. Boske's helmet was opaque, so she'd just have to take the glare on faith. Julia had armored up when the marines had, so Boske was just as in the dark about her own expression.

"Dammit, Highness," the marine noncom sent over a private channel. "What the hell do you think you're doing?"

Julia slowed to a stop in front of the other woman, doing her absolute best to convey nonchalance with her posture. To avoid giving the other woman an advantage, she kept her armor's ability to project her face onto the outside of her helmet turned off as well.

"I'm making certain these marines have the best chance they can get at surviving this encounter," she said firmly. "We both know those horsemen are going to have a lot of the antiarmor weapons. The more firepower you have, the better the chances are that you'll take them out before they kill our marines."

"Those marines are *my* responsibility, Highness. Don't you think that your unexpected presence would make their survival *less* likely? If you just pop up with no warning in the middle of a fight, someone is likely to shoot you or get shot at because *you* surprised them. You need to go back to the column."

"Not going to happen," Julia said firmly. "I brought along enough heavy weaponry to do my part. You don't have enough people in powered armor to be picky. Let's do both of us a favor and not waste time that we don't really have. I'm going to be part of this fight. You might as well make use of me, because I'm going to be there whether you like it or not."

The other woman spent a full ten seconds cursing but caved to the inevitable. "Fine, but you do this *my* way. I give the orders, and you follow them to the letter. We don't have time to argue about who's in charge, so it's going to be me. If you can't handle that, I'll have my marines hold you down, strip that armor off of you, and make you run your little ass right back to the column. Am I clear?"

Julia's initial reaction was to tell the woman that she'd like to see her try. That, however, wouldn't be very helpful—particularly if she carried out her threat—so she decided to be cooperative.

She wondered if the marine would be so bold while talking to the Kelsey from this universe. Probably not.

"We'll do it your way, Corporal," Julia said. "How can Big Bertha help?"

With that, she tapped the large weapon that she'd commandeered for use with her armor. She'd picked up the name from one of the other marines when he was explaining how it worked to her, but she wasn't precisely sure where the phrase came from. It sounded mildly insulting, but the marine didn't seem to take it that way, so she wasn't sure.

What she did know was that the weapon was more than capable of doing its part in the upcoming fighting. It was a plasma rifle built for powered armor. In the scheme of things, it wasn't that large, but had an outsized ability to damage people, equipment, and the landscape.

They didn't have a lot of ammunition left for it, but they needed something that could take out a large group of riders before they could scatter. Which, based on their previous behavior, was exactly what they'd do. Then they'd keep shooting at the marines until they killed them all before heading on to attack the column.

"How many shots do you have for that thing?" Boske asked.

"Six. It was all I could find. Most of the ammunition didn't survive the crash."

Boske nodded. It was hard to see while she was in armor, but the slow tilt of her head gave Julia the clue.

"I'd rather keep that weapon in reserve, but I understand the need to take out as many people at once as we can. I'm authorizing you to fire *two* shots. That's it. We need to save the rest of the ammunition for later because we might desperately need the ability to use plasma at some point, and if we use all of the ammunition too quickly, we could be screwed."

"What if they get past us?" Julia asked. "They're going to catch our people out in the open. We've got to use whatever firepower we have to take them down while we can."

The noncom raised her hand slightly. "I don't have time to argue with you. You're authorized to fire *two* rounds, and if you see a large grouping of personnel after that, you may fire *one* more, but I don't expect that to happen. Right now, they're clumped together because they don't think we know they're coming. As soon as they realize they've been discovered, they're going to scatter.

"Frankly, I'm not even sure that you'll get that second shot off before they've separated enough to render the plasma blast zone too small to make a dent in their numbers. All we can hope to do is to take out as many of them as we can and try to get them to engage us.

"If they decide that they're going to ride on, nothing we can do can stop them. We just have to make ourselves the target they want to take out. Otherwise, Colonel Talbot and the rest of the marines are going to have to deal with them, and that'll mean a higher number of casualties that I'd rather avoid."

That was what Julia hoped to avoid, too. The horde wouldn't have sent such a large force against a group protected by high-tech armor if they didn't think they could handle the problem. That meant they had some kind of surprise hidden up their sleeves. One that she was certain that no one would like.

They'd have to adapt and overcome. They really didn't have much of a choice.

* * *

TALBOT HAD to admit that the attackers had hidden themselves well. If he hadn't had access to drones with infrared and ultraviolet capability, he would've missed their hiding places in the grass.

It seemed that they'd dug shallow holes and then dragged mats of woven grass across themselves. The cover perfectly matched the grass around them, which impressed him a great deal.

However they'd gotten themselves into position, they'd done so without disturbing the living grass enough for him to notice. In fact, he'd wager that they'd done well enough to fool even Captain Beauchamp and her people.

"So how do we go about this?" Adrian Scala asked from where he lay beside Talbot. The two of them were a short distance in advance of the column, peering through the tall grass at the crest of the hill they were on. The smell of the earth and grass felt like it was helping conceal them, too.

"I think the best way to get this started is to drive them out of hiding before we engage," Talbot said in a low voice. "We have a pretty decent idea of how many people we're looking at, based on the infrared signature, but I'd rather see them running around so I can be sure. Besides, we won't be able to see what kind of weaponry they have unless they're out and about. I wonder what they did with their horses?"

There were no horses anywhere within the tactical drones' range. If he had to guess, Talbot would wager that the horde had brought extra people to lead the horses away. Off to the right of their hiding place, set way back from where the column could see it from the ground, there was evidence that a large number of horses had recently been there, so the ambushers must've ridden in from off to the side of the known path, allowed the riders to dismount, and then had the horses led away.

No doubt the people with the spare horses were waiting somewhere in the distance, likely ready to come in once the ambush was sprung. Just one more thing for him to keep an eye on, but one with a potential upside. They could always use more horses, either for trade or for their own use. They still had fifteen hundred kilometers or so to travel, and extra horses would make that journey easier.

"So how do you want to spring the ambush?" Scala asked.

Talbot grinned. "We use our technology to our advantage. We have the drones start buzzing their position, out of reach of their hand-to-hand weaponry, and see if that gets them to come out and do something ill-considered.

"The drones will be inside bow range, and potentially even a thrown spear, but I'd wager the odds of a hit are low. The drones will be moving quickly and using at least a little bit of jinking to keep from being an easy target, so we won't get very many hits."

Scala nodded. "Okay, let's say that works, we spring the trap, and everyone comes running out. They have other forces in the area that they might be able to signal. If we get bogged down in a heavy fight, and more forces come in to pin us in place, a lot of people are going to die."

Talbot nodded grimly. "You got that right. So, we make sure we deal with these guys quickly. Most of the marines are back at the column, but with the flechette rifles our people here have, we should be able to take care of most of them. We'll have the drone coverage up, and if we see other attackers coming in, we'll modify the plan on the fly to deal with them. No matter how we play this, it's going to be quick and ugly."

He looked across what he could see of the plain and felt sad that such a beautiful area was being used for such a bloody purpose. Under other circumstances, he could imagine these fields filled with crops tended to by large machines, like the ones they'd found in the building.

This place had once been the breadbasket of Terra. Maybe at some point in the future it would be again, but until then, it was going to have a little bit of blood soaked into the ground.

He opened a communication channel back to Carl Owlet, who had a number of people controlling the drones for the marines, so that the fighters could be focused on what they needed to do.

"Carl, execute plan bravo."

"Copy that," his young friend said. "We've got some drones coming in from a couple of different angles and we'll buzz them as close to the ground as we can, then circle around and come in from other directions. With the pattern we're working up, it's going to seem like a lot more drones than we actually have. We've also arranged a little surprise for them that I think will probably help get them out into the open."

His friend's words filled him with a little bit of dread. "What are you planning? This isn't going to cause any big explosions, is it?"

Carl laughed. "Nothing like that. We took some of the smoke grenades that your people recovered from the crashed pinnaces, and we've attached them to the drones. Once the bad guys start moving around, we'll drop smoke into the middle of them to confuse their situation even more. That shouldn't obscure them from your advanced optics."

Talbot thought about that for a moment and then nodded. "That sounds like a good idea. Make it happen."

He switched channels to the general marine frequency. "Squad Charlie, this is Talbot. As soon as the drones come onto the scene and flush our ambushers, you are cleared to take them down. Make sure you hit your targets but be sparing with the ammunition. We need to take all of these people down as quickly as possible, but we don't have many reloads.

"We're going to drop smoke into the middle of them, so don't get excited about anyone you can't clearly see. Wait for your targets. Use the drone feeds to figure out who's going where and keep engaging them.

"Squad Delta, circle around and be ready to keep them from getting away. Once we lay enough firepower into them, they're going to make a break for it, and there are other fighters from the horde out there. We've got to be ready to interdict them."

Even as he finished speaking, the drones flew in from seemingly every direction and began buzzing over the target area. For a moment there was no response, and then large swaths of grass flipped over.

Screaming men and women came boiling out from under the mats and charged toward where the column would be, only to find Talbot and his marines on the hill between them.

There were more dismounted horsemen than he'd expected. At a guess, he was looking at over a hundred people. Maybe as many as a hundred and fifty. His ability to count was disrupted when the drones began dropping smoke into the middle of the charging enemies.

That disturbed them a lot. The smooth charge of the armed men and women was quickly turned into a chaotic rush, as people were both charging forward to fight while others ran away from what they thought was deadly danger.

Talbot didn't notice any of the antiarmor weapons, but visibility was crap. He had to assume that they had them until he knew for sure they didn't.

"All marines," he said in a flat tone. "Open fire."

Every marine with him on the low rise opened fire, sending flechettes into the screaming confusion below them. With that kind of firepower, it wouldn't take long to mow down the fighters they were facing.

"Enemy contact!" Chloe Laird shouted over the command frequency. "There's a second group just off to the side of the column popping out of concealment. Holy hell, there has to be two hundred people there. We're engaged. We're *heavily* engaged and need backup ASAP."

"Hold them as best you can," Talbot said as he stood. "Adrian, stop these bastards here while I go back and help the column."

"Got you covered, boss."

Talbot took off at a run, using his powered armor to build speed. This was an unmitigated disaster. With that many bad guys, the column was going to be overrun no matter what they did. The chances of keeping them off the civilians and unarmed Fleet personnel were effectively zero.

Talbot hoped the admiral had a good plan, because he didn't know of anything that he could do that was going to change the outcome now. All he could do was fight. With any luck, he'd make it back to Kelsey, so that they could stand back-to-back when the horde rolled over them.

21

J ared was watching the ambush play out over his implants when disaster struck. He heard shouts of alarm off to his right and turned in the saddle to find a lot of fresh enemies coming out from under grass mats barely fifty meters away from the column.

The new attackers were leading off with bows and arrows, shooting at Captain Beauchamp's warriors. They also paid particular attention to anyone with a rifle.

The marines quickly turned their flechette rifles—those that had any—onto the attackers. Captain Beauchamp's mounted forces charged toward the intruders, drawing weapons as they moved. There was a lot of yelling, screaming, and whooping in the air.

Jared turned his attention to the noncombatants and started ordering them to the other side of the column. He had to get armed warriors between the ambushers and the people that couldn't defend themselves.

He saw Kelsey racing toward the attackers, her powered armor making her leaps seem effortless. She had both of her swords out and seemed prepared to go in swinging. He wasn't sure it was going to be enough, considering how many people the horde had coming in.

This group looked at least as large as what Talbot had reported ahead of them, and they also had the mounted column that the ready response team was attempting to deal with. If that group also managed to disengage and get to the column in fighting order, he and his people were in *extremely* dire straits.

"How the hell did we miss these people?" Elise asked as she moved closer to him. She had a small flechette pistol in her hand, but she was obviously not confident that it was going to be enough.

Neither was he, though he drew his own weapon.

"I don't know," he said grimly. "Maybe we'll have time to figure it out after we've dealt with them. We've got to form everybody into a circle so that we can protect the group from every angle."

He sent out orders to that effect over the implant coms, and his people coalesced into a ball with all of their weapons pointing outward.

The situation had changed so quickly. They'd gone from almost being to the outpost to being caught in a deadly ambush just a few kilometers away from supposed safety.

He wanted to think that they were going to come out of this okay, but the situation seemed too ugly for that. It didn't seem as if they were going to have an opportunity to get this situation sorted out in their favor. Their enemy had been far cleverer than he'd imagined possible.

A number of them had already begun firing antiarmor weapons at Kelsey, but she seemed to be everywhere. She dodged left and then right, allowing the explosives to fly past her as she waded into the enemy. Her blades flashed out, severing arms, heads, weapons, and anything else that got in her way.

A crashing off to his left brought his attention around as Talbot came thundering out of the grass, barely pausing as he rushed toward the fighting in his powered armor.

He wasn't as lucky as his wife. One of the antiarmor weapons smashed into the ground right in front of him, exploding in a bright flash and sending the marine tumbling through the air to slam into the ground hard. A number of the enemy cheered his fall and rushed toward him.

"Kelsey," he said over the command channel. "Talbot is down off to your left."

His sister whirled in place, cutting a man down to clear the way for her to jump forward. With her powered armor, she was able to achieve an impressive height and came down on another warrior, crushing him in place as she sprinted toward her husband. She planted her feet near him and diced anyone that came close.

Jared felt a very bad feeling. As the enemy was massing to overwhelm Captain Beauchamp's forces, they'd split off a good chunk to face Kelsey as well. Several of them were already bringing antiarmor weapons to bear.

This was not going to end well.

* * *

KELSEY DREW her neural disruptor with her off hand and began shooting the men holding antiarmor weapons. The bolts sent them spasming to the ground, dead before they fell. She couldn't hit them all, unfortunately and at least one person managed to fire before he went down. Thankfully, his aim was somewhat off, but that was no reprieve.

The warhead flew past her and impacted in the middle of the column with terrible effect. It sent Fleet personnel and civilians flying in every direction, dead or wounded. Mostly dead.

Captain Beauchamp's people were also heavily engaged with the ambushers, but the odds were stacked against them.

To add insult to injury, that's when Major Scala called on the general com channel with word that while the ambushers had lost a lot of people, they'd split around the marines and were making their way toward the column. The marines were in pursuit, but the enemy had left a force to slow them down. They weren't going to be able to keep the horde warriors from reaching the column.

Perfect.

She didn't have a chance to check Talbot, but her implants told her that he was still alive. He wasn't even terribly injured. The impact had just knocked him out. The problem was that she couldn't move him while still defending their position. She was stuck by his side or she'd have to abandon him, something that she would never do.

A quick check of the drones revealed that the force coming in from the ambush site was going to hit the circle of Fleet personnel and civilians, and they were going to do it hard. She sent a quick warning to Jared and focused her attention on using her weapons to the best of their ability.

She'd sheathed her swords even as she was running for Talbot and had a flechette pistol in one hand and a neural disruptor in the other. Both were taking a toll on the enemy, but the power supply for the neural disruptor and the magazine for the flechette pistol weren't infinite. She'd have to put one weapon away to reload the other.

Even though she was cutting down swaths of the enemy, they didn't seem inclined to retreat. The deaths of their fellows only pushed them to charge her harder. It was almost as if they were suicidal.

Even as she was being forced to choose which weapon to reload, she saw something else happening back where the ambushers had concealed themselves. Several of them were dragging a large device out of the pit where they'd been hiding.

She didn't recognize what it was, but it had to be something bad.

Choosing her flechette pistol, she smashed one of the attackers out of her way with her other hand and emptied the small magazine at the enemy working on the machine. She took them down, but unfortunately, she didn't kill them all. One managed to crawl his way back up to his knees and continued doing something to the machine.

Kelsey fired her neural disruptor. Too bad he was out of range.

The top of the machine opened, and a metallic ball shot into the sky. She had no idea what it was and no time to figure it out because when it reached about fifty meters in height, it glowed as brightly as the sun and the world around her went dark.

* * *

JULIA HAD CIRCLED AROUND JUST like Corporal Boske had instructed her to and found a good hiding place in the tall grass. She'd opened fire on command with the plasma rifle, sending the two unbearably bright spots of coherent light flashing into the middle of the column of enemy horsemen, where they'd detonated with tremendous explosions.

The blasts not only threw horses and people in every direction, it had incinerated those closest to the point of impact. Much like Boske had anticipated, the horsemen had immediately split apart and began fleeing in multiple directions.

Julia fired the third authorized blast from the plasma rifle at the man who seemed to be in charge and took out him and the half a dozen riders still too close to avoid destruction.

Her three shots had started a fire that would likely rage out of control in the flat grassland. Luckily, the wind wasn't blowing in their direction, or toward the outpost. It would end up being a crisis somewhere, but it wasn't something she could worry about now.

With that, she backed away from the fighting, as ordered. She raced around to the left, using a slight rise in the ground to hide her movements from the enemy. Her new course took her to a seasonal stream bed and toward a low hill that the water had cut into the base of.

When she was right beside it, she leapt as far onto it as she could and caught herself at the top of the incline. That sounded impressive, but it wasn't much of a hill. She'd only cleared a dozen meters over the base of jumbled rock.

When she was on the top of the rise, the additional height gave her the perspective to see where all of the horsemen were. She settled down into a good hiding spot and started calling off the locations to Boske.

She'd barely gotten started when a bright flash off to her left seemed to slam against her with psychic force. It didn't move her body, but it still knocked her out.

An indeterminate amount of time later, she blinked as consciousness returned. She was immersed in complete darkness. What the hell had that been? She tried to get her mind to work, but her thoughts were as slow as molasses.

She tried rolling over, but her armor refused to cooperate. Thankfully, she had the internal musculature to force it.

Only her artificial muscles weren't working either. She pushed, but nothing happened. She felt as weak as a kitten.

A quick check showed that her implants were offline. She'd never experienced that before. The armor wasn't transmitting any visuals to her implants, or her implants weren't receiving them.

Based on the evidence in front of her, she thought both of those things might be true. Somehow the enemy had managed to disrupt not only her armor, but her implants and her Raider augmentation.

Her armor was made so that it could be opened manually, so she reached up and found the manual releases for the helmet. They weren't made to be easy to manipulate, because no one wanted an enemy to get their armor open while they were inside it.

Still, Kelsey had trained her hard on knowing that part about her armor. The woman seemed to know *everything* about Marine Raider this and Marine Raider that. In this case, Julia was happy that she hadn't argued.

It took a minute of fumbling around to finally get the helmet to come free. The fresh air slammed into her face, cooling her immediately. She had no idea how long she'd been out, but the sun was still shining brightly down on her face.

The view showed her she had another problem. Her artificial eye wasn't working. The only vision she had was through her natural eye.

She needed to get out of her armor and figure out why her implants and hardware weren't working. She closed her eyes and tried everything that she could to access her implants. No dice.

Was there any way to force them to reset? That wasn't something she'd ever needed to know. Her implants were always on. They'd never turned themselves off before. She hadn't even suspected they *could* be turned off.

After having a lot of conversations with Ralph Halstead on board the destroyer, she knew that almost every piece of equipment had some type of reset. One could never count out having some type of critical error freeze everything in place.

There'd be something that would allow her to restart her implants. At least that's what she hoped. As much as she loathed the things, she absolutely needed them right now. Their enemies were all over them, and if she couldn't get herself back in motion, a lot of people were going to die.

While she kept thinking about that, she managed to roll herself over. Having her helmet off made that a little easier because she could see what she was doing. It took a supreme effort of will and force to get herself onto her stomach, but she managed.

Once she was there, she brought her hands to her torso and found the covers that went over the manual releases. Like the helmet, they weren't easy to manipulate, but she managed to remember what needed to be done.

With a loud click, all the latches that held the various pieces of her armor together disengaged. They were mechanical and so allowed the torso to split apart in the back where she'd normally get inside.

Arching her back, she forced the panels apart and extracted herself from her dead armor. Finally, she sat on the ground, covered in sweat, and looking at the armor beside her.

What the hell happened? What had that flash been?

Probably some type of electromagnetic pulse or something. Whatever it had been, it had obviously been designed to work against Imperial technology that was hardened to stop that kind of thing.

Julia spent another ten minutes attempting to manipulate her implants and Raider augmentation but was unable to get *anything* to work. There had to be a way, but she didn't know what it was.

Out of options, she rose to her feet and stared out over the plain where she'd been looking earlier. Before the blast, she'd been tracking a number of horses and riders. They were all gone now. However long she'd been out, it had been enough for them to leave.

If everyone in the party had had their implants affected this badly, it was a disaster. It meant that the horde had won. There was no way that Captain Beauchamp's people could have held them all off.

And considering how bloodthirsty they'd seemed, her heart was filled with dread at what she'd find when she got back to the column.

Clumsy and lacking the strength that she'd subconsciously begun relying on, Julia made her way down the hill and onto the plain. It was going to take her at least half an hour to get back to Boske.

She wasn't even wearing her marine fatigues or boots. Those were still in her saddlebags. She'd put them there when she'd gotten into the armor. All she was wearing was a skinsuit.

Her feet were going to be torn to pieces walking on the rough ground if she hurried at all. It might take her two hours to get back to the column, and that would certainly be too late to help, unless she could find her horse.

She prayed that everyone was still alive, but deep down she knew that was unlikely. She dreaded what she was going to find when she got there.

Resolute in spite of what she knew was coming, Julia began walking back toward where she'd last seen Boske. If the marines were still alive, maybe the group of them could still make a difference. Somehow.

22

Talbot woke groggy and disoriented. He immediately realized that he was riding, but the last thing he remembered doing was fighting. He blinked dazedly down at his hands, which had failed to move when he'd tried to raise them to his face. Someone had bound them tightly to the saddle horn.

His feet were similarly secured to the stirrups, when meant that any attempt to dismount would end with him being dragged by the horse. As he wasn't a skilled rider, he'd be an idiot to even *try* to get his feet free before his hands.

It would be child's play to use his Raider augmentation to break the rope securing his wrists, but he looked around to see what their situation was first.

A relatively small group of prisoners were being moved on horseback. There were dozens of enemy warriors around them, a number with bows out and arrows already nocked. Any precipitous action on his part would result in immediate bloodshed.

It felt like he couldn't completely wake up, and he shook his head trying to clear it. That's when he noticed that his implants weren't responding to his mental calls. They were offline.

His blood ran cold. He'd never heard of anything like that before.

Surreptitiously, he tried to flex his augmented muscles and found that his enhanced strength was also gone. He didn't know if that was because his implants were offline or if there was some kind of damage to the augmentation itself. He wasn't precisely certain what happened.

The last thing he remembered was being thrown into the air by the explosion of an antiarmor warhead right at his feet. His armor must've saved him, but it was nowhere to be seen now. Someone had stripped it off, and he was only dressed in his skinsuit, not even having any shoes on his feet.

Giving up on the idea of an immediate escape, he focused on what he could see. He needed to know what the situation was so that he could create a plan of action.

His captors seemed content to allow him to look around, so long as he didn't make any move they didn't care for. Talbot craned his head around and finally got an accurate count of just how many of their people were with him.

There were thirteen horses being led in the center of a group of about four or five times as many armed and armored enemies. None of the prisoners wore armor—either Imperial or local. All of them were stripped down to their uniforms, if they had them, or their skinsuits if they'd been in powered armor.

Talbot was relieved to see that his wife was at the front of the group. She was unconscious, but she was bound upright in the saddle just like the rest of them.

He knew it wasn't Julia, because he'd taken the precaution of memorizing their hairstyles. They were almost identical in appearance, but not indistinguishable, if one paid close attention to the details.

He also could see Admiral Mertz and Commodore Meyer directly behind his wife. A quick check ahead of him revealed Commodore Stone, Commander Cannon—the assistant tactical officer from *Athena* —and Chloe Laird.

A glance behind him showed Captain Beauchamp, Elise Orison, Olivia West, Austin Darrah, Ralph Halstead, and Carl Owlet. Only Beauchamp was semiconscious. From the blood and bruising on her face, she'd been brutally beaten.

Thirteen prisoners out of just over a hundred marines, Fleet personnel, and civilians. Whatever had happened, they'd lost the fight. The horde wouldn't have all of the senior people if that weren't the case. It worried him that none of the marines under his command and none of the regular Fleet personnel were present.

Were they being kept in separate caravans to prevent an uprising? He wished he knew for sure, but without his implants, he couldn't see anyone's status, contact the drone network, or even assess his own condition.

The next person to start moving was Admiral Mertz. His head came up abruptly and he also had weapons aimed in his direction, but since he wasn't enhanced, he wasn't going to try to break his bonds.

The other man blinked owlishly around himself before he turned in the saddle and his eyes locked on Talbot. They were separated by a couple of horses, and Talbot wasn't certain that their captors would be pleased with them talking to one another.

He wished he could open a com channel with the admiral and tell him to stay where he was, because they were in exceptionally dangerous circumstances right now.

The admiral was bolder than he, because he used his heels to urge his mount to slow. Their captors watched him but didn't interfere. Perhaps they thought that the display of weaponry was enough.

After all, wasn't it? They'd won the fight. No one here was in a position to resist them. If the prisoners made any kind of move, they'd be slaughtered. Without reins, they couldn't even really control the horses they were bound to. Not that they had the skills to do so, in most cases.

Admiral Mertz finally made it up beside him. "What's going on? My implants aren't responding."

Talbot shrugged slightly. "I was unconscious when whatever it was happened, so I'm not really sure."

"It must've been that big weapon they fired up into the sky," the admiral said quietly. "I think it was some kind of EMP device. Maybe one tailored to operate against Imperial equipment.

"My implants are offline. Maybe burned out. The last thing I remember was that weapon going off. It must've knocked everyone with implants out. We're in deep trouble."

"I'd say that's something of an understatement," Talbot said with a grunt. "Do we have any idea where everyone else is? I find it peculiar that the people here are mostly what I'd call our senior staff. There are a couple that are a little lower in the hierarchy, like Commander Cannon or Chloe Laird, and the science types, but everyone else is what I'd say is a major player. How did they get all of us gathered in one place? Hell, how did they get me out of my armor?"

The admiral shrugged. "I don't know, but I think we're about to find out."

He gestured with his chin toward where Captain Beauchamp was edging in their direction. It looked as if she were awake enough to talk. She looked like hell. Whatever she had to say, it wasn't going to be good.

* * *

MAKING her way across the grasslands barefoot and half blind wasn't anything close to easy, but Julia managed to get back to where she left the marines. It took her a while to circle around the fire that her plasma shots had started. What she found when she got there was devastating.

Whatever had taken her down had also taken out the ready response team. Each of them lay where they'd fallen. Or at least where their armor had fallen.

Someone had removed their helmets and then slit their throats.

Julia went from person to person until she found Corporal Boske. The woman lay on her back, her eyes closed and her expression peaceful. She'd probably never even felt the cold kiss of death, which Julia supposed was a blessing.

She stumbled a few feet away and threw up as she sobbed. She'd known these people. She'd fought beside them. Now they were gone.

Julia wiped the tears from her face, found a canteen to wash out her mouth, and gathered what weapons she could find. The final tally was half a dozen marine knives, flechette rifles made for the armor, a couple of flechette pistols, and a couple of stunners.

None of the advanced weapons worked. They were just as dead as the plasma rifle that she'd left on the hill. That flash had to have been some kind of extremely powerful electromagnetic pulse.

That left her with the marine knives. Very old school, but they didn't require any power source at all, other than her muscles. Not her strongest asset, but they'd have to do.

There were a couple of ration bars and a pair of maintenance slippers that someone had kept in one of the suits of armor. They weren't very tough, but they'd slip over her bare feet and give her *some* protection as she made her way back to the column.

Julia took a small bag from another set of armor and stuffed the food that she'd recovered inside with the knives in their sheaths. Her skinsuit had no place to strap on a knife, so she carried the final one in her hand, still sheathed because she wasn't an idiot.

She'd use it if push came to shove, but without her augmentation, any kind of confrontation was going to be heavily one-sided against her. Her very best option was not to be noticed at all.

With a final look at her dead comrades, Julia set out toward the column.

It took hours to get back into the general area where the column had been. She found it because a little bit of smoke smudged the clear sky in that direction. The smoke from the fire she'd started was a pall off to the side. Someone was burning something ahead of her.

Or maybe cooking something. If so, they were charring it badly because the smell of burnt meat was overpowering.

Julia moved as carefully and cautiously as she could. Where possible, she used grass where others had gone before her. It was helpful that she'd found the area that the invaders had come through because the grass there made less noise as she passed. She had no ability to do any kind of stealth, so every noise she made sent her heart bounding into her throat.

She arrived at what was obviously some type of hastily dug concealment pit with mats of grass that had been thrown aside to allow ambushers to attack the column. She didn't know how the ambushers had known where the column was going to be, but they'd done damned well at placing them. The column was only about fifty meters away.

Rather, what was left of it.

Dead bodies lay everywhere. Based on the few people she saw moving through the carnage, the horde had won. It looked as if they'd killed *everyone*.

Taking slow, deep breaths to calm herself, she ducked into one of the pits and started counting the enemies that she could see, trying to figure out what they were doing.

There were seven people searching for things to load onto pack horses. All the horses that had come with the column were either gone or being held ready to leave. The people she was observing were perhaps making a final pass to gather anything that they considered worthwhile.

One of the men, a tall, powerfully built fellow with his dark hair drawn back into a ponytail, shouted at the others to mount up and get moving. They obeyed his orders quickly, finding their mounts and climbing aboard. They quickly tethered the cargo animals to them and moved out.

That just left the one man who waited patiently for them to leave. She wondered what he was doing. Why hadn't he left with his friends?

The answer came when he seemed satisfied that they were gone and he moved over to a different area, bent down, and uncovered something.

When he rose, Julia recognized what she was looking at. Those were Kelsey's swords. The ones made of the same material as the marine knives. The ones that could cut through just about anything. It looked as if the man intended to claim them for himself and didn't want any of the others to know that he'd done so.

He had a horse nearby and started heading toward it. Julia knew that if she wanted to get a ride out of this place and not be completely unarmed, she needed those swords and that horse.

She dropped the bag with her food and spare knives, rose quietly to her feet, and moved forward as quickly as she could, hoping that he wouldn't hear her coming. She unsheathed the marine knife she'd kept and made the best speed she could toward his back.

Sadly, she wasn't good enough.

When Julia was about ten meters away, he whirled in place and spotted her. Before she could rush him, he dropped Kelsey's swords, bent his knees, and grabbed a spear off the ground.

"Well, well, well," he said with a grin as he hefted the probably more familiar weapon. "It seems we have one final survivor. You're pretty. Perhaps I'll save killing you until I've had some fun."

With that, he stepped toward her, his weapon held ready to attack or defend. It gave him a lot more reach than she had. He could stab her or use the blunt end to beat her.

This wasn't looking good at all.

23

All it took was one look at Clarice Beauchamp's face for Jared to know that their situation was grim. She sagged in the saddle, her face badly bruised and swollen. Her hands and legs were tied like his own. If they hadn't been, she might've fallen off her horse.

"Tell me," he said quietly.

"We fought as well as we could, but there were too many of them," she said, her voice slurred. "We couldn't stop them. Once they deployed whatever that weapon was, all of your people collapsed. It was just my warriors against many times our number when the enemy finally coalesced around us. I tried to get riders free to go for help, but the horde killed them all.

"The raid leaders questioned my surviving people and myself closely, since we were the only ones awake. They asked who the most important of your people were. I had no choice but to tell them. I enhanced the roles of a few of your people to save more of them. It was all I could do."

Jared felt his throat constrict. "What happened to the rest?"

"Dead," Beauchamp said softly, her head falling forward. "They killed them all, your unconscious people and my own survivors both. We few are all that is left."

The news was like a kick to his groin. He was responsible for those people, and he'd led them to their deaths.

"What about Julia?" he asked when he could finally make himself speak again. "Or the marines that went with her."

The local shrugged. "I don't know. None of them were brought back, so I assume that whoever they were fighting killed them where they fell. I saw some of the people take your sister and her husband out of their armor, so they knew how to remove it. Nothing would've stopped them from getting to the people that went hunting them."

"I don't see Commander Roche," Jared said. "Didn't you give them his name as well?"

She shook her head. "He was killed in the fighting. I saw him go down with two arrows to the chest."

In a way, Jared hoped that Julia was dead. He knew that if she wasn't, the death of her friend would break her.

"What happens now?" Talbot asked. "Where are they taking us? What are they going to do to us?"

Again, Beauchamp shrugged. "Nothing good. They're taking us to their capital city. It sits on the outskirts of one of the ruined megacities. They're going to torture us, put us on trial, and then execute us.

"They'll do their best to extract what information they can from us first. That's where the torture will come in. They'll want to know everything they can about you, what you can do, and where you came from. For me, they're going to want to know everything I can tell them about my people's defenses. They'll want to know how to destroy us utterly.

"That's why they've got our arms and legs tied, to make certain that we can't somehow kill ourselves. The strapping held you in the saddle while you were unconscious, but they're not going to remove it until we stop for the evening, and then they'll secure us again once we've taken care of our necessary business. They'll take no chances with us being able to get away or take our own lives."

The news made Jared feel hollow inside. Not only had he failed his people, everyone he cared about was going to die in the most horrible manner imaginable. He had failed the Empire utterly.

"Where's everybody else?" Talbot asked. "There have to have been a lot more of them than this."

"Gathering everything that we salvaged and chasing down all the horses that got away," she said. "They're also burning their dead. They'll leave ours where they fell."

"No doubt there are groups of pack animals somewhere around us. That will have the majority of their forces acting as guards because they don't want anyone to take all their new toys. They'll also have people back at your camp breaking into your crashed ships and securing everything for their own use."

"That had to be some kind of EMP weapon," Talbot said slowly. "My implants are offline, and so is my augmentation. I'm not sure if it's fried or if it simply needs to be reset in some fashion. I had a manual that explained how it all worked, but it was stored in my implant memory. Maybe Kelsey knows more. I'm a little worried that she hasn't woken up yet."

"One of the invaders took special pleasure in making sure that she was unconscious once they removed her from her armor," Beauchamp said. "He kicked her in the head several times. She was still alive, obviously, or they wouldn't have strapped her to the horse, but she may be gravely injured.

"I was warned that we can talk amongst ourselves when we wake but that we are not allowed to approach anyone that is unconscious. I know you want to check on her, but we're going to have to wait and see if she wakes up on her own. If you try to violate their rules, they'll hurt you badly. They only need a few of you alive to talk.

"I hesitate to mention this, but gelding is a favorite torture of theirs, so I would be *very* careful not to get on their bad side any more than you already are."

"We have to assume that Julia and the other marines were killed after the bomb went off," Jared said, wanting to go to his sister in spite of the risk, but not daring. "The only people that could help us are right here. I doubt that any of your people will be coming for us. Is that right?"

Captain Beauchamp nodded. "They'll find the bodies left on the field once all the fighters are gone, but they're not going to send anyone after us. The horde is too strong. The only help that we can count on now is right here, so we're as good as dead."

* * *

JULIA FROZE IN PLACE. Without her augmentation, she didn't have a chance against a trained warrior. His spear had reach on her knife, and she didn't have even a third of his strength without her artificial musculature. She had no speed advantage, and she couldn't even turn her combat over to the implants in her head. She was outclassed in every way imaginable.

There was no way she could win this fight.

He'd obviously come to the same conclusion, because his grin only widened as he advanced toward her. He casually twitched his spear with nimble fingers so that she couldn't be sure from which way a jab or strike might come from. His movements definitely left the impression of a predator playing with its food.

"I'm not certain how the outriders missed you, but I'm glad they did," he said with a dark chuckle. "You're a luscious piece of fruit just waiting to be plucked and savored. What secrets do you know? How does one as pretty as you serve the monsters in the sky? The ones who killed our world."

His playful tone had vanished by the time he'd finished his little speech, replaced by a cold sneer. Obviously, he didn't like the Rebel Empire any more than she did. Perhaps Julia could use that to her advantage.

Though she didn't drop her knife, she raised her empty hand. "I don't serve those monsters. None of us do. We're fighting them, trying to stop them. There's been a terrible misunderstanding."

The man laughed without the slightest bit of humor. "I'd say so, because you should never have come here. Your kind is not welcome. You might not think you serve those things, but you do. They have things in your heads that control your every move. We know.

"Don't worry, we'll make sure and cut it out so that they don't ever have the chance to do that again. We might even let you live once we've finished, if you're *very* cooperative.

"I hope that you yield completely, because you'd make an excellent addition to my household as a comfort slave. You don't look like the kind that would survive as a drudge, so if I were you, I'd start learning how to please me right now."

Yeah, that wasn't going to happen. She might as well die right here and now. She'd never give herself over to someone like this. Better to bleed out than to be a sex slave. Or worse.

She was just about to throw herself at him and take her chances when a cry from just off to her right captured both their attentions.

Staggering up out of the grass, Scott Roche rushed toward the man, a flechette pistol in his hand. "Die!" he screamed as he raised the weapon.

Julia knew damned well that the pistol had to have been fried. There was no way it was going to work as anything better than a rock.

Deep down, her attacker had to have realized the same thing, but his trained reactions betrayed him. No warrior would allow a charging enemy to get to him with a weapon that he knew was deadly, even if subconsciously he knew the weapon was useless.

With one smooth motion, her attacker turned to face Scott and met his charge with the tip of his spear. The primitive weapon easily knocked the flechette pistol away before plunging through her friend's chest.

"No!" she screamed as she charged forward. She held the knife in her hand low and used her short stature to come in at a lower angle than the man might expect.

He immediately tugged on the spear and made to turn toward her. Unfortunately for him, Scott had his hands wrapped tightly around the spear and wasn't letting go. The man's weapon was hopelessly tangled and couldn't possibly stop her charge.

The warrior released his spear and drew his sword, using that motion to slash it toward her head, but she was already rolling on the ground at his feet.

She came up blade first, and the wickedly sharp knife cut through his armor and flesh both, opening him from groin to sternum.

The stench of blood and offal was almost a physical blow to her senses as she threw herself back from the fatally wounded man, watching for him to collapse in death.

Only he wasn't done yet. Holding his guts in with one hand, he staggered after her, seemingly determined to kill her before he fell.

If she could keep him at arm's length until his wound dragged him down, she'd survive. If he caught her, she was dead.

Even though her attention was fully on her attacker, she saw Scott Roche do the impossible out of the corner of her eye. He pulled the spear from his chest, turned it so that the point was facing toward her attacker, and hurled it with his remaining strength, even as he collapsed to his knees.

His aim was off, but the spear still struck the man in the back of his head with its shaft, once again distracting him at a critical moment. Julia took advantage of his distraction to race inside his sword's reach until the two of them were almost touching.

He grabbed her with his free hand, yanking her hair back painfully, but it didn't stop her from plunging her knife through his chin and into his brain. Hot blood spattered across her face as he quivered. Moments later, he collapsed and she let him go.

Certain that the man was dead, Julia raced to Scott's side just in time to catch him as he slumped. A quick look showed her that he had two arrows buried in his chest, as well as the horrific wound that the spear had caused. Without modern medical facilities, her friend was dying.

Already he was coughing blood and had trouble breathing. She wasn't sure how he'd survived as long as he had.

"You shouldn't have," she whispered as she stroked his upturned face.

"It's my duty... and privilege... to trade my life... for yours," he gasped out between coughing fits. "They took... Mertz and... the others... alive. Save them. Make them... save our people."

With a final gasp, he went still and stopped breathing. She sat with her dead friend's head in her lap and cried until she had no tears left inside her.

She wasn't a warrior, but she'd track the horde down and kill as many of them as she could. She'd save her new companions, no matter the price. Then she'd do whatever it took to save her people. Scott's sacrifice demanded no less.

The horde had chosen the wrong person to make an enemy of. She'd make them pay for what they'd done. Terra would run red with their blood. She swore it.

24

When Kelsey woke, her head hurt terribly, and her face felt almost as bad. A glance around revealed that her greatest fear had come true. Somehow, she'd been captured. There'd been some kind of weapon, she remembered foggily. She'd tried to stop them from setting it off but had failed.

It only took her a few moments to realize it must've been some type of electromagnetic pulse weapon. Her implants were offline, and her augmentation wasn't working either. That was patently obvious because her face still hurt. If her medical nanites had been functional, they'd have already taken care of the cuts and bruises, and her pharmacology unit would've stopped the pain.

A look around her revealed most of her friends scattered around her, but they were all prisoners. She didn't see Julia, which might be very good or very bad. There was also no sign of Commander Roche either. She hoped they were okay and had gotten away.

Everyone else seemed to be in just as bad a shape as she was, but they were all awake. She was obviously the last one to wake up, which was an unusual state of affairs for her. She felt as if someone had beaten her, and that might not be far from the truth.

With as many people as she'd killed, it was entirely possible that they'd taken out some of their wrath on her. It felt as if her ribs might be cracked, although that was impossible. The Graphene coating would've kept the bones from breaking, but she was certainly bruised in all the wrong places.

As soon as it was obvious that she was awake, her husband made his way up to her. Since his hands were tied to the saddle horn and his legs were secured to the stirrups, his pace was slow. The warriors guarding them seemed to be okay with him getting close to her, but had their bows prominently displayed. She was certain that if anyone made a break for it, they'd catch several arrows in their back and would be dead before they got outside bow range.

Hell, the horsemen probably could ride faster than any of them under the circumstances. They might just cut them down with swords. She and her friends were helpless to resist at this point.

"It's bad, isn't it?" she asked Talbot when he got beside her.

He nodded grimly. "I'm not going to hide this from you. That EMP weapon took everyone with implants out. The horde then overwhelmed Captain Beauchamp's people, started figuring out who the important people left alive were, and executed everyone else. We're all that's left."

His words were like a sledgehammer to her gut. She almost whimpered in the pain of knowing that so many of the people she was responsible for had died. All because they'd inserted themselves into someone else's business.

"We should've just kept going," she said softly. "We should've ignored the group heading toward where the pinnaces were and run. We stuck our noses where they didn't need to be, and now they've chopped them off for us. Where are we going now?"

Her husband took a deep breath and let it out slowly. "From what I understand, Captain Beauchamp seems to think that they're taking us to their capital city. It's built next to one of the ruined megacities.

"Once we get there, they're going to torture us for whatever information we have and then execute us. Apparently, this isn't something that even cooperation is going to change. Unless we figure out how to get away, we're going to be put through some of the most horrific things you can imagine and then they're going to burn us alive. That's their form of execution, just in case you need extra motivation to come up with a brilliant escape plan."

Kelsey's stomach roiled. She *had* to figure out a way out of this. She was a damned Marine Raider and the Crown Princess of the New Terran Empire. There was no way in hell that she'd let these barbarians kill her and her friends.

She looked around at the guards shepherding them. "It looks like we've got about fifty guards. We're tied up, but they have to stop sometime. We need to at least try and escape. Even if we fail, what's the worst that can happen? We get a clean death in battle. That's a hell of a lot better than torture and immolation."

Kelsey looked up at where the sun sat in the sky and tried to guess the time. It wasn't easy without her implants, but it seemed like evening. They probably only had another hour before the sun set.

She had no doubts that the guards would keep them tied up for as long as they could, but they had to cut them loose to use the bathroom and eat, if they wanted to get them back to their city so that they could be questioned.

Kelsey knew that they'd be under heavy guard, but surely they could do *something*. Maybe not tonight. Maybe it would be tomorrow night. She had to figure out what the horde's patterns were before she could find a way to subvert them.

"Are we sure that Julia and Scott are dead?" she asked.

"Scott is," he said. "Captain Beauchamp saw him with a couple of arrows in his chest. I'm sorry, Kelsey, but he's gone. As for Julia, she was off with the ready response team. None of them were seen or heard from again, so I can't imagine that any of them escaped."

His words infuriated her. How could they have misjudged the situation so badly? How could *she* have misjudged the situation so badly?

She cast a glance over at where Jared was talking with Captain Beauchamp. Since none of the woman's people were with her, the horde had butchered her entire command.

What would they do if they escaped? There had to be more horsemen scattered around than those she could currently see. These people were doing things that she didn't know about, and that put every plan that she came up with at risk.

If they broke out of this camp, they'd have to somehow evade the other horsemen, figure out how to get clear of this entire area, and still make the fifteen-hundred-kilometer journey to the Imperial Palace. All by themselves with no advanced gear or even basic supplies. On foot while evading horsemen who would no doubt be determined to capture and kill them all.

Simple, right?

The thought of all that made her frown. The EMP had probably fried the Imperial Scepter. It was the physical key to get into the vaults. They also didn't have possession of it anymore. Could they even access the Imperial Vault without it?

There was probably a way in without it, but they didn't have their implants, so how could she activate computers to try to bypass the security system?

The odds stacked against them seemed overwhelming. They had no outside help, and even if they managed to resist the people holding them captive, they could expect extermination in the ensuing fight.

Maybe one or two of them could get away from this, if the rest gave up all hope of escape and fought, but that was probably wishful thinking.

It certainly seemed as if everything they'd fought so hard to accomplish was for nothing. The artificial intelligences would win. They'd eventually bring the Omega Plague back to Terra and exterminate every living being on the planet, which she supposed was a kind of pyric revenge on the horde, but that wouldn't help the New Terran Empire.

Humanity's best hope of beating the AIs was lost, and she had no idea how they could possibly survive, much less win.

* * *

IT TOOK every bit of her strength, but Julia managed to drag Scott's body to where the horde had been burning their dead. It broke her heart to heave him onto the smoldering flames in the hastily dug pit, but she did it. She wasn't going to leave him out for the animals to eat. He'd been her friend and loyal supporter for years, and he deserved the final care she now showed him.

The stench of burning flesh made her stomach heave, and she threw up as soon as she'd accomplished the task and staggered away from the hellish scene. Then she sat on the ground and wept.

When she finally regained control over herself, she set about searching the remaining dead for clothes she could wear. Her skinsuit wasn't going to be helpful in what she needed to do. Her pack horse was gone. Probably taken by the raiders as a matter of course, so none of her own belongings were available.

She gathered some marine uniforms and some boots that she could use with several layers of socks to take up the extra space her small feet would leave, but that wouldn't do for the first part of what she needed to do. She had to blend in, and that meant she needed local clothes, armor, and weapons.

It took a while, but she managed to find one of the warriors who was almost as small as she was. The man was thin and wiry, and it looked as if he'd specialized in the bow.

In fact, his weapon was exquisite. Its polished wood looked strong and its bowstring was taut, but that hardly began to tell the story of this weapon.

Its surface was polished from use, and the wood almost glowed under the protective coating that the man had applied often to keep it pristine. The length of the short bow was etched with all kinds of detailed patterns. They were very similar to something that she'd seen in the library on the destroyer. Something called Celtic knotwork. It was simply gorgeous.

The weapon was obviously made to be used from horseback because of its short length. That had the added benefit of reducing the pull on the string to the point where she could use it. The arrows the man carried were a bit thicker than she was used to shooting in her youth, and the heads had wide, razor-sharp blades of metal that would cause great wounds, likely killing the targets quickly.

The challenge would come when she needed to use it. With only one eye, her aim would be put to the ultimate test. Thankfully, she still had her dominant eye, so it wouldn't be impossible.

Julia stripped the man before dressing in his clothes, which was a disgusting and gross thing that she wished she didn't have to do. Then she put his armor on over them. At least she was able to keep her skinsuit on underneath everything, so it felt like a layer of mental insulation from wearing a dead man's things.

The man had died of a neck wound, so even though his armor was stained in blood, it wasn't damaged in a way that would stand out to anyone that saw her. At least until they got close enough to see her clearly. Or smell her. Ugh.

She took a few minutes to wash off the blood with water salvaged from the dead. She'd need to take enough to survive on, and some food as well, when she departed. One more thing added to her mental checklist.

That done, she pulled the man's sword from its sheath, once she had it belted on. It was almost as much a work of art as his bow. The blade was made of brightly polished steel. The wavy marks of folded metal were vaguely familiar to her. Something called Damascus? That sounded right.

Her brother had an interest in knives and had raved on about this kind of weapon, telling his very disinterested sister all about it in excruciating detail. It had bored her to tears, but she was now grateful that she had any frame of reference at all.

The man also had a pair of long daggers of the same metal. Based on the mark at the base of the blades, the weapons were probably forged by the same smith.

She took them all. They were no use to the dead man, but they might make the difference between her life or death. She hoped the dead man would have approved.

Not that she had a lick of skill with either weapon. Their excellence wouldn't save her if she fumbled when she had to use them.

Julia moved back to the horde raider that she'd killed and recovered Kelsey's swords. She'd strap them to the horse and use them if push came to shove. They might make up for some of her lack of training. No matter how good other blades were, one strike from a hull metal blade with an almost monomolecular edge would shear it off.

Kelsey would want them back whenever she caught up with her. That was fine. The other woman would be far deadlier with them. In the meanwhile, she'd use them.

Once she had all her newly acquired weapons in place, she gathered every bit of food and water she could find. Running out of either while trying to cross the plains would be a recipe for death, and she had no idea how many people she was going to be chasing.

She also found a plasma grenade on a dead marine. It was Major Scala, she thought, though with the damage to his face, it was hard to say.

The weapon might not work, but she took it anyway.

All that done, she mounted the captured warhorse and turned him in the direction that the horde had ridden away in. He was surprisingly willing to have her as a rider. The other man must've been a jerk to him, too.

The tracks were already diverging as she left the scene of the battle, so she suspected that the horde warriors might've split apart to cover more ground. She'd know for sure once she got closer to them.

Her best bet for survival would be to avoid contact altogether until she'd caught up with them. If she could skirt the groups ahead of her, she could figure out where the prisoners were, and perhaps find a way to release them.

She was their ace in the hole, a gambling reference she actually understood. Without the horde expecting any survivors, they'd be focused on their prisoners. With any luck at all, she'd make them deeply regret that oversight.

Julia put her heels to the horse's flanks and set off in pursuit of the others. It was time to try and snatch victory from the jaws of defeat.

25

By the time they'd stopped for the evening, Talbot was exhausted and sore all over again. His lack of riding skills was magnified by the fact that he couldn't even move around on his saddle. His captors also didn't appear to be the kind of people that liked to give breaks, so his ass was a mixture of lead and pain. Much worse now that his medical nanites were down.

Four warriors came to untie him, two holding swords, while a third covered him with a bow from a different angle. The fourth person used a knife to cut the rope binding his legs and hands before gesturing for him to dismount.

Talbot barely managed to get off the horse without falling over.

His captors almost dragged him over to a moderately secluded place and allowed him to use the bathroom. One of them poured water over his hands and handed him a small sliver of soap to clean up.

The lack of toilet paper was somewhat disturbing, but they had a coarse cloth that they dropped into a bag when he'd finished his business. Then they bound his hands tightly behind his back again.

The rest of the marauders were setting up camp and guarding the remainder of the prisoners. All of the horses were picketed off to the left, several fire pits were being dug, and people were gathering wood from the scraggly trees around the area.

One of the marauders sat in a folding chair, watching Talbot. She was dressed in armor like the rest, her helmet set off to the side of her chair next to her sheathed sword.

His captors dragged him before her, forced him to his knees, and stepped back. He didn't look, but he was certain they were all covering him with weapons as the woman examined him.

"So, you are one of those that serve the sky machines," she said, her voice low and melodic. Her tone was one of cold fury.

"No," Talbot said firmly. "We're not. We were fighting them when we came to Terra. They destroyed our ship in orbit. We're no allies of the machines."

The woman threw her head back and laughed mockingly. "If only you knew how many people just like you said the exact same thing, or so the histories say. But that all changed when we put them to the question. The *truth* came out then.

"I don't know why you've come back to Terra after so long, but you'll meet the same fate as your predecessors. First, though, you're going to tell us everything that you know about what the computers intend."

"I don't suppose there's anything I could say that would change your mind?" Talbot asked sadly.

"No. I've determined that you're most likely the leader of this particular expedition. You seem to be the strongest warrior, and you were captured inside forbidden armor. That makes you someone that knows much about what the machines intend.

"My associates at the capital are going to ask you many questions. It would go easier on you if you cooperated. In that spirit, I'll give you the opportunity to save your people some pain. Why are you here, why did you bring those ships from the sky, and why did you crash them so that you couldn't leave again?"

Talbot snorted mirthlessly. "The crash was unintentional. The last ship failed right before landing. If things had gone according to plan, we'd have gotten to the ground without the machines—or you—knowing that we were here at all."

The woman made a face that showed she didn't believe a word he'd just said. "You tell a fanciful tale, but it will not save you in the end. Do you know how the horde questions recalcitrant prisoners? Would you like a demonstration?"

Talbot's stomach clenched at that, but he stood firm. Well, knelt firm. "No."

The woman chuckled darkly. "Understandable, though I still think you deserve to know what awaits you. Observe the fire off to our left."

One of the warriors there held up an iron bar whose handle was thickly wrapped in leather. He stuck one end in the fire and grinned at them.

Talbot's skin grew cold. That didn't look good at all.

"We use hot pokers to convince you to tell us what we want to know," the woman said conversationally. "Even the bravest warriors break after a while. It doesn't matter how long you lie to us, eventually you'll tell us what we want to know, or you'll die screaming under the question. Frankly, either one of those outcomes is satisfying.

"It's our tradition, if you will, to start with those who are not warriors to convince the warriors to speak. You'd be surprised how many strong men and women break when seeing those they're supposed to protect being tortured. Though I have a different idea.

"Perhaps I'll start with the blonde that caused us so much trouble. We found her in armor standing over you, so I think she cares for you. How much do you care for her? Will you save her from that fate? Or will you watch her scream until she dies?"

It took every bit of Talbot's will to keep his expression blank. He wanted to snarl, leap to his feet, and attack the woman, but he couldn't do that. They'd know for sure how important Kelsey was to him then. Not that they didn't already know.

The woman sat there letting the silence drag on as the sun touched the horizon behind her. She seemed content to stay that way until the sun had completely set, then she rose to her feet and stepped over to Talbot.

She leaned close and smiled darkly. "I will take great pleasure in conducting the questioning once we return to the city," she said in a low, throaty voice. "I will start with the woman, and then I'll move on to the weakest among you. You won't feel the heat of the poker until all of your friends are dead, warrior. Will you break when you see those under your care screaming in agony?"

Talbot tried to headbutt the woman, but she hopped back and laughed as her men began beating him. With his hands tied behind his back, he was helpless to resist as they pummeled him into unconsciousness.

* * *

JULIA RODE in the direction that the horde had taken when they'd left the area. She had no idea how many people were ahead of her, or even which subgroup contained people she was looking for. And she was going to have to look through subgroups, because the horde force had definitely split into different parties.

Unsure of how to proceed, she stopped for a moment to consider her options. She had no skill in tracking, and each of the subgroups left what looked to her like identical sets of prints. While she had a lot of riding experience, telling different sets of hoofprints apart was something she wasn't knowledgeable at.

Yet, if she was going to find her friends, she was going to have to locate the appropriate group and follow them. She was going to have one chance at this, and she needed to make certain she did the very smartest things she could. This wasn't the time to go running off killing people. She had to think this through and act cautiously.

The answer, when it finally came to her, seemed blindingly obvious in retrospect. The cargo horses were heavily laden, and thus their prints were deep. Those who were riding regular mounts without that kind of load tended to move faster than the cargo horses, so their strides were longer. She found one group of tracks that had relatively light hoofprints, yet the distance between prints was short, as though the horses were moving slowly.

While that certainly didn't mean that she'd found the group with her friends, this at least gave her a logical starting point.

It was impossible for her to judge just how many riders there were, but the interior group had a few different sets of markings on their shoes. These were obviously beaten metal, and there were some differences in the shaping and texture on them. That led her to believe that there were at least six people in the center of this group, though there might be twice that many. Again, she had no way of knowing for certain.

The surrounding group seemed significantly larger than many of the other sets of tracks she'd found. To her mind, that meant that it was far more likely that this was a prisoner convoy. That meant she was likely following the people that she most wanted to find.

Julia got back on her horse and started after the group. She rode cautiously, because she wasn't sure if they'd leave someone riding behind as an early-warning system. If it was her, that's what she'd do.

Still, there'd been the one man left behind to go over the site of the battle. That meant they'd expect at least one person to follow along behind them. Since she was dressed in similar armor and riding one of their horses, it was likely that they'd initially believe she was him.

If someone came too close though, the game would be up. She probably didn't look exactly like their comrades and didn't know enough about them to spot what she might have wrong on the armor and such. She also didn't know their idioms, so any kind of conversation would likely give her away.

The worst thing that could happen was if a group of horsemen approached her. If any of them stayed at a distance with bows trained on her, she was screwed. If there were only two people close in, she might be able to cut one down by surprise and then deal with the other one, but even that was chancy.

She didn't have her Marine Raider augmentation to help her win this fight, so stealth was a much better option than fighting. She had Kelsey's swords, but those would be a one-trick pony. She might kill a single warrior by surprise and *might* even beat a second. Three? She'd be a dead woman.

To her relief, she didn't see anyone as she traveled. She didn't rush, but she didn't dawdle either. She had some distance to make up. They'd have to stop for the night, and that would give her a chance to see if she was after the right group.

If so, and if she could get to them while the camp was quiet, it was possible that she could free one of the warriors. Her search of the battle site hadn't shown any of the senior people, so if she could find Kelsey or Talbot, that would be ideal.

One of the advantages that she had was skill with a bow. Nothing like the one she'd captured, but she'd grown to love shooting the bow while growing up and still had a modicum of skill with one. If she had to use a weapon, she'd be much more comfortable using her new ranged weapon.

If she could get to Kelsey and back her up with a bow, perhaps the woman's husband could take the other sword, and the two of them could cut the rest free.

It was almost dark when she finally spotted something promising. There were wisps of smoke rising from just over a small rise ahead of her. That probably meant that there was a campsite somewhere on the other side.

If so, they probably had watchers out. They wouldn't want to be surprised in the middle of the night. She had to approach carefully and cautiously, so as not to alert them to her presence.

Julia hobbled her horse behind another small rise so that no observers would see him. She'd have to sneak up on foot once the sun had fully set.

They wouldn't have night vision goggles, so they wouldn't be able to see her coming, so long as she didn't make a lot of noise or do something that caused them to spot her. These guards would probably think they were in a relatively safe place.

After all, they'd killed the group that they'd been after, she thought bitterly They were on their way home all safe and sound.

In actuality, the best time to move would be sometime early in the morning, but she needed to scout. Insertion and extraction would take time. She had to assume that this was the wrong group, simply because if she assumed it was the right one and made a mistake, then she was screwed.

She found a good place to wait and spent the next several hours trying to think about what she needed to do. She ate and drank from her supplies but didn't dare take a nap because she was afraid that her exhaustion would overwhelm her.

Without her augmentation, Julia's body wasn't nearly as resilient, and without her implants, her mind was already clouded with fatigue. It was like she'd been before the Pale Ones forced the change on her and she was having trouble readjusting.

When she finally decided that she'd waited as long as she needed to, she made one final check to be certain that nothing on her armor would make noise. She then circled around to approach the campsite from a different angle.

If she were the guards, she'd be watching along their backtrack, so her best angle of insertion would be from somewhere off to the side of that. This was a plain, so there was high grass and scrub brush that she could use for cover, but she had to move slowly because she didn't dare cause any motion or noise that would attract their attention.

That meant getting into position to see what was inside the camp took far longer than she expected. Luckily for her, she'd approached near where they were keeping the horses. So long as she didn't spook them, their soft movements and noise would cover hers. With that in mind, she kept enough space so that they didn't react to her.

It only took a few minutes to figure out that she was in the right place. There were a few banked fires that had enemy soldiers sleeping around them. It was hard to tell in the darkness, but she thought there were perhaps forty people sleeping there.

Some distance away from the fires, sleeping in the chill air, were the people that she was looking for. Their captors had their arms and legs tied, and they were under guard. Two men with bows stood watching from a safe distance, each on opposite sides of the group. She almost missed the second one in the dark, but he coughed and drew her attention to where he was standing near a scrub tree.

His presence made her stop and look around more closely. She couldn't afford to miss any other guards in the dark. Even one left alive would raise the alarm.

If her guess was accurate, there were probably between six and eight other people scattered around the camp acting as sentries, and the two she'd seen keeping watch over the horses. She wasn't certain how she would deal with them, but the glimmering of a plan started working its way into her brain.

It was dangerous, but if she could pull it off, they might all be able to slip away before the people around them even realized they were gone.

If stealth failed, she always had plan B, which was risky because of the EMP. She'd recovered that one plasma grenade. If it was dead like all the rest of the Imperial equipment, then using it would be futile and stupid.

But those were primitive devices with little or no electronics. Basically, you pulled the retaining pin, threw the grenade, and it blew up. It should still work. Theoretically.

If the plasma grenade went off, she'd kill at least two thirds of the enemy. At the very least, that would slake some of her bloodlust and reduce the fighting to a manageable level. She hoped.

Still, her preference was to let Kelsey make that decision. To do that, she had to take care of the guards and get to her.

Well, there was no time like the present.

She held her bow with an arrow comfortably nocked against the string in one hand while she had a marine knife in the other, carefully hidden behind her thigh. She strolled directly up to the first guard. They were going to see her coming, no matter what she did, so her best defense was to look exactly like the rest of them.

Perhaps she could pretend to be their relief for that one critical moment. Dealing with the other guard was still going to be problematic, but she'd have to trust in her own skills and hope for the best.

As it happened, the guard she was approaching had his back directly toward her. She actually managed to get right at his back without him being aware that she was even there. She was pretty sure that his partner across the fire had seen her approach, but he hadn't had any reason to be alarmed.

That was about to change.

She jammed the knife into the back of the first guard's skull as soon as she was within arm's reach. The blade entered with an audible—though soft—crunch, and the guard fell like a puppet whose strings had been cut.

Not giving the other guard a chance to react, Julia brought up her bow, drew the arrow back, and fired at his head. She was already grabbing for another arrow and getting ready to fire the next shot, because she was certain the first one wasn't going to be enough. No one was that lucky.

Except that today she was.

The arrow struck the man right in the eye, and he collapsed without a word. His fall was almost as noiseless as his partner's.

Julia slowly turned in a circle, her bow ready to fire, making sure that no one else was responding to what she'd just done. Miraculously, it seemed like her insane plan was working. No one seemed aware of what had just happened.

She had to act quickly, since time was not on her side. None of the prisoners had woken up during the attack. They were probably exhausted from everything they'd been through, and now things were about to get a *lot* more hectic.

Julia retrieved the marine knife from the skull of the dead guard and wiped it clean on his shirtsleeve. Then she stepped quietly through the prisoners until she was standing next to her doppelgänger. Julia bent over and placed a hand across the woman's mouth.

Kelsey's eyes flew open, but with her hands and feet tied, she was unable to do anything. It only took a moment for those eyes so like hers to narrow, then the other woman nodded.

Julia removed her hand and spoke very quietly in Kelsey's ear. "I've killed the two guards watching over you, and I'm going to cut your hands loose."

Cutting through the ropes with the marine knife was easy. The most difficult part was making certain that she didn't accidentally cut Kelsey's hand off. She repeated the work on the woman's legs.

Once the ropes were gone, Kelsey rubbed her wrists and feet, probably to help restore more circulation, and then rose.

Julia turned so that Kelsey could see her swords strapped low on her back. She hadn't dared wear them where the silhouette could've been seen. That might have given her away.

Kelsey slowly drew one of the swords from Julia's back. "Give Talbot the other one," her doppelgänger said softly into her ear. "Then we need to get everybody else cut loose and get out of here."

Julia handed the plasma grenade to her. "I have no idea if this will work, but I figured I'd bring it along."

Julia repeated the process with Talbot, and he was just as quick on the uptake. Once she'd freed him, he rose to his feet and took the second sword.

The two of them went from person to person, quietly waking them up and cutting them free while Julia kept watch, her eyes scanning for sentries or waking enemies near the fires.

Clarice Beauchamp retrieved the weapons from the two dead guards. She'd be best trained in the use of them, so that would be helpful. She'd also take one of the bows, and Olivia or Elise could take the second.

Once the entire group was awake, Kelsey gestured toward where the horses were being kept. "If we can get the horses saddled and get going before they realize that we've escaped, we might actually get away."

Of course, that's when someone near the fire stood, saw what they were doing, and started screaming that the prisoners were escaping.

Well, so much for the easy way.

26

K elsey reacted instantly, pulling the pin on the plasma grenade and hurling it toward the fire. While she didn't have her usual Marine Raider enhanced strength, her normal muscles had gotten stronger with use, and the grenade made it the full distance without any trouble.

Her aim was true, and it landed almost in the middle of the group of scrambling enemies, rolling to a stop just at the lip of one of the pits. It sat there for one extended heartbeat even as Kelsey was turning her back to the impending explosion.

"Fire in the hole!" she shouted. "Cover your eyes!"

She hoped to God that the grenade worked because otherwise no one would be looking at the enemy as they came to kill them.

The grenade's explosion made it sound as if the world had ended. It was only then that she realized that her augmentation was no longer protecting her hearing. Her ears rang, and she felt as if she'd been kicked in the back as she staggered forward, almost falling.

She'd been a little too close to the explosion, she decided. But if it was bad for her, it was going to be *really* bad for the enemy.

Kelsey turned and saw that while the grenade hadn't killed everyone, it had certainly maimed most of the survivors. No one was standing, and those that weren't dead looked as if they were seriously injured. Hell, many of them were on *fire*.

The grass all over the camp was also on fire, and she expected that was going to mean a big blaze since no one was in a position to control it. The smell was already spooking the horses, she was sure. Like the explosion hadn't.

Even though that took care of almost everyone in their general vicinity, it had certainly attracted the attention of the camp sentries. She didn't know how many of them there were going to be, but she'd have to be an idiot to think that those warriors wouldn't be rushing toward them even now.

"To the horses," she shouted over the ringing in her ears. "Anyone with a weapon—particularly a bow—shoot at anything that moves."

Julia ran beside her. "Based on what I saw, there's probably six or eight sentries out there. Two more near the horses. They'll be ready for us."

"You've got a bow. Help cover us."

"Good idea, Princess Obvious."

Kelsey smiled a little as she watched Captain Beauchamp hand the final bow to Olivia. She found a place near the back of the group as they made for the horses. The sentries would be coming from every direction.

They had a real chance of getting away, but only if they broke contact completely. Any pursuers would find a way to signal other groups to come after them. She had to make sure that nobody survived this fight.

Julia and Captain Beauchamp engaged the guards ahead of them before Kelsey saw anyone. She had no idea how effective their fire was in the dark and confusion, but she hoped they were good. Otherwise, someone was going to die.

Two guards came running in from the left, and Olivia brought her bow up and snapped a shot off at one of them. He grunted and went down, but it didn't look like he was completely out of the fight.

Kelsey ran forward, even as the second guard fired an arrow at her. She managed to successfully throw herself to the side enough for him to miss.

She'd do a lot better if she still had her Marine Raider augmentation, but in this case, even a few centimeters were enough for the arrow to fly harmlessly past her with an audible "thwap."

Olivia hadn't been idle. She'd already drawn another arrow from her quiver and fired it at the second guard. Her aim was true, and the arrow caught him squarely in the chest, dropping him on the spot.

She could hear Talbot and Captain Beauchamp fighting somebody on the other side of their small group as they continued toward the horses, but she couldn't spare them any attention. The wounded guard had thrown aside his bow and drawn his sword. He wanted to fight it out man to woman.

Kelsey wasn't obliging. She let Olivia shoot him in the stomach. He went down writhing and groaning.

Unfortunately, her focus on those two had allowed a third to slip close without her seeing him. The man seemingly appeared out of nowhere with a sword in hand, already swinging at her.

Kelsey's reflexes were exceptionally good, even without her Marine Raider augmentation. She'd also been practicing the Art for quite a while now, and that included weapons. She blocked the attack at the last moment.

She'd intentionally used the flat of her blade so as not to cause the piece of steel flying toward her to snap off and continue on its merry way. That would be almost as bad as not blocking it at all. Her hull metal blade was more than strong enough to take a hit on the side.

The unexpected blocking of his blade put the man off-balance enough for Kelsey to swing around and take his leg. In one stroke—even with her reduced strength—the blade's edge was more than sufficient to cut through his leg, armor and all. He went down screaming as blood gushed from his gory wound.

Looking around as she stepped away from the writhing man, Kelsey saw no further signs of guards, so she risked a glance at where Talbot and Captain Beauchamp were fighting. Talbot was using her other sword and engaging two foes while Captain Beauchamp fired arrows at several more that were threatening the group.

Kelsey raced toward them as Olivia turned her attention to the new threats.

Talbot was a lot stronger than she was, and even though his use of the sword wasn't as good as hers, he managed to hold his own while the archers dealt with the more distant threats.

She intervened and quickly killed one of his attackers. Talbot followed up with an immediate strike on his man that decapitated him.

With that, the fight was over.

There might still be a guard or two out there, so they stayed watchful, but the other members of their party were able to secure the horses they needed and scatter the rest.

Captain Beauchamp searched out the wounded enemies that were still alive and finished them off. That might've seemed cruel because they were technically prisoners at this point, but the wounded were so gravely injured that there was no chance that they'd be able to do anything for them. What medical supplies they had were gone, lost somewhere in the gear that had been stolen from them.

More disturbing, Julia was going through the main camp doing the same thing, her face cold and merciless. Kelsey didn't know if that was because of experiences she'd had as a Pale One or simply the loss of Scott Roche and so many others, but the woman never hesitated as she strode from body to body, her expression blank and her eyes cold, making sure they were truly dead or ending their suffering with firm thrusts of her captured sword.

Kelsey took a deep breath and regretted it. The mixture of burning grass, spilled blood, and cooked flesh was nauseating.

She turned her back on the carnage and considered what they needed to do next. They had to figure out exactly where the scepter was if they were going to retrieve it. They simply couldn't complete their mission without it.

Unfortunately, not knowing which group had the damned thing, the only place they could be certain they'd find it was the city where all of these bastards were going.

That was going to mean going deeper into enemy territory. Not exactly a plan for guaranteed survival. Still, what choice did they have?

She'd talk it over with Jared and see what his opinion was, but her thought was they were going to have to follow the enemy right straight into their lair.

* * *

NOT KNOWING how long they had, Jared made certain they gathered as much food, water, weapons, and other supplies as they could find before they fled the area. It was still dark, so they weren't going to be traveling fast, but the plasma grenade blast would've been a big, bright neon sign to everyone within line of sight that something terrible had happened.

There were probably scouts from various groups of horde riders already on their way to figure out what had happened. He and his people need to be long gone before they arrived.

Beauchamp helped get everything secured to the horses, since the majority of their personnel weren't skilled riders and none of them really knew the esoteric secrets of packing lots of gear on the beasts. If somebody came across them and they had to make a run for it, that would not be the time to find out that their packs were going to come undone.

They also gathered up any armor they could find that might fit somebody in their party. Most of the people had been killed in the explosion of the plasma grenade or had caught fire from the effects of it. Their armor was a bit more resistant to that sort of thing, but it would still look totally scorched if anyone examined it closely. They'd have to make do with what they could find.

He wasn't looking forward to riding in the dark, but it beat the hell out of being on his way toward torture and execution. Right now, he still couldn't tear his mind away from how many of his people had been killed.

When the EMP weapon had knocked them all out, it had made them completely vulnerable and the horde had executed virtually all of them. It was so inconceivable that he still couldn't get his mind wrapped around it.

Beauchamp was in the same position. Her people had fought to the end, but they'd been greatly outnumbered, and all of them had been killed or executed except for her. Now here they were, a small group trying to figure out what they were going to need to do to survive in the middle of enemy territory.

After the fighting, Julia had disappeared for a short while and then returned with her horse. They all immediately mounted up and set out, moving slowly in the darkness.

As the group rode, he pulled the people he needed as close together as they could get and went over the situation with them. When he was finished, he looked at Clarice Beauchamp.

"What are the chances that we can get back to your outpost without the horde hunting us down?"

The woman shook her head. "They're going to be swarming the general area come morning. We need to be gone by then. If we turn around and go back, we're going to discover that they've sent parties back to stop us. We just don't have the numbers to fight off an attack.

"Besides, that group you sent off with your sister-in-law started a grass fire, like the one that your sister started tonight. The first one is between us and the outpost, and the second will cut off some of the enemy coming to search for us, which is a good thing. There's no easy way to get past either of them. I'm afraid that the only way open to us is forward."

Jared grunted, not really surprised to hear that. "They're going to know that we're loose. They'll do a search around the campsite, and they won't find our bodies. Worse, they're going to find the people we killed and know it was us. We can assume that means they're going to be hard on our tails once they figure out what happened."

Beauchamp smiled. "There's a reason that we scattered the horses back in the direction of the outpost. That's going to make them initially think we fled in that direction. If we're lucky, the morning winds will push the fire across our path and hide which direction we actually went.

"We can't count on that, but we're going to get a little bit of time because of their uncertainty. I suggest we use it wisely. If we can change into armor and clothing that the horde wear, they won't realize that we're not another search party unless they close with us."

He was still thinking about that when Carl Owlet spoke. "The

Imperial scepter is somewhere out there, and it's being taken toward our original destination. If we're going to get into the Imperial Vault, we have to have it."

"Is it any use now?" Jared asked. "The EMP probably junked it, just like everything else electronic, including the implants."

The young scientist smiled. "It has safety measures built into it to prevent it from frying. If I can get my hands on it and access to some tools to get into its interior, I can probably reset it. Also, our implants have a reset, too, although it's going to be a *lot* more difficult to get to. They were designed so that they would resist EMPs of almost unimaginable strength, but being so close to that huge weapon overloaded ours.

"I'm afraid this is going to require Doctor Stone's help. She's going to have to make an incision to get to our implant nodes—a specific one—and then I can apply a specific frequency of power to it. I'm afraid that it's not something that's going to be simple, because as we all know, the implants are inside our skulls. But if we can get our hands on her medical gear—the stuff that wasn't ruined by the EMP —it's not out of the question."

Jared thought about that and shuddered a little. Brain surgery in the wilds of Terra with no implants to guide their way would be hard. If they couldn't find Doctor Stone's surgical kit, it would be impossible, and they'd have to make do without their implants.

Lily confirmed that fear when she shook her head. "We have to find my spare medical kit—the one I left at the pinnaces—if we're to have any chance of doing that. I don't dare open up anybody's skull without it. Admiral, we need to recover that as badly as we do the Imperial Scepter. Hell, anything at all that we can get back is going to increase our chances of success. We need to do what we can to make that happen."

Jared rubbed his face as his horse moved forward in the darkness. "So, what you're saying is that we're going to have to sneak into an enemy city right under their noses, find where they've stashed all of the gear they've taken from us, all without them raising the alarm? Then we'll need to get out of the city and somehow escape what is probably the seat of their power. That doesn't sound difficult at all."

Difficult or not, they really didn't have a choice. If they were going to succeed in their mission, they had to have the scepter. They'd find a way to sneak into the horde city without raising the alarm, steal what they needed, and then somehow escape again without being noticed.

And that was only the first step. From what he knew, the horde city was actually farther away from the Imperial Palace than the campsite where they'd crashed the pinnaces.

They had no advanced weaponry, were down to just over a dozen people, and Terra was a hostile world that seemed determined to kill them. He just didn't know if they could make it.

Still, he wasn't going to give up. This wasn't his kind of fight, but he was going to make it work. The New Terran Empire was counting on them, and he wouldn't let them down.

No matter the cost, they'd do what needed to be done. And that started with getting into the horde city without being captured.

27

A fter five days of riding, Julia was exhausted. They'd traveled mostly by night, terrified that one of the horde search groups would catch them. To help mitigate that, they'd chosen not to head toward the horde city directly.

Instead, they'd slipped away from the direct line between Captain Beauchamp's outpost and the city, looping far off to one side and only turning toward the latter two nights ago.

The first day she'd been terrified that the horde would come down on them, but they didn't see a single rider. Beauchamp seemed to believe that the direction they'd taken might have fooled them. She believed that there were so many riders out there, that their tracks were being confused with the rest of the search groups.

It probably helped that the grass fire Kelsey had started had cut a huge slash behind them and the smoke filled half the sky. That had to be distracting. They'd caught a break that none of them had had any reason to expect.

Beauchamp had worked with her to make some modifications to her armor that she'd said would make it blend in more seamlessly with the horde, should they be spotted. Julia didn't really understand the significance of the changes, as they all seemed cosmetic, but anything that kept her from blowing their cover was a good thing.

As she worked, Beauchamp had told her stories about the man who'd once worn the armor that was now hers. He'd been a practical joker, but fierce in battle. A loyal friend that would trade his life for his comrades without a moment's hesitation.

A truth the local knew firsthand as he'd done exactly that during the fight, saving her life at the cost of his own.

She couldn't understand how the other woman was just calmly talking about her man. She seemed reflective and at peace. Not unhurt, but not as if she'd just lost so many people she'd known and commanded.

Julia was a wreck in comparison. The pain of losing Scott squeezed Julia's heart tight in her chest. She couldn't stop replaying the last fight over and over again in her mind. What could she have done differently? What actions would've allowed them both to have survived?

Her brain knew that he'd already been dying and nothing she'd done would've changed that, but her heart still wailed at her failure to save him. His death would always lie heavy on her soul, a stain that she would never fully wash away.

Though she intended to try. The blood of their enemies would make for a satisfying start. If it would ease her pain, she'd bathe in it.

They'd entered a light forest early yesterday, which had slowed them down, but also served to conceal them from any pursuers. That gave her hope that they might finally be in the clear from the most immediate threats.

She certainly hoped so, because as tired as she was, the rest of them were infinitely more exhausted. None of them were trained riders except for Kelsey, Elise, Olivia, Carl, and herself. Oh, and Beauchamp. So almost half of their number. Yet the other half desperately needed some rest. They also needed to plan.

By the best of Beauchamp's estimates, the horde city was just over twenty kilometers away. The other woman thought that they'd start seeing the tallest of the buildings in the megacity in the morning, if they found a suitably clearing.

"Why not just live in the megacity?" she asked Beauchamp as they drank water and ate cold rations in the chill dawn the next morning. "If they're going to build their city right next to it, why not just go ahead and take the extra step to move into the larger accommodations? I understand that they wouldn't have power, but something could probably still be done to make it work."

"The ruined megacities have their own inhabitants," the local woman said. "To journey into one is to risk being captured by those people, and they're significantly more paranoid of outsiders than the rest of us, which is saying something. They don't want contact with others. In fact, they'll use force to drive others out of the megacities. Those that they don't kill outright.

"Yet the megacities are such rich sources of salvage that other groups can't help but go into them. They don't go in unarmed or in small numbers, though. It doesn't take long for the inhabitants to start shadowing them. No one else could possibly know a megacity like its inhabitants. So, such excursions are brief and heavily armed. Those that aren't are never heard from again."

Well, didn't that just sound peachy?

It was probably best that they didn't make any plans to go into the megacity, then. There really wasn't any reason to do so, but knowing their luck, something would come up and force them to retreat there.

That might be negative thinking, but they had to plan for the worst-case scenarios. If their raid inside the horde city went off without a hitch, they could ride away. If it didn't, they were going to need a handy place to retreat to because the horde city would become an anthill of people searching for them. They had to do everything in their power to avoid being recaptured because nobody wanted to be tortured and then burned to death.

If that meant retreating into the megacity and hoping that they could evade the inhabitants long enough to find a way to escape again, that's what they needed to plan for.

Going inside the megacity would likely be the worst of all worlds. None of the technology would work, and the inhabitants would be hostile. They'd know every square centimeter of the city they lived in, and it would be impossible to find where they lived without capturing some of them, which would enrage the rest.

Based on what she'd heard, it sounded as if anyone captured there was dealt with harshly. Perhaps as harshly as the horde dealt with their prisoners. Though it was possible that the captured invaders were kept alive as labor, or worse, it would be best to consider how the horde treated their prisoners.

Though, to be fair, she wasn't sure that held for run-of-the-mill captives. Those might just be enslaved. Which, on reflection, might be a worse fate than even a painful death.

This could easily be a "from the frying pan into the fire" sort of moment. Yet another catchy phrase that Kelsey had shared with her. Considering that the form of execution the horde favored was immolation, it had an ironically grim meaning as well.

Julia took a few moments to look over the rest of the party, many of whom were still asleep. They'd travel again today and make it close to the horde city by dark. Tomorrow, they'd have to figure out how they were going to sneak inside the damned place.

One thing was for sure, the horde would never expect them to come wandering right up to their seat of power looking to sneak in. That kind of behavior was insane.

She wasn't exactly happy that that's what they had to do either. They'd have to observe the horde city before they could make any decision about how to get inside it. Once they did get inside, they'd have to find out where all their gear was being kept, which she was sure would be under heavy guard. Then they'd need to get access to it without the horde knowing, and finally slip away unseen.

At any point, they could make a critical mistake and their goose was cooked. Yet *another* catchy phrase with a double meaning from her doppelgänger that involved fire. She was just a font of gruesome sayings.

Julia sighed. It was no use complaining. Their situation was what it was. She really hoped they could get Doctor Stone's medical supplies —maybe even the spare medical kit that had been left at the pinnaces —because she'd love to have her augmentation back online. That would make escaping the city at least possible.

If they could scrounge up their gear and find a place inside the city to hide while they recovered, then they could come up with a plan to escape completely. Perhaps once they'd left horde territory, the rest of the trip would be easier.

That overly optimistic thought made her mentally laugh. It was almost guaranteed that the trip was going to get harder with every single step.

Thankfully, figuring all this out wasn't her problem. She could give Kelsey and Mertz—Jared—advice and opinion, but in the end, those decisions rested with them.

As she chewed the last of her meal, she wondered what they'd decide to do. Would it be a straightforward plan that she'd never have considered, or would it be some kind of crazy mission that was bound to get them all killed?

Knowing her doppelgänger, Julia was betting on the latter.

Well, it was time to get the rest of them up and start that planning. They had some more riding to do and then someone would have to scout the city. Probably Talbot, since marines had that skill set.

It was crunch time, and everything needed to go just right, or they'd all be dead, just like Scott and the rest.

* * *

THE NEXT MORNING, ten minutes after her husband had left to scout the area toward the horde city, Kelsey forced herself to stop worrying about him and what he might find on his search. She couldn't afford the distraction. They needed to have a plan of action once they found a way into the city.

Which they would, one way or another.

The information that Talbot brought back would certainly help them figure out the details of what needed to be done, but they'd need to have a plan already firmly in mind before then. They were only going to get one chance at this.

Their newest hideaway in the woods was well concealed, and they'd stashed the horses in a thicket where they'd likely not be discovered. Kelsey was well aware of how much noise a horse made as it went about its life, but these seemed preternaturally quiet. It had to be part of their warhorse training.

If they hadn't been quiet, they'd have had to stash the horses much farther away from themselves and hope that no one came along to discover them.

With only a dozen of her friends left alive, she felt empty inside. She couldn't stop thinking about all the people she'd known or was responsible for that the horde had killed. So many people.

Yet here they were, about to give the horde another chance to kill them. Worse, this wasn't for revenge. It was only to get their equipment back before trying to slip away undiscovered.

A big part of her wanted to see these bastards bleed. To make them pay for all the pain and suffering they'd caused. But revenge wasn't something that they could afford to dish out right now. The cruel sons of bitches were going to get away with everything they'd done while she and her friends fought the AIs to save humanity, including their sorry butts.

"Once we get inside the city, we'll need to get under cover quickly," Beauchamp said. "Every interaction we have with one of them is an opportunity for them to figure out that we don't belong. It will only take one person sounding the alarm for us all to die.

"One thing going for us is that we're going to look like warriors from inside their own society, so I'm hopeful that we can make our way deeper into the city without the regular populace disturbing us. The horde has a terrible reputation about how it treats its people— almost as bad as they treat everyone else—so the average man or woman on the street is unlikely to interact with a horde warrior, much less a dozen of them."

Jared nodded his head slowly at that. "I'd imagine they have a seat of government of some kind. Probably a palace. Right?" At her nod, he continued. "They're going to have people in charge that want to see everything that's been captured. That means everything being brought in on pack horses will be taken to some kind of central repository to be sorted and identified.

"That location is going to be heavily guarded, and we're going to have to get inside without raising the alarm, take what we need, and then get away without them being any the wiser. If anyone has any ideas about how to make that happen, I'm all ears."

Before anyone could respond, the sound of horses riding sounded in the distance. The noise was faint, but it was clear that they had visitors. Thankfully, they didn't have a fire burning or anything else that might give away their position.

Kelsey rose from where she was sitting, picked up her bow from where she'd set it beside her, and headed for the trees in the direction the noise had come from. If they were going to have to fight, she was going to be ready.

Of course, if they had to fight, they were all dead anyway. They couldn't allow a single person to get away with word of where they were. Even missing people would raise the alarm sooner or later. Any sign at all that something unusual was happening would give them away eventually.

She made her way through the trees using a path that she'd discovered early this morning. It brought her to the exterior strip of this stretch of forest and allowed her to observe what was going on out on the plain.

About two hundred meters away, a group of horsemen rode along the edge of the forest. At her rough count, there seemed to be about three dozen riders and about twice that many pack horses.

One of the pieces of equipment strapped on the outside of one of the packs was a computer that the science team had brought with them. It looked as if she'd spotted one of the groups that had ambushed them heading back to the city.

The good news was that they weren't in immediate danger, so she relaxed a little. Once they'd safely passed, she wormed her way back to the clearing and told the others what she'd seen.

"We might have made a mistake in sending Talbot off alone," she ventured while they digested her words. "We're a little exposed out here. It might make more sense to follow along behind him.

"All we're abandoning are the horses, and they can pull themselves free because I made certain the knots in their reins would give way with any kind of determined tugging. If something happened to us, I didn't want them to starve to death."

"We're going to need the horses to escape the area," Beauchamp said. "We can't afford to have them discovered while we're gone. Still, I agree with you doing that."

"With any luck at all, we'll be in and out of the city before they have a chance to be discovered. If we lose the horses, that hurts our chances of survival. If we get captured, we're dead."

"Neither of those options is very appealing," Jared said. "Do you think we should just head down the path after him? He's not going to be expecting us, and we really don't want to surprise him."

"We also don't want to be spotted out here," Kelsey countered. "We're committed to this, Jared. We need to follow him so that we can take advantage of whatever he finds. Honestly, we should never have let him go alone. Time is not on our side."

Her brother sighed and rubbed his face. "You're probably right. Let's pack our gear and make it look as if no one was ever here. We'll follow along behind Talbot and see what we can find. Hopefully, he won't run into any trouble and we can make contact without any fuss.

"If we miss one another, we'll need to leave a note here telling him that we decided to follow him. Put it under some stones in a pattern so that he'll know it wasn't here when he left."

Kelsey hoped her husband wouldn't run into anyone, that they'd get close to the city and find some way to make this damned plan work. This was a make-or-break moment. They had to get the scepter and get away again, and the clock was ticking.

28

T albot moved slowly through the forest, keeping an eye out for any sign that the horde had been there before him. Any path leading toward the city was likely to be either observed or possibly trapped. He absolutely didn't want to be a victim of something he could've spotted long before he chanced upon it.

He was approaching both the horde city and the ruined megacity, as they were seated next to one other and both perpendicular to his position. The ruined megacity was significantly larger and taller. Even in its present condition, many of the buildings still stretched an unimaginable height into the sky, and he caught glimpses of the towers through the closely set trees and the leafy canopy.

The horde city was significantly more primitive, though much newer in construction. If he had to make a guess, it was probably only fifty or sixty years old. It would've been constructed after the AIs had crushed Terra. No one would have been comfortable building a city so close to the dead megacity if some time hadn't passed to make them feel safe in doing so.

The occasional clearing allowed him an unobstructed view of the megacity, and he was hoping for a better look at the horde city, if he could find a hill with a view. It irritated him that he'd once had access to drone video of the two cities, but it was now locked away in his implants. His personal memory of the details wasn't good enough to plan with.

Relying on his implants had made him sloppy, and he vowed that future Marine Raider training would include more working without implants. Basic skills needed to be maintained, even if new recruits thought they no longer needed them. This situation had *thoroughly* proven that.

There were animal paths crisscrossing the underbrush, so those were what he mainly followed. That brought risks, but it was significantly more difficult to move through the foliage without using them.

Not being familiar with the normal sounds of the forest life, every movement of leaves or snap of twigs on the ground made him freeze. He saw a few small creatures with bushy tails. Some of them chittered indignantly at him.

Once, he saw a larger four-legged creature, but it was obviously an herbivore, even with the magnificent rack of horns on its head. It stared regally at him for a few seconds once he tried to move, and then bounded off with far more grace and beauty than he'd expected.

He'd thought travel through the forests would be easy. Wrong. The travel time projections for getting to the Imperial Vault would need to be extended. Rather than speeding their journey, the horses might slow them even further. At this point, six to eight months might be optimistic.

He continued on his way, focused on the area around the trails as he moved. If he were the enemy, this kind of chokepoint was where he'd put any traps or observation points. That meant he had to go slowly and be exceptionally careful.

They'd discussed this before he'd left the temporary camp, and he'd decided that his look around would take as long as needed to make sure this was done right. If that meant he stayed overnight, he'd prepared the rest for that option as well.

Talbot found his first sign of other humans maybe two kilometers from the horde city. There was a small blind set up away from the path, but within view. It was almost a pillbox set into the side of the hill, made of logs covered over with dirt and foliage.

He probably wouldn't have spotted it, if it'd been well maintained. Whoever was in charge of making certain that it wasn't visible hadn't kept the plants atop it alive, so the dead growth tipped him off.

Perhaps it was only occasionally manned. If the horde didn't have a full-time force working in the forest, then they'd rotate between observation blinds similar to this throughout the area around their city.

Its presence told him something important. The horde expected people to try to sneak up on the city. That meant that there was going to be more difficulty getting in than they'd hoped for.

Or perhaps the observation posts were to keep people from leaving. From his point of view, it was difficult to tell. They knew virtually nothing about the horde, other than their murderous intent. Maybe they had slaves. Or something worse that he couldn't imagine at the moment.

To satisfy his curiosity, Talbot headed closer to the blind.

He moved cautiously, trying to stay away from the path so that he wouldn't be easy to spot as he moved through the undergrowth. Since it had been a damned long time since he'd trained at moving through the wilderness, he certainly hoped nobody was inside the damned thing, because there was no way they could miss hearing him coming.

He really wished that the marines had taught more ground operations of a covert sort during his training. There'd been a couple of exercises and classes over the years, but whatever he learned in them was long out of practice. He made more mental notes to adjust the as yet theoretical Marine Raider training that he was supposed to be helping formulate.

When he got close to the observation post, he could see the door leading into the back of it. No one had bothered trying to disguise the thing from the rear.

He wondered what made this particular path more viable for travelers than the other animal trails that he'd seen. It didn't look any larger than the others. Perhaps it was because it moved more directly toward the city. Or perhaps they were all monitored at some point.

The door leading into the bunker was manually operated and didn't seem to have a lock. He considered the possibility that it was protected by some kind of alarm but dismissed that.

While it was obvious that the horde had some of the means to generate power and construct high-technology items—as demonstrated by the EMP weapons and the antiarmor rockets—he doubted very seriously that they used such technology for anything as pedestrian as an alarm system so far from their city.

Looking inside was going to be a risk, but only a small one that might pay dividends down the road. He tested the handle and found it unlocked, just as he'd suspected. He opened the door and looked in, his hand on the hilt of Kelsey's borrowed sword.

It was dark inside, but he could make out the general details from light filtering through the observation slit on the far side of the structure. As he'd suspected, there was no power, no lights, and no indication that this post had been occupied anytime recently.

In fact, based on the debris that had been deposited inside the small, low structure—likely by bad weather—it had probably been at least a couple of weeks since the last time anyone had been inside it. Maybe a month. Assuming, of course, that they cleaned up after themselves.

There were two chairs and a slender shelf built into the wall beneath the observation slit. It was likely that the observers were stationed here during times that the horde suspected there would be unauthorized travelers moving around the city.

The slits weren't useful for firing bows—being laid out horizontally rather than vertically—so he suspected anyone stationed here was meant to simply observe and warn someone else about what they saw via a runner or some other low-tech method. As there were no signs of any kind of communication device, that would be the only way they could do it.

He was still thinking about how the horde would carry out those tasks when he heard the sound of a branch snapping somewhere outside the observation post. It was probably an animal, but he needed to be on his guard. If somebody spotted him now, they were all in very deep trouble.

Moving as quietly as he could, Talbot exited the observation post and eased the door closed behind him. The slight squeaks that the hinges had made when he'd opened the door the first time now sounded like screams in his ears. He certainly hoped that if that was someone out there, they wouldn't hear it.

Talbot eyed the surrounding forest and tried to judge which direction the noise had come from. There was a path—though it wasn't well-defined—leading away from the observation post and deeper into the forest. It sounded as if something or someone was coming down it.

He needed to get out of there and do it now.

Even as he started moving, he saw some of the branches farther up the path move and caught the outline of a human form. No, two human forms.

The horde had finally sent people to watch the trail, and he was directly in their way. He was moments from discovery.

* * *

No MATTER how quiet he tried to be, Jared felt as if he'd stepped on every single twig and brushed against every branch as he'd moved. Each noise sounded incredibly loud in his ears, though he knew most of them were too soft to carry. Most of them.

He tried to emulate Captain Beauchamp, but he'd never capture her grace and skill at moving through the forest like a ghost. For someone who he'd only ever seen ride a horse, she had a lot of grace at moving through the forest.

None of the rest of them did, that was for sure. Each and every one of his people seemed unable to miss anything that made noise, and the animals around them quickly went silent as they passed. If any trained woodsmen were lurking out there, they'd immediately know something was wrong. He just hoped they didn't figure out exactly what the silence meant while he and his people were still here.

Even as he was thinking that, Beauchamp froze and held up a hand to halt the rest of them. Everyone else shambled to a stop, though their eyes were all darting around, looking for what had caught her attention.

She took two steps back and placed her lips directly next to Jared's ear. "There's someone up ahead. It might be Talbot, but I'm seeing some kind of movement on the side of the hill. There's too much underbrush in the way for me to get a clear look, but the man I see seems to be about the right size for him. I'm not sure what he's doing, but it feels like he's hiding from something. If so, we should do the same."

Taking a risk, Jared stepped forward until he could see what she'd seen. It took him almost ten seconds to spot the man on the side of the hill. He was crouched behind what could have been a low wooden wall, so there was some kind of structure up there.

Beauchamp was right. It was impossible to tell exactly who it was without getting a little closer, but Jared's years with the marine made him feel certain that it was Talbot.

"It's him," he said softly back to Beauchamp. "What's he doing?"

"Hiding," she said with more than a hint of tension in her soft voice. "There's someone else up there."

Jared motioned for Kelsey and Lieutenant Laird to join them. In a low tone, he explained what was happening in front and above them.

"Chloe, I want you to take point on this," he said when he'd finished. "Kelsey will assist you because she's got the best hand-to-hand skills of any of us. I'd put her as the lead, but you have better tactical training than she does. Sorry, Kelsey."

His sister shrugged slightly. "It's all going to come out in the wash. If there's trouble up there, both of us are going to be involved. Talbot has one of my swords, so if he has to come out swinging, he's going to be effective. With his training in the Art, he has a good grasp of melee combat with a blade and his body.

"The key here is that we can't let anyone report our presence. We not only need to ambush the people he's looking at, but we need to make sure that even someone who gets away is taken out before they get back to the city."

"I think that's where Captain Beauchamp and Julia come in," Chloe said, brushing her tangled red hair out of her eyes. "We need to let them take the other side of that building Talbot is behind. They're both experienced with bows, as are you, and they'll be able to pick off people that are fleeing at a distance.

"But even that isn't going to be enough. If we start chasing someone through the forest, they're going to lose us unless we stay on their heels. Bows are going to be useless beyond a fairly short range in this environment. This is going to be blade work."

"Yes, it is," Jared said grimly. "Once you engage, we'll come up behind Talbot and provide a backdrop behind him with extra bodies. None of us are trained for this kind of fighting, but we've all got swords and marine knives. If we have to help with the fight, we'll do it. We'll just hope it doesn't come to that."

At his nod, Kelsey, Chloe, Julia, and Captain Beauchamp moved out. The rest of them stayed where they were for the moment, because they didn't want to risk making any noise until the fighting started. They'd make their way up the hill as quickly as possible once things got rolling and come in behind Talbot.

With any luck at all, they'd be able to silence whatever patrol Talbot had spotted. That was only a short-term solution, though. Someone would eventually miss those people.

At this point, they were committed to making this crazy plan work. Even if killing the patrol set off a search for them, it wouldn't happen immediately.

But the clock *was* ticking. It was time to make the magic happen.

29

K elsey followed Chloe Laird up the hill. They both moved slowly because neither one of them was skilled at woodcraft. They couldn't afford to make any loud noise because that would alert whatever group Talbot had spotted to their presence. If that happened, whoever they were, they'd have too great a chance of warning the city that they had intruders.

By the time they'd reached the top of the slope, at least some of the people up there had moved into the structure. Her husband had slipped around to the closer side of the low building but hadn't noticed her presence yet. His attention was focused on the back of the structure.

She didn't know if that meant there was no one else outside but decided to take the most pessimistic view. They'd assume there were more people in the woods and that it was *her* responsibility to take them out.

As she was edging onto the area above the slope, Talbot sheathed his sword, drew his marine knife, and darted inside the structure. There was a muffled shout and the clang of steel on steel. Well, hull metal on steel, which was pretty close to the same.

With the attack in progress, Kelsey immediately discarded stealth and raced toward the forest behind the structure, her bow up and ready to engage targets of opportunity. Laird had a captured sword and was standing beside her side, scanning the forest for threats.

Farther across the hill, Kelsey caught a glimpse of blonde hair and spotted Julia and Beauchamp, who were both using their bows to seek out potential targets. She ignored them and continued to scan for any enemies.

She didn't see any.

With a gesture, she sent Chloe deeper into the forest to see if she could spot anything. Beauchamp was moving forward to do the same thing.

Kelsey watched their backs, ready to fire her bow or race after them, but she also kept an eye on the structure. The sounds of combat had already ceased, so she certainly hoped her husband was victorious.

She really *should* check just to make sure.

Keeping the majority of her attention focused on Laird, Kelsey edged closer to the door leading into the strange, low structure. "Talbot, tell me you're okay," she said, pitching her voice low enough to carry inside, but softly enough not to warn everyone in the general vicinity.

"I'm fine," he answered with a hint of a growl. "I got a cut on my arm, but it's not serious. Both of the people I spotted are down in here."

Kelsey considered passing that information along to Laird but decided against it. They should treat this as if Talbot had missed some of the enemy. Instead of fretting about it, she kept watch while she waited for Talbot to come out.

He stepped out of the short building a few moments later. He had his right vambrace off and was using a piece of cloth to wipe at a bleeding cut about five centimeters long on the back of his forearm. He was right. It didn't look too bad, so the armor there had mostly stopped the blow. The gash would need stitches but didn't seem immediately dangerous.

She half snorted at how her conception of what made for a serious injury had changed over the years. This kind of cut would've freaked younger her out. Now? Losing a finger *might* qualify as a moderate injury.

"Tell me what you've got," she said, keeping her eyes on the woods. "We spotted you from down below, so we have no idea what's going on up here."

"Two warriors came up the path from deeper into the forest. This observation post seems like it's only manned intermittently and isn't very well maintained. The plants on top are dead, so its camouflage is gone. They may've been coming to repair that rather than actually performing observational duties.

"At this point, it hardly matters. Now that I've killed them, somebody is going to be asking questions about them soon enough, and then they'll start looking for them."

He frowned toward her. "Aren't you supposed to be back at the camp waiting for me? Did something happen? Is everyone else okay?"

"We had a group of riders come past, likely heading toward the city. It made us feel a little exposed, so we left the horses tethered where they were and followed you in. Our window of opportunity is closing faster than we'd have liked. We need to get inside the city, get what we need, and be gone before they start looking for us in earnest. Once that happens, getting clear of the area is going to be a lot harder."

He grimaced at her words. "It's going to be hard no matter what we do. Those bastards will be all over us. I haven't gotten close enough to the city to see much yet, but I'm sure it's well guarded. I'll bet that it has a wall and plenty of roving patrols to make sure that nobody gets in or out without being challenged. These people strike me as the kind that don't want their 'citizens' wandering off, if you know what I mean."

"Yeah, I get that impression too," she admitted.

This wasn't the time or place to rush things, but the situation had been out of their control from the moment they'd landed. They just hadn't known it. Now they did.

Laird and Beauchamp came out of the woods with their weapons lowered, shaking their heads. Julia joined them as they converged on the observation post.

"There's no sign of anybody else out there," Beauchamp said. "It doesn't look as if that path is well traveled. Sending two people out into the woods like this isn't really a patrol. These men must've had some kind of task that they were performing."

Talbot nodded. "I've got some ideas on that, but it doesn't really matter what they were doing. Whoever sent them is going to be wondering why they don't come back once it gets dark. We're going to have to get rid of the bodies and clean this site up so that no one can tell anyone has been here.

"The goal of this is to leave them wondering exactly what happened. If we could arrange for an animal to eat them, that would be great, but we can't count on that. We're going to have to stash them somewhere and hope they remain undetected for a couple of days."

The local woman shook her head. "No matter what we do with them, crows and buzzards will feast upon their corpses, and that means that they'll be visible circling over this area. Anybody with half a brain will follow the carrion birds to see what they're eating once the missing people are remarked upon.

"This definitely shortens our timetable. We're going to have to get into the city tonight, if we can. By tomorrow, there will be search parties all through these woods and it will not take them long to find the bodies, since we have no tools to bury them. We'd be better off expecting the horde to seal the area sometime tomorrow. If we can get in tonight, find what we need, and then get back out before dawn, that would be best."

"We'll just have to make this work," Kelsey said glumly. "Chloe, make sure that everyone gets up here safely. We'll move the bodies into the woods and hope that buys us a day. Then we'll follow the path and see where it leads."

The clock was running out far faster than Kelsey had hoped, but their goals hadn't changed. The chances of failure were huge now, but they'd make it work. They had to.

* * *

JULIA FOLLOWED Captain Beauchamp as she made her way along the path that the two dead men had been traveling. The two of them were scouting ahead to see where it led while the rest of the party took care of the bodies.

They didn't have a lot of water to clean up the blood that Talbot had spilled, so she wasn't sure how well they'd do, but that was someone else's problem.

Beauchamp moved slowly, taking deliberate steps, and making certain that her feet didn't land on anything that was going to make noise. Julia tried to follow her example, though with less success. A *lot* less success.

The forest around them was filled with unidentifiable noises, and she felt her eyes darting back and forth, always concerned that what she was hearing meant more men coming to attack them. None materialized, however.

It took them half an hour to make their way to a hill that gave them a decent look at the horde city. Shorter than the abandoned megacity beside it by a significant margin, it was still somewhat larger than she'd expected.

Definitely low tech, but with high walls made of stone and wood, and patrolled by what looked like a strong force of armored warriors. Outside the walls in the cleared area between it and the forest, groups of horses rode along the perimeter of the city, either to keep intruders out or to make certain that the populace stayed inside. She wasn't sure which.

There were fortified enclosures along the wall that she suspected held weapons, based on the way they could be opened outward. That might mean low tech weapons, but Julia suspected there were advanced technology killing devices behind the covers. Hopefully, they wouldn't find out the hard way.

The two of them found a place to crouch behind the ever-present underbrush and observe the operations around the city without being visible themselves. Beauchamp was obviously watching what was going on with the guard patrols, but Julia found her attention focused on the dead megacity.

It was an amazing thing. She'd seen the implant tour of Imperial

City from the destroyer's library as part of her preparation for this mission. The abandoned megacity seemed very much like it. Innumerable buildings reached impossibly high into the sky, and it dwarfed the collection of primitive structures beside it.

The megacity, whatever its name had been, wasn't as big as Imperial City, but it was far larger than anything on Avalon by many orders of magnitude. She could only imagine what her home world would look like when they'd advanced to that point. If they survived the oncoming war with the Rebel Empire.

"Getting inside isn't going to be easy," Beauchamp finally said. "They've got a lot of guards on the walls, and those roving patrols are going to be a real pain in the ass to get by. You can bet they've got observers watching everything from those towers spaced along the walls, too. I'm not sure how we're going to slip in."

Even as they watched, a group of pack horses accompanied by warriors was approaching the massive gate set into the intimidating wall. They couldn't hear anything being said from this far away, of course, but whatever exchange there was, it was brief. The pack horses and riders were passed into the city with barely a glance.

"Maybe we need to find one of the groups with some of our salvaged gear, kill them, and go in disguised as them," Julia said thoughtfully. "They're expecting those kinds of groups and aren't checking for identification. People tend to see what they expect to see, after all. The guards at the gates can't possibly know everyone."

"There is some risk in doing that," Beauchamp said after considering the idea for a minute. "Though I will admit that I like the audacity of it. If we try an ambush, we can't let even a single person get away. If they do, they'll spread the alarm, and the hunt will be on. This close to the city, they'll find us in short order."

Julia nodded. "As I see it, we don't have a lot of options. Whatever we're going to do, we need to do it quickly. Any type of stealthy insertion is going to take time to set up, and even more to execute. We need to be inside the city today. It seems to me like the most direct path to success is walking in right under their noses.

"Besides, they're going to take the cargo right to where we want to go. That means we'll be able to find what we need much more quickly.

If we have to search for where they're holding it, we might never find it in time. If we're expected, they'll let us right in."

The warrior sighed. "We're going to have to convince your compatriots of that, but I think you're probably right. If we can get our hands on a group of pack horses, we can probably bluff our way in. Getting back out is going to be a lot more difficult, but perhaps not impossible. Now all we have to do is find a group that we can eliminate."

Julia heard a noise coming from off to the side of the area they were hiding in. It wasn't coming from the path they'd taken to get there. She strained to see what was making it but couldn't see anything through the trees.

She picked a handy tree whose species she couldn't identify and climbed up as far as she could get. She'd become a much better climber over the last few years. She credited all the exploration that she'd done inside the ships she'd been on. The maintenance tubes had lots of ladders, and navigating those translated well into climbing trees, so long as she made sure that the branches weren't going to break under her weight.

The climb gave her a view of the area just on the other side of the strip of forest they were in. Crossing through that open space were two dozen horses packed high with gear, shepherded along by six riders.

That seemed like a small number of people to be escorting something as valuable as that, but it suited her purposes better than what she'd been expecting. As Kelsey had once said—with a phrase that was oddly appropriate for this situation—"never look a gift horse in the mouth."

Whatever *that* meant.

The group she was watching would have to go around to the right-hand side of the woods to get into the cleared zone around the city. That would take them an hour or so at their current pace.

If she could convince Mertz and Kelsey that they could take this group out without making too much noise, they could then use the pack horses as cover to get inside the city. This might be their best chance to make something happen.

Unfortunately, they wouldn't have time to retrieve their horses. That meant some of them would have to stay outside the city. That might actually be a plus, because the noncombatants could go back to the horses they'd stashed and have everything ready for them to retreat once the deed was done.

Or to get away when their last stand made the horde go nuts.

"We need to get back to the group," Julia said once she'd climbed back down, her hand still resting on the rough bark of the tree. "I think I see an opportunity coming our way. If we take advantage of it, we might just be able to get inside the city undetected and get what we need."

Of course, if they screwed up any part of this, they wouldn't get another chance to try again. This was going to be one of those things where they had to succeed on the first try. Like skydiving.

Talk about an incentive to do one's best.

There was always the chance that someone in the city would realize that they didn't belong. Every word they said, every gesture they made, was an opportunity for someone to figure out that they were outsiders. If that happened, they were all dead.

In a lot of ways, she was facing something very close to what she'd faced with the mad computer on Erorsi. If the horde got their hands on her, they'd torture her just as badly—or possibly even worse—than the AIs' damned electronic henchman that had implanted the damned augmentation into her without anesthesia.

And unlike in the machine, the horde would then set her on *fire*. While the end would be relatively quick, it would be horrific beyond measure.

She'd do *anything* to make certain that didn't happen. They all would.

As rough as this first leg of the journey had been, how difficult was it going to be when they got closer to the Imperial Vault? Or even partway there?

This mission was just like one of the adventures she'd read when she was a kid. As her father had told her, adventure was something very bad happening to someone else, very far away, or a long, long time ago. Even so, she'd always wanted to go on an adventure.

Her younger self was an idiot.

"We need to get back to the rest," she finally said. "We've got a lot of work to do if we want to capitalize on this, and we'll need every second to make sure we don't screw it up."

With that, the two of them headed back to where the rest were going to be as they followed along the path behind them. She'd seen a decent ambush spot while up in the tree. All she had to do was convince the others to back her play.

30

J ared listened to Julia's plan, but started shaking his head before she was halfway done explaining it.

"That's too risky," he said when she'd finished. "*Anything* can go wrong, and then we'd be totally screwed. First of all, if even one person escapes the ambush you propose, we're dead. Second, if the gate guards don't recognize someone in the party, they might have us right there. If that's the case, we'd never get away, and once again, we're dead."

He took a deep breath and continued. "Third, after we get into the city—if we're that lucky—then any interaction at all will be dangerous. The chances of us being discovered go up dramatically with every word we speak or gesture we make."

"It doesn't matter," Julia said firmly. "Within a day—perhaps two at most—this entire area is going to be swarming with people looking for us. We have to plan on that happening sometime tomorrow, or we'd be crazy. That means we've got to get inside the city today, and preferably get out before dawn with what we need.

"If you can come up with another plan that accomplishes that, I'd be happy to hear it. Unfortunately, I don't think you're going to. The city is heavily guarded and well patrolled. We're not going to sneak inside without someone seeing us. That means we have to go in under their eyes. I think my plan is probably the best option to do that."

At that point, Kelsey stepped in and put her hand on his shoulder. "She's right. This situation requires bold action, and she's come up with a viable plan. Perhaps the only one possible at this point."

Talbot sighed and nodded. "We don't really have any choice, Admiral. We need to get inside that city today, and if they lock everything up at night, that means we're limited to just a couple of hours to make the magic happen. We have to go for it."

"Just give me a second to think about this," Jared said tiredly, rubbing his eyes with his right thumb and forefinger.

As much as he wanted to reject this crazy plan out of hand, he knew that they were right. They'd run out of time and options. They had to have the Imperial Scepter, and they really needed Lily's spare surgical kit to reactivate their implants and augmentation.

Everything else they could do without, but those two things would make or break their chances of making it to the Imperial Vault and then getting inside it.

He was going to have to go with Julia's plan. He had no choice.

It worried him because he knew that the slightest miscalculation or bit of bad luck would see them dead in minutes—if they were lucky. Hell, even success might still mean that most of them died before the rest got away. This was easily the grimmest situation he'd ever been in, and that called for taking an insane risk for even a slim chance to get away.

He tilted his head back for a moment and stared up toward the hidden sky. The intertwined branches overhead formed a green canopy that mostly blocked the sun from getting through, except in dappled shadows. How he wished he had time to enjoy the scents, sounds and sights of nature, but he didn't.

Putting the almost wistful thought from his mind, he looked at Julia intently. "Tell me where the ambush has to take place. We need to get there as quickly as possible, because we'll need every second to improve our chances of taking them down. Do you have any ideas on how to most effectively do that?"

Julia crouched down and brushed the dead leaves and branches away from a small area, leaving a spot of open ground. She picked up one of the sticks and began drawing on the earth with it.

"This is the outline of the forest as I saw it from up in the tree. This 'X' is where the enemy was. They were coming around this section of the woods to get to the cleared zone around the city. Do you see this indentation in the forest right here?"

Jared nodded when she looked up. "You think they're going to go inside there? That would be odd."

She shook her head. "No, but if we put some of our archers on the far side of this gap, they'll be hidden in the woods right next to where the enemy is going to pass. If we spring a trap at the right moment, I think that there's a better than fifty percent chance they'll dodge into this cul-de-sac and be trapped inside.

"What I'm recommending is that we put our archers here to take out the outermost riders while we have a couple of our own troops move to block them from going forward. They only have six riders in total. If we can take out half their number at one go, and they also see a blocking force in front of them, they're going to try to get away.

"We'll post archers at the back in the first section of forest that they've already passed as well, so that if anyone tries to reverse course, they can take them out.

"It makes me sad to say this, but horses are easier to hit than human beings. We can take our initial shots directly at the people, but they're armored and our best chance of stopping anyone from getting away is to remove any possibility that they can outrun us. We don't have the horses with us, so we have to target their mounts. I'm sorry.

"Also, with only six riders, we can only take that many people inside. Our horses are too far away to be of help. They'd spot people on pack horses right away and think that was too odd to pass unremarked. These people know horses and riding.

"We'll already be taking a risk just having any of us that can't ride along. We can't chance it. The ones we leave behind can head back to our camp and wait for signs of our success or failure."

"This situation just keeps getting worse and worse," Kelsey grumbled. "I get the possibility of hurting or killing the horses. I don't have to like it, but I get it. If that's what we have to do to survive, that's what we have to do. We should get moving."

Jared watched his sister stalk back down the path. He was no happier than she that they might have to kill innocent animals, but he understood the stakes just as well as she did. The horses were combatants in their own way, at least while the enemy was on their backs.

They'd do whatever they had to do. Far too many people were counting on them for them to cut any corners. There's be time for regrets later.

* * *

TALBOT CROUCHED JUST inside the tree line and waited. He couldn't hear the approaching horses yet, but he suspected that they were close. It wouldn't be long before they were fighting. He and Chloe were going to be the non-ranged response force in front of the group. The admiral and Commodore Meyer were doing the same thing on Kelsey's side of the opening.

Kelsey had given Jared her other sword, so if they had to fight, they'd have that one advantage. They had to keep the riders from getting past them at all costs. Her swords gave them an edge—if one could forgive the pun—that the enemy wouldn't expect and couldn't counter.

He'd made certain that the admiral knew about the dangers of directly blocking a sword swing. Kelsey's weapons would shear off the other blade in a heartbeat, and it would just continue on flying toward him.

That reminded him of his arm wound, though that wasn't how the injury had occurred. His arm still throbbed where the enemy's dagger had cut him earlier. They had no medical supplies, so he'd washed it out as well as he could, wrapped it in cloth, and then put his vambrace back over it.

Lily was worried about him getting an infection. Without his medical nanites or access to his pharmacology unit, that was a very real possibility. One that could render him unfit to fight in short order, or even kill him. If it got that bad, they'd have to take his lower arm off without any anesthesia, probably using one of Kelsey's swords.

Kelsey hadn't figured out that she needed to be worried about that, and he had no intention of telling her. They'd either have access to the medical supplies soon, or they'd be dead. Losing his arm to amputation because it was infected was the least of his worries. He had to focus on the moment.

Looking out into the area that the small caravan would be passing through, he could see how Julia's plan might play out in a perfect world. While this wasn't a chokepoint by any means, their enemy's options would be severely limited during the attack. The enemy would be pinned between the forest he was hiding in, the forest a hundred meters away on the opposite side of the open area, and the forest on the other side of the cul-de-sac, with only three paths to ride away in.

It was possible they'd manage to ride around Chloe and himself, and make a break for the city, but Captain Beauchamp, Elise, and Olivia would do their very best to make sure they didn't get past them in the front with their bows.

The horde fighter's second most dangerous option was retreating back the direction they'd come. If they did try to reverse course, Kelsey and Julia were back there with bows to make certain they didn't get anywhere, with the admiral and Commodore Meyer backing them up with swords.

That left any survivors of the initial attack the option of fleeing directly into the cul-de-sac. That's where the majority of their people were waiting. They had the swords that they'd captured, though they weren't skilled in the use of them. Still, quantity had a quality all its own.

There were six riders with this group, so with any luck, their initial shots would take out at least two. The follow-up arrows might take out another one. That would leave three figuring out which direction to flee.

If they tried to go past Talbot and Chloe, the archers would take a toll on them. He didn't think the enemy riders had a great chance of making it past three skilled shooters. If they retreated, that was going to be more problematic. The admiral and Commodore Meyer had no skill with swords to stop them if they directly engaged.

Commander Cannon was in charge of the force inside the cul-de-sac. The redheaded tactical officer had basic hand-to-hand skills, as did most Fleet officers. Hopefully she and her team wouldn't have to deal with more than one or two riders, while the main fighting team raced in to cork the bottle behind the enemy.

Well, this was either going to work out or it wasn't. Worrying wasn't going to change the outcome.

Talbot glanced over at Chloe and found her watching him.

He raised an eyebrow. "What?"

"I'm just trying to figure out how you do it," she said softly. "It seems like disaster after disaster is falling on top of us, and you're handling every blow like it's no big thing. How do you stay so calm?"

He chuckled. "It's getting to me too, but I've got more experience at keeping my worries buried. It's all my time as a noncommissioned officer, I suspect. Officers could run around with their hair on fire, but the noncoms had to be steady."

She smiled slightly and shook her head. "They frown on officers running around with their hair on fire because it's bad for morale. At least that's what they said at the academy. I think most of us do okay, but you're a rock. No matter what happens, you're there doing your part to make things work out.

"I've learned a lot by watching you. If I survive this little adventure, I think I'm going to be a better officer because of it."

"I think you're a fine officer as it is, Chloe. It wouldn't surprise me at all if you get bumped to major once we get off Terra. Hope you're ready to command a company."

She blanched a little at his words. "I'm not ready to command a company. I think I need more seasoning."

"This may surprise you, but you're getting that seasoning right now. There's an old saying, 'good judgment comes from experience, and experience comes from poor judgment.'

"While I haven't seen you exercise any poor judgment, you've certainly seen *everything* that can go wrong, and that's almost the same thing. Most officers never consider how bad things can get until they're in over their heads.

"After this mission, you're going to be thinking about all the curveballs that life and combat can throw at you. That's where success lies in our line of work. Preparing for all the possibilities, good and bad. If you've considered the good breaks, you can capitalize on them. If you've gnawed over the unpleasant surprises, then you can try to mitigate them."

"I've been thinking about that, actually," she said. "We're about to get into one of the most important fights we've been in since we landed on this damned planet. There are so many things that could play out badly, even though this is only a small action. If even one person gets away, we're screwed."

He reached over and put a hand on her shoulder. "Planning out the things that can go wrong doesn't mean we let them paralyze us. Sometimes you just have to trust that the dice are going to come up in your favor. If they don't, well, to mix metaphors, you'll just have to play the cards you've been dealt."

"You really need to work on your motivational speaking, Colonel."

Before he could respond, he heard the sound of horses approaching in the distance. It was time. They'd either stop the enemy in their tracks and move on to the next phase of their crazy plan, or they'd blow it and go from the frying pan into the fire.

He watched and waited until the caravan came into view. What he saw was like a blow to the side of his head. There were more riders than Julia had indicated. At least a dozen, possibly a few more.

That was going to make carrying off this ambush significantly harder. The chances of some of his friends being killed in the process also went up significantly.

Well, he'd just told Chloe that one had to learn to roll with the punches, and he'd been worried that this sounded a little too easy. There wasn't much they could do to improve their odds, so they'd just have to fight harder.

This was all Kelsey's show now. As soon as she gave the word, they'd kick this party off and hope for the best.

31

K elsey watched the horses as they began riding past and felt her heart sink. There were more people than Julia had said there would be. At least double the number, in fact. The one group her doppelgänger had seen must've met up with a second group. Now, with their numbers bolstered, taking them all out went from challenging to seemingly impossible.

That sucked, but there was nothing she could do about it now. They were going to have to carry off the attack just like they'd planned, because there was no way to make any changes to it.

She waited until the group had ridden past her hiding place and then kicked off the party by shooting one of the trailing riders in the back. The woman she'd targeted screeched and fell off her horse to writhe on the ground, her arms futilely reaching for the length of wood that had plunged into her back, which was just out of reach.

Julia had been waiting for that and fired moments after she did. Her arrow struck one of the men on the far side of the caravan, taking him in the torso. He didn't fall off his horse, but he didn't look like he was in very good shape either.

The three archers positioned with the forward group opened fire, taking down two of the riders directly ahead of the caravan, potentially killing them both. The third shot must've missed because Kelsey saw no sign of anyone else being inconvenienced by an unexpected impalement.

Even as Talbot and Chloe were running out in front of the group, Jared and Sean were doing the same on her end. Jared had her blade, so he was going to take the brunt of the hand-to-hand fighting. Her worry now was that there were too many enemies to stop them from retreating back past her. She had to make it her mission to stop that from happening.

"Target anybody running back our direction," she told Julia. "If they're not running, shoot anybody that goes for a bow."

Julia's answer was to fire another arrow even as Kelsey was tracking her next target. The other woman's shot flew right past one of the warriors as he jinked his horse to the side. Unfortunately for the other team, there was a second man right behind the first, and that rider caught the arrow in the throat. He pitched backwards off his horse and fell to the ground, lying there unmoving.

Kelsey's next shot caught one of the trailing riders as they turned to retreat. The arrow struck the man in his chest but must not have penetrated very far. Though he staggered in the saddle, the experienced horseman kept moving forward. She had to rush her third shot, but it did catch him in the side before he could get past her.

While he didn't fall out of the saddle, the way he was sagging to the side led her to believe that he was dead or critically injured. They'd have to catch up with his horse before it got too far, assuming they won this fight.

The archers up front had been just as busy as she was, so all three of them were peppering the vanguard of the caravan with shots. Kelsey had no time to count how many people went down, but it was at least two more.

Several of the riders raced toward Talbot and Laird, even as two more turned and bolted toward Jared and Sean. With the speed of their horses, they were on her friends before Kelsey could fire again.

Sean proved unable to strike at the man racing toward him. It was obvious that he meant to strike the horse, but the rider was very well trained. His mount seemed to leap to the side, and in a flash, he was past the officer, striking down with his sword as he passed. Thankfully, Sean blocked the strike even though it knocked his sword out of his hand.

As the escapee blazed past their blocking force, Julia fired an arrow into the man's back.

Or rather, she tried to. He dodged, not even seeing the first one until it flew past him, but her follow-up shot struck him in the spine, and he fell off his horse.

The one that attacked Jared found out immediately that that was a bad idea. Jared had paid attention to Talbot's instructions about her sword and so he struck from the side at the descending blade, seemingly aiming to break it off just above the hilt.

His aim was off, and he ended up taking the man's hand instead.

Well, that worked, too.

The pure shock on the man's face at what had happened to him didn't slow him down from trying to escape, though he was having to use his knees to control his mount as he tried to staunch the flow of blood from his severed limb.

That slowed him down quite a bit and made him an easier target. Kelsey's next shot took him in the side, and over he went.

Up front, Talbot and Laird had done their part to stop anyone from getting past, and the three archers had put down everyone on that side. Kelsey saw that their side was doing just as well, with a couple of people on the ground wounded, and two wounded men that had ridden out of sight around the curve of the forest.

She raced out of concealment and leapt on the nearest horse that she could catch. It gave her some grief, but she firmly put him in his place. All those years of riding were paying off now as she was able to get the recalcitrant beast headed after the people that had retreated.

As she came around the bend in the forest, she saw that one rider had fallen off his horse and his mount stood nearby, looking nervously toward Kelsey.

The second mount was standing a little further away, but Kelsey couldn't see any sign of his rider. It was possible the other man had fallen off his horse as well, and that his body was hidden by the grass, but she wasn't going to assume that was the case. This could be some kind of ambush.

A quick glance up the open area between the tree lines showed no sign of the man running, so if he wasn't lying in the grass somewhere ahead of her, he was in the woods somewhere to her left. The trees on her right were too far away for even an unwounded man to make it to them in the time that he'd been out of her sight.

Since the man in the open was between her and the second horse, she dismounted, drew the local sword she'd appropriated, and approached him carefully. He was still breathing but was only twitching sporadically. He tried for a knife at his belt, but she planted her boot on his wrist to stop him.

Kelsey considered finishing him but wasn't sure she had that in her. She'd hunted men down and killed them, but the idea of killing someone she'd already defeated turned her stomach. She settled for kicking the knife a short distance away and stepped clear of the dying man.

That's when the man hidden in the grass nearby chose to strike. He seemingly rose out of the ground less than a dozen meters away and rushed toward her. He had his long blade out and was already slashing it toward her head.

He was *huge*, taller than Talbot and much more muscular. He outweighed Kelsey by more than three to one. Without her Marine Raider augmentation, he was significantly stronger than she was too, and he was also a trained warrior. The scars on his face proved that.

His first slash, though powerful, was a little high. He was probably used to fighting people that were significantly bigger than her. For once, her short stature was working in her favor.

Kelsey managed to duck and used her blade to nudge his over her head with a loud clang of metal on metal. That put her near the man.

Seeing an opportunity that likely wouldn't come again, she jumped inside the arc of his blade, drew the marine knife from her belt, and plunged it through the armor on the side of his torso. The armor was thick and scarred from other blows, but it didn't even slow the almost monomolecular point of the hull metal blade.

The wound didn't stop the man from jerking back and pulling the knife's grip right out of her hand. He brought his blade back around, and it smashed into hers hard enough to knock it out of her grip. It went flying somewhere off into the grass on her left.

Suddenly disarmed and knowing that she didn't have time to search for her weapon, she went on the attack. If she'd just had her body and no skills, she'd be dead in the next five seconds. Thankfully, the Art gave her something to work with.

Lacking any strength to go along with the moves she was going to execute, she wouldn't be able to do any throws or body checks. She was going to have to bring him down to her level as quickly and efficiently as possible without any of that.

Even as he was drawing back to strike at her again, she lashed out and connected with his right knee. There was an audible pop, and the man's leg gave way. He didn't fall, but he staggered to the side like a drunken sailor.

Following up quickly, Kelsey ran two steps forward and launched herself into the air. His blade was already in motion, coming to strike at her—low this time—and she used her armored forearm to slap it away as it slid beneath her flying body.

She planted both her feet right in his face. The impact was sufficient to send him crashing to the ground with blood spraying from his nose and mouth. Momentarily stunned, he seemed unable to figure out how to move for just a few critical seconds.

Kelsey hit the ground a bit off-balance, but continued her roll forward, grabbed the knife still protruding from his side, and plunged it back into his throat.

Even mortally wounded, he tried to hit her with his sword one last time. She was far too close for the edge to hit her with any force but ducked close to him just in case.

The pommel of the weapon struck her leather helmet hard enough to throw her to the side with her head ringing, but there was no follow-up. The man gurgled, writhed beside her, and died.

Kelsey stood, her legs momentarily unsteady. Her face was covered in blood, but it wasn't hers. The foul iron stench made her want to throw up, but she managed to control her stomach.

That was of course the moment the man she'd spared stuck his recovered knife into her left calf.

The sharp, bright pain made her yelp as she hopped away from him. He lay there unmoving, his hate-filled eyes already starting to cloud over.

She knelt and looked at the wound. The puncture wasn't bad. The knife had probably only penetrated a couple of centimeters. Not enough to cause her more than inconvenience. It was bleeding freely, but there was no bright-red arterial blood. She'd live.

This damned fight reminded her far too much of the battle at the Imperial Retreat where she'd stalked and killed the assassins associated with her dead brother. It had been just as brutal and bloody. Thank God that her experience there had hardened her for what was happening now.

Kelsey staggered toward where her sword had fallen. She didn't have time for weakness. The fight might still need her.

Even as she searched for it, she made a mental note to practice fighting with her augmentation turned off. She'd been very lucky this time. The next fight might kill her.

A moment later, she had her sword in hand, had mounted her horse, and galloped back toward the fight.

Which was over by the time she came back into sight. Talbot and Laird had almost made it to the bend of the open area closest her, and Julia—now mounted—was also headed her way.

Kelsey slowed and made a gesture for the others to slow down. No need to rush now.

Their reserve force had come out of the cul-de-sac, and it seemed that all of the enemy was accounted for. After making sure no one else seemed badly wounded, she made her way over to Talbot and Laird. His torso was liberally coated in blood, though his posture didn't speak to any serious wounds.

"Are you hurt?" her husband asked with a note of worry.

She shook her head. "I was just a little too close to someone having the worst day of their life. Did we get them all? Are you hurt? Is anyone else?"

"All the enemy is down, and no riders bolted, other than the two you chased. We're okay. Did you get the two you were after?"

"I finished them off," she answered grimly. "We're going to have to hide the bodies, though thankfully we won't have to worry about them being discovered until tomorrow. It's already late in the day, and the horde warriors won't have time to become concerned about any birds, if they see them at all."

He nodded. "The archers took care of most of the ones here, but there were a couple that were still alive. They weren't going to survive, so Captain Beauchamp finished them. It makes me sick to my stomach having to do something like that."

She pulled him into a hug. "Harsh times call for harsh measures. It's not like we killed them out of hand. They fell in battle, and she made certain they didn't suffer. After what they did to the rest of our people, I don't have much sympathy for them."

He shook his head slowly. "Just because they're monsters doesn't give us a right to be monsters as well. I agree that she did exactly what needed to be done and that it was a mercy. We just have to be careful that we don't become hardened to this kind of thing. I'm a little worried about Julia on that front."

She looked over at her doppelgänger. She'd joined the captain in killing the wounded back at the campsite where she'd rescued them, and she'd been cold-blooded and methodical about it. Not cruel, but still something to watch. If they survived the day.

Talbot gave her one final squeeze and then stepped back. "Let's move the bodies into the cul-de-sac. We'll load them onto their horses and dump them a couple of dozen meters inside the forest. Hopefully no one will discover them before we make our escape."

Relocating the bodies was going to be a grisly task, but Kelsey threw herself into her work. Talbot was right that they couldn't afford to become monsters, but she wasn't going to lose much sleep about the indignities and unfairness of cutting down bastards like these. These men and women had chosen to butcher her unconscious people. They more than deserved what happened to them.

It looked like all of the pack horses were gathered in a clump— almost twice the number Julia had originally reported, which matched well with the idea two groups had merged. A couple of their people made sure that they didn't run off. As soon as they'd taken care of the bodies and washed the blood off their new mounts—and themselves —they'd see about getting into the city.

Ready or not, it was time to confront the enemy in their lair.

32

J ared felt naked as he rode out into the cleared area around the horde city. They were now in plain sight of both the guards on the walls of the ominous place and the mounted patrols that circled it. They were now fully committed to this crazy plan because there would be no backing out.

Even though he was near the front of the caravan, he wouldn't be doing the talking. He'd leave that to Beauchamp. She understood more about the horde than he did. She'd at least heard them speaking before and knew how to get the inflections right.

While everybody still spoke Standard, pronunciation of certain words had changed over time here on Terra. And on Avalon, too. The linguistic drift might kill them if someone got suspicious.

As a group, they'd discussed what they'd do if their ruse was discovered. As grim as it sounded, everyone had the means to make certain that they weren't captured. They all had knives that they could use on themselves.

None of them wanted to commit suicide, but if the other option was torture and immolation, he'd slit his own throat without a second's hesitation. The next few minutes were going to determine if that was necessary.

If their journey ended here, the New Terran Empire was doomed. Humanity itself was probably doomed. The AIs might have been satisfied with ruling over humanity before, but their development of the Omega Plague told him that they were now prepared to start eliminating their creators.

Beauchamp had gone over some basic ground rules of their behavior for this meeting. No one was to speak except her, unless directly spoken to. Even then, they were to keep their responses as brief and basic as possible.

Not that the woman expected the guards to question everyone. Based on what Julia and Beauchamp had seen, conversation was minimal. After all, what kind of idiot would try to sneak into the city right under their very noses.

His heart was pounding as the group approached the gate. None of the guards stationed in front of it or on the walls above seemed overly concerned at their approach.

Nor should they. A dozen people—even if they'd been trained warriors—would pose no threat to the city.

One of the guards standing in front of the gate stepped forward as they approached and raised his spear into the air, point first. "Hold. What news of the escaped prisoners?"

"We haven't seen them," Beauchamp said with a grimace. "If we had, you'd see them strung out behind us. Someone else will catch them. They won't get away."

The guard grinned at that. "True enough. Pass."

Jared was starting to breathe a silent sigh of relief when that same guard narrowed his eyes and once again raised his spear.

"Hold." He was looking directly at Kelsey. "Take off your helmet."

Jared tensed. This was it.

The man looked her up and down once she'd removed her head cover, revealing the bruised and battered face she'd gotten when she'd been captured. He eyed her suspiciously for a moment, and then he smiled.

"How can a little thing like you be a warrior? Did you steal

Daddy's armor, little girl? Maybe you need a real man like me to show you how to use that sword and not get beaten up like that."

His companions rumbled with laughter, and he visibly preened a little.

Kelsey slowly smiled in a way that made Jared's blood run cold.

She edged her horse closer to the man and leaned over toward him. "That assumes you could even find the sheath with that short sword of yours. You look a little... clumsy."

"Oh, my mistake. That's just a dagger with a dull edge. So, is that what this is? You're looking for a real woman to sharpen that thing for you because your whetstone has grown worn from overuse and you think I have a firmer stroke than you? I hear that comes with age, old man."

There was a brief moment of stunned silence before the guard's companions roared in laughter. Many of them had doubled over, unable to contain their mirth.

The man's face flushed a deep red as he scowled. "You have a saucy mouth, girl. Do you just use it to talk? Did you mouth off to the wrong man and he beat you like a drum?"

Kelsey gave him a disdainful sniff as she turned her horse to return to the formation. Her horse's tail flipped almost dismissively.

"I set him on fire, so I think I came out ahead in the end. Shall I climb down so that we can compare blades? I promise not to look disappointed when you come up... short. After all, I'm sure it's cute for its size."

The guards roared again, and the man's flush deepened even further.

"I'll give you this, woman, you've got a quick tongue," he ground out. "Get inside before I'm tempted to teach you some manners," the guard said as he gestured with his spear for them to proceed. "And don't be surprised if one day I make you call my name with that sassy mouth."

"Keep dreaming, big man," Kelsey said with a toothy grin as she rode past him. "Keep dreaming."

The exchange had made Jared feel as if he was having a heart attack. Once they'd crossed through the gate and into the city itself, he motioned for Kelsey to ride up beside him. That was easier than trying to redirect his horse to meet hers.

"*Have you lost your mind?*" he demanded quietly as she fitted her helmet back on. "You deliberately provoked him."

The corner of his sister's mouth quirked up. "Once he'd singled me out, I didn't have a choice. It would've been out of place for a warrior to take that kind of challenge without responding. Yes, I upped the provocation by mocking him that way, but trust me when I say that I had to. Anyone who has spent any time around the marines would know that."

"She's right," Beauchamp said from his other side as they rode through the city, the sound of the shod hooves loud on the cobblestones beneath them. "I'm glad she reacted the way she did because no woman of the blade would allow that kind of talk about her without striking back. Not all combat is physical. Her silence would've raised their suspicion."

She grinned at Kelsey. "And that was well said. I'll have to remember that when I next need to put an uppity man in his place."

Jared wanted to rub his face but that would've seemed out of place, so he just allowed himself a single sigh. Instead of responding, he looked at the buildings they were passing.

Most were made of wood, though some stone was used in their construction. They all looked primitive, but not because of the materials they'd used. He'd seen the Imperial Lodge where Kelsey had stayed for a while on Avalon once they'd put down Ethan's regicidal insurrection. It was wood and stone but built by true craftsmen. These buildings were… sloppy.

He wondered if they'd built the structures themselves or used slave labor. There was no telling, and honestly, he didn't even want to know at this point. Some things were best not thought about.

A much more pressing concern was where they were going. Wandering the streets would not serve their purposes. In fact, if they didn't figure out where they needed to be very soon, someone was going to get suspicious, of that he was certain.

At the moment, they were on a wide street that led deeper into the city. The smaller, packed dirt alleys that led away from the cobblestones were narrow and seemed to only serve the areas just off the boulevard. That wouldn't be where they were keeping anything valuable.

For the moment, he thought they were safe heading directly into the city. The powerful lived in the centers of such places, and that would be where these caravans were heading. The trick was going to be finding the right building, and then fooling whoever guarded it into thinking that he and his people had the right to go in.

Jared looked up at the sun with a hand shading his eyes and estimated that they had an hour and a half before dark. He had no idea what the city guards would do at that point, but he was willing to bet that everything would be locked down for the night. This seemed like the kind of place where they didn't like the idea of random people wandering around in the dark.

At this pace, moving through the timid crowd that hurried to get out of their way, he estimated that they'd arrive at the city center in twenty or thirty minutes. If it took much longer than that to figure out their ultimate destination, they were going to end up fighting in the middle of a hostile populace with nowhere to go.

Jared gritted his teeth and gently used his heels to urge his horse to go just a little faster. He had to be careful because he didn't want it breaking into a gallop, and he still wasn't that good at controlling it, but every second counted. They had to get to the right place and get under cover, and they needed to do it right now.

JULIA GUIDED her horse along the cobblestone street almost on autopilot as she watched the crowd move around them. And it *was* definitely moving around them. The people looked terrified of her party, and that told her all she needed to know about how the horde treated its own people. The bastards that ran the horde were brutal.

She wished she had the ability to overthrow their regime but knew that that wasn't in the cards. They'd be lucky to get out of the city with their skins intact. Her thirst for their blood wouldn't be slaked today.

The crowd parted around them, rushing to be as far away from the horses as possible, and allowed the group deeper into the city at a fairly decent pace. Once they'd left the gate, the quality of the buildings began slowly improving. The rough wooden structures were replaced by stone, even though that was still just as slipshod as the buildings behind them.

With every block they traveled, the quality of the construction continued to improve until they were finally in an area that looked somewhat prosperous. The crowds had changed here as well. While they still had a fearful aspect to them, they didn't seem to be completely terrified of her party.

This section of the city had a lot of shops, and the people around them were either conducting business or making things. The scents of hot metal, burning wood, and odd chemical smells seemed to dominate the air. Maybe this was where the horde merchant or service classes lived and worked.

Interestingly, there were carts here that were being used to move goods of some kind. They weren't being pulled by horses, she noticed. Everything was human powered. That had to impede the ability to move large quantities of goods, so there had to be some kind of societal reason for it. Maybe the horses were reserved for the higher classes.

As they rode, they passed other warriors on horses. There were also some that patrolled on foot, but those seemed to be of a lower class than the ones on horses. It looked as if there were strata in the warrior class. She filed that information away as potentially useful.

On the other side of the merchant quarter, they entered a portion of the city that seemed to be much more finely designed and constructed. The streets were of higher quality, the cobblestones fitted more tightly together and easier to ride on. There were even horse-drawn carriages that moved people from place to place on their unknowable business.

The carriages were of very fine construction. The play of dark and light woods used, as well as the intricate carvings and bright painted surfaces, spoke of wealth. The drivers seated atop them dressed in bright clothes that seemed oddly designed to Julia. There had to be some kind of ceremonial aspect to that, as all of them dressed in a similar manner.

The buildings they traveled between were imposingly tall and extremely well-built. Where wood was used, it was planed down to flat surfaces, sanded to smoothness, and then painted in bright colors. If there was stone—which most buildings here used stone in parts of their construction—it was shaped and smoothed to be aesthetically pleasing as well.

Definitely a high-class neighborhood.

She was still admiring some of the houses—though in many cases the word "house" seemed trivial when used for the buildings in question—when she saw another group of horsemen approaching them from directly ahead.

There were warriors, but there were also pack animals. The packs were noticcably empty.

This group looked like the same kind of caravan that they were pretending to be. Perhaps these people had already been to the repository of the stolen gear. If so, she and her companions were definitely headed in the right direction.

She hoped the others passed by without trying to converse but wasn't shocked when one of the horsemen edged over and changed direction to ride directly beside her. He was examining her armor, and he had a slight frown on his face.

"Your armor is very well constructed, but it's made for a man," he said, his frown deepening. "Why don't you have one more fitted to your form?"

That sounded like a personal question, but she wasn't sure she should challenge him like Kelsey had the guard. That had been *insane*. She should probably just answer the question.

Sadly, it was one that she hadn't been prepared to answer. She'd hadn't considered that there might be different styles of armor for men and women.

There had to be, she belatedly realized. While she wasn't well-endowed, other women were. Lieutenant Laird, for example had a generous bosom. So did Commander Cannon. Their armor—which they'd probably salvaged from dead women—must have a more expansive chest segment to allow for that, so they could be protected yet comfortable.

She'd gotten hers from a small man because her options at the time had been limited but hadn't realized there was a difference in construction for gender. Now she might have gotten them all killed because of her ignorance.

For a couple of seconds, her brain ran in every direction searching for *anything* that she could say that would make sense and seem innocent. Then the perfect answer struck her. In fact, it was so perfect that she had to resist the urge to smile.

She shrugged her shoulders at the man. "These are my brother's hand-me-downs. You know how it is, the first son always gets the good stuff. I suppose I'm lucky to have this. One day—maybe soon now— I'll buy my own gear."

At her words, the man slowly nodded. "I hadn't realized that happened across gender lines, but I've done the same thing for my younger brothers."

He examined her torso closely, likely trying to imagine how small-breasted she had to be to fit into such tight confines. There was nothing sexual in his gaze, just cold-eyed professional curiosity.

She was glad the warrior couldn't see the weapons she'd taken from the dead man whose armor she wore. The fine steel blades were safely in their scabbards, and her bow was on her back. Those were definitely not hand-me-downs.

Julia turned slightly in the saddle so that her torso obscured the bow a little better. It's exquisite artistry might catch the man's attention.

He started to say something else, but someone from his own group shouted at him to hurry up. The man shot an irked glare back at his group but did pull away and start after them.

"Once you drop off your cargo, do me the honor of joining me at the Tavern of the Elk. I'm there most evenings. I'd like to learn more about you, and I believe I can recommend an armorer that can help you."

His tone indicated that he was giving her an instruction rather than requesting she do as he asked. He was someone with natural authority. She wondered who he was in this society.

Without waiting for a response from her, the man hurried after his fellows, leaving Julia and her party blissfully alone.

She wondered if her armor implied that she was of a lesser social standing than him or if he was a higher-ranking member of whatever they called their horsemen. If something on the armor indicated rank, she didn't know what it was.

Thankfully, she had no intention of ever seeing the man again, so it wouldn't matter. Whether he had been hitting on her or giving her an order that he expected her to obey, he was going to be sorely disappointed when she not only didn't show but turned out to be one of the people that had escaped their clutches.

That complication dealt with, she focused on where they were going. They just had to find the holding place for all the captured gear and deal with whoever was guarding it. Somehow. And they had to do it fast.

33

T albot grew more antsy the closer they got to the center of the city. The number of guards around them had been steadily increasing over the last few minutes, and it now seemed as if they were everywhere. They outnumbered the civilians in their now opulent clothing by a significant amount. That meant they dwarfed his party's numbers.

Off in the distance, a larger structure rose above the buildings around it. He'd seen pictures in books on various planets of the Old Terran Empire. Kelsey loved reading about that kind of thing and always had a few printed up from the ship's library in their quarters. What he was looking at was a castle.

Most of those structures in the Old Empire were recreations of what had existed on Terra back in the prespaceflight days, but the building in front of him, though similarly constructed, had a brooding, brutal look about it. It wasn't just for show. It was a working edifice meant to stand off a determined attack. It looked strong enough to even survive some advanced weapons.

Though his party was still making its way through the crowds, he noticed that the civilians were less inclined to hurry out of their way. These more affluent people believed that they had the right-of-way, and that implied a level of power in their stratum of the social fabric of the horde. These were movers and shakers in their society.

Or at least they thought they were.

It was hard to believe that these people had been an industrialized, advanced civilization only a century ago. They looked as if they belonged in the Middle Ages, of which Kelsey had also read a few books. The clothing styles were strange, but none of them would've known anything different during their lifetimes.

It was interesting. Even on Avalon, when the AIs had used their EMP weapons and destroyed all advanced technology, his people had never devolved into this kind of primitive society. They'd remained one civilization, under the rule of Emperor Lucien. They'd kept the manners and education that they could and pulled themselves back out into space. It had taken a while, but they hadn't lost their identity as a people.

To him, it certainly seemed as if the people of Terra had abandoned their identity in favor of this more primitive and warlike mode of living. He wondered if that was because the AIs were still above their heads and ready to blast any civilization that became too advanced with their kinetic weapons.

In the end, he finally decided that that might be a mystery that he'd never solve.

He was still thinking about that when he noticed another emptied caravan coming around the corner ahead of them. The warriors surrounded the empty pack horses and pulled them down the street back in the direction that Talbot and his people had just come from.

Talbot inclined his head toward them as they passed, and one of the warriors in the group did the same. No words were exchanged, which was just fine by Talbot. He'd rather not risk saying the wrong thing, and frankly, he just wasn't as bold as Kelsey or Julia. Those two leapt in where angels feared to tread.

He urged his horse to move faster and made a hand gesture to the admiral that they'd be changing course. The other man nodded.

Once he'd made his way around the corner, Talbot saw what he was sure was their ultimate destination. The building in question was squat and made of thick stone blocks. He wasn't certain what its original purpose had been, but it was now surrounded by guards that were keeping even the entitled populace of the horde city at bay with stern looks and occasional shoves.

The latter was greeted with cries of outrage, but the guards seem unimpressed. A few were forced to show a few inches of blade to send the most pompous scurrying away.

To Talbot, that told a tale. These powerful people were not used to being treated so cavalierly. That meant that whatever was going on here was new. Otherwise, everyone would already be aware of how defensive the guards would be. That made this place the most likely repository of their stolen gear.

As their horses approached the building, one of the guards on foot walked out and held up a hand. This man was older than many of the guards that Talbot had seen so far, his hair iron gray and his beard only containing a few strands of black. His face had two wide scars that went from his hairline on the left side of his face down close to his chin. Both wounds were red and ropey.

"Hold, there," the man said gruffly. "You must wait until the current group finishes unloading before you can enter."

Talbot nodded and contented himself with edging closer to the admiral after the guard had returned to his companions.

"With the number of guards around this place, I don't think we're going to be able to fight our way out," he said softly. "Whatever we do inside, we're going to have to come back out looking as if everything was normal. That might be a little bit difficult if we have to kill a bunch of guards in there."

The other man smiled sourly. "It's not as if we have a choice. I doubt very seriously that Lily could get Kelsey's Raider augmentation back online in just a couple of minutes, even if we found her surgical kit. We'd still never get out of the city alive.

"Our only chance of success is to find the scepter and the supplies that we absolutely must have, stash them in our saddlebags, and then just walk out just like every other group that we've passed. Unfortunately, there *will* be guards inside to keep people from doing *exactly* what we plan on doing. Count on it."

Talbot pursed his lips. "Maybe not so many. The people that we're pretending to be have already been trusted to bring everything in that they've captured. I think the mounted warriors are a different, higher caste than the foot soldiers. Maybe even nobility. That might give us the break we need.

"We have to get a jump on the next part of the plan and secure the inside of this building while we conduct our search. I doubt very seriously that the guards on duty are going to allow us to look for what we need.

"Once we do, we're going to have to figure out how we get out of the city before they discover what we've done. I think we can get out of the general area before someone comes along and starts screaming, but that's not going to get us out of the city.

"We'll have to get over the wall and past the mounted patrols outside. Once we do, where do we go from there? If we make a break for open country, you can bet they'll have riders running us down before we get even an hour away."

Jared looked over toward where the towers of the megacity rose in the distance, dark and empty. "I think the answer is sitting right in front of us. If we can get outside the city walls, we're going to have to make a break for the megacity. Even with all the bad things we've heard about places like that, at least it offers us a chance of survival."

Talbot had already come to that same conclusion. It wasn't a happy idea, but no matter what they did, there was going to be a bad outcome. At this particular moment, he'd be happy if they survived to see the sunrise.

Before he could say anything more, another caravan of warriors and packhorses began coming out of the building through the opened doors.

This was it. They'd have one chance to carry this off, and if they failed, each and every one of them would die fighting or at their own hands to avoid capture. The only avenue to survival was success, and he was going to do everything within his power to make sure that his wife and the admiral got away, even if it cost him his own life.

* * *

JARED EXAMINED everything he could as covertly as possible as they entered the squat building. The exterior walls were significantly thicker than he'd expected, and he'd been expecting them to be thick indeed.

It looked as if the stone blocks used to construct the outer shell were at least a meter thick, and the wall was made up of them stacked four deep. The passage through the wall was about two meters wide. He'd think of it as the foyer, though the term seemed off in the context.

He couldn't imagine what they were defending against in this primitive environment. Lesser walls would stop most basic attacks, but nothing would stop a kinetic projectile from orbit.

Well, it didn't matter. What was important now was making note of every guard he could while trying to determine the best method to conduct this operation.

Once they were through the narrow foyer, they came into a larger room with the ceiling supported by pillars of stone even thicker than the blocks that made up the walls. The room seemed to take up the entirety of the building. Lighting inside was provided by a number of smoking torches that cast a flickering yellow glow over everything.

Their smell wasn't as acrid as he'd have expected. It was actually somewhat pleasant. It made him wonder what they used for an accelerant.

A glance upward showed that the smoke went out through narrow vents in the ceiling. From the amount of soot up there, no one had bothered cleaning inside the room for quite some time.

Half a dozen guards were stationed along the walls at equidistant locations. They weren't the most interesting contents of the room, however. It looked as if a lot of his people's gear had already been brought in and stored. Piles of everything imaginable were stacked high in every open portion of the floor except for that directly in front of the large, reinforced wooden doors they'd just passed through, the cramped foyer, and the area where the horses now stood.

Searching through those piles to find what they'd need was going to be a huge pain in the ass, and there was absolutely no way they could accomplish that while still under the watchful eyes of the guards.

Even if they took the guards out of play, there was no telling how long it would take to find the Imperial Scepter, much less Lily Stone's spare medical kit or the requisite supplies for even simple brain surgery.

Interestingly, the center of the room was taken up by what looked like a huge, ornate altar of some kind. The flat surface was made of stone that had been smoothed flat by whatever artisans had created it. The side panels were carved with intricate designs that he couldn't make out from this distance, but they looked ceremonial.

The purpose of the altar was unimportant. It was a mystery they didn't have time to solve.

Jared looked over his shoulder and saw a huge wooden beam leaning against the wall in the foyer nearest the doors giving access to the interior of the building. That probably meant the doors could be barred from the inside. That might be useful, if things went downhill.

He wasn't certain how they could possibly get what they needed and still escape. With the doors open, the exterior guards would certainly hear the sounds of combat. And with no means of silently disabling the interior guards, he wasn't sure they could even find what they needed, much less escape. It seemed like an impossible task.

Captain Beauchamp edged up beside him and casually dismounted. "Do you see the stone cover at the center of the room?" she asked quietly.

He nodded as he got off his own horse. "It's some kind of altar, isn't it?"

The woman shook her head. "It's a protective cover. I believe this is the treasure house for the horde. That cover probably leads to stairs going deep underground to where they keep their most revered and valued artifacts."

Jared thought about that and felt his eyes narrow. "Do you think that they dug out the area beneath here specifically for that, or would they have used something that was already present? With the megacity adjacent to this city, there are probably old tunnels down there."

"Almost certainly the latter. If I were a betting woman, I'd suspect that they walled off an old tunnel and are using part of it for their own purposes. It wouldn't be accessible to anyone above ground, and not even the people living inside the megacity would be able to break down a formidable barrier."

Jared smiled. "Then I think that I have a plan. You're not going to like it. Hell, *I* don't like it, but it's the only chance I see for us to succeed. If I'm right, we can get away clean. If not, well, we're totally screwed."

34

K elsey tried to make sense of the piles of equipment and supplies that surrounded them but couldn't. It seemed like there was no rhyme or reason about how anything was placed inside the room. It was just unloaded wherever happened to be convenient for the person placing it there. That was going to make searching through the mess much more difficult.

She stepped over and joined Jared as he eyed the guards around the room. "We need to have our noncombatants start unloading, or they're going to get suspicious," she said softly. "I can't tell where anything is in this place. It looks like they brought a bunch of stuff from the crashed pinnaces as well as what we were carrying with us. Sadly, we don't know if we're the last caravan, so some of the stuff we're looking for may not even be here."

"That's true," he agreed. "It's even possible that something like the scepter was taken to their palace rather than being brought here. That seems like the kind of thing a ruler would be interested in.

"Maybe it's just me, but it also seems odd that they'd have their treasure vault outside their castle. That's what Captain Beauchamp thinks that formation in the center of the room is, an access to an underground treasure vault in a walled-off tunnel from the ruined megacity. Well, I think it's in a section of tunnel. At least I hope it is."

She shrugged slightly. "If that's what it is, they must have some reason to do it, because no one would just put their stuff out in the open without a good reason. How are we going to do this?"

As the noncombatants started unloading the horses, Jared covertly directed her attention back toward the doors they'd come through. "See that bar? I'm pretty sure that locks the outer doors from the inside.

"It's thick, so it'll hold until they can bring something significant to break it down. The doors are heavy and braced with metal as well. I'd imagine that's because they'd rather not have somebody stealing all their stuff.

"Commander Cannon, Sean, Carl, and I will get the doors closed and the bar in place. Austin and Ralph can back us up and help with the bar if it's heavier than it looks."

He turned slightly to face the interior of the room. "That leaves Julia, Captain Beauchamp, Talbot, Chloe, Elise, Olivia, and yourself to deal with the guards. You got enough ranged firepower that you should be able to take them out before they know what's going on. Lily will be on standby to help anybody that's injured. Did I miss anyone?"

She shook her head. "No, that's everybody. I'll brief my team on what they'll be doing. You take your group."

Kelsey casually walked to each of the designated fighters and told them in short, quiet sentences exactly what she wanted them to do. Each was assigned a specific guard to target with their ranged weapon, if they had one. Talbot had one of her swords, so he should be able to deal with the last one with a few strokes.

With five people wielding bows, they should be able to eliminate the half dozen guards before anyone was hurt. The initial shots would be a complete and utter surprise, so the targets wouldn't be dodging.

She was much more concerned about Jared and his people getting the door closed and locked. It looked stout, but she was certain that the horde had the means to get in. She'd seen plenty of old Terran vids where doors like that were cracked open with battering rams.

Of more concern was what they'd do once the plan was in motion. If the strange stone structure in the center of the room did lead downstairs, would they be able to get out of this supposed treasure room? If not, then they shouldn't attack at all.

Yet she already knew that they didn't really have a choice. This would be their one and only chance to try to recover what they needed and get away, if they could. If the vault was in one of the old tunnels that once had served the megacity, they might even succeed.

Jared was probably right. There had to be hundreds of tunnels running around beneath the ground this close to the place. Maybe thousands. It was very easy to dig deep and place things underground when you had high technology. The towering structures of the megacity were testament to the skills of the builders, and so were the less visible aspects of the old place.

Once she and her people were in position, Kelsey kept an eye on Jared as he and his team stopped unpacking the remaining horses and moved as casually as they could toward the reinforced doors. The guards seemed somewhat confused by their actions but didn't do anything more than glance at one another.

The one thing she and her people couldn't do ahead of time was draw or prepare their weapons. That kind of thing would spark a response. They'd have to draw fast and make their first shots count.

The moment that Jared made a gesture to his people and they rushed the doors, Kelsey drew her bow from across her shoulder in one smooth movement, her free hand already grasping an arrow from her quiver and bringing it up to the string.

The guard she'd selected for herself seemed stunned and was slow to react. Her shot took him in the center of the chest. Though his armor did an admirable job of stopping much of the force, at this range the arrow still won. Just to be certain, she fired another one into him even as he fell.

Not everybody had been as lucky with their initial shots, but their follow-up arrows were keeping the guards busy even as the enemy drew their weapons and shouted in alarm.

Talbot was rushing his target. She was tempted to fire an arrow at the guard in front of him, but that might be a mistake. She'd have to let her husband fight his own fight. Instead, she shifted her aim to one of the remaining guards and helped bring him down quickly instead.

None of the guards were able to reach her team, except for the one fighting Talbot. That man discovered how outclassed he was after two blows from her man. One of them took the guard's arm off at the wrist, and the other struck off his head. God, but that was a bloody spectacle.

With all the guards down, she turned and rushed toward the doors.

Jared and his people had them closed and were holding them tight while someone—or more likely several someones—pushed hard on the other side. The tech team was struggling to get the massive bar into the metal holders that secured the doors from opening, but it seemed a little heavy for them.

Without her augmentation, she wasn't exactly made for the task, but she figured that every little bit would help. Together, they managed to get the massive bar into place with a loud "thunk."

Everyone stepped back from the door and eyed it warily as the people outside continued slamming against it and shouting. The heavy wooden planks didn't even quiver.

"That should hold until they bring in something significant to break it down," Jared said in a tense rush. "Everyone split up and go through the piles. We need to find the Imperial Scepter, Doctor Stone's spare medical kit, Carl Owlet's tools, any equipment Carl could find from the pinnaces that hadn't been burned out by the EMP, and anything else small enough to carry with us while we're moving fast, but that might help us get to the Imperial Vault.

"Throw anything that we don't need into the foyer leading toward the doors. That might keep them from getting in for just a little bit longer."

Kelsey raced around the other side of the room and started digging through a pile. She was too far away from the foyer to throw anything into the tunnel, but Ralph Halstead was at her side, grabbing everything that she tossed away and racing back toward the tunnel to dump it.

A glance at the rest of the room showed that others were

emulating his example so that the searchers weren't slowed by having to also help barricade the doors. That was smart. If they could get some large, heavy items directly behind the doors, that would help wedge them shut, even if they did bring in a battering ram. The horde troops would have to completely demolish everything.

Captain Beauchamp was recovering the arrows they'd shot. She'd done that every time they'd been able to after fighting. Kelsey approved, because once they were out, they were left to fight at close range.

"We should take the biggest things and put them directly behind the doors at the hinges," Kelsey shouted. Anything that gained them a few more minutes was worth doing.

In fact, the stone slabs covering what they hoped led to a vault below might be more massive than anything that had been brought from the pinnaces.

"Ralph, come with me," she said. "I want to check something out."

The stone edifice in the center of the room was even larger than it had looked from the entryway. It was at least three meters long and a meter and a half wide. It stood about waist high for a normal person, so chest high for her.

The top was unadorned, but the sides were heavily engraved with scenes of what looked like battle. A closer inspection revealed horsemen fighting against what certainly looked like Rebel Empire marines in powered armor.

Interesting, but she didn't have time to examine it.

The top slab seemed to be unattached to the sides, so she pushed on it. There was the sound of stone grinding on stone as it shifted maybe a centimeter to the side. It was *heavy*. The slab was as thick as her fist and seemed to weigh a ton. Which might be the literal truth. Getting it to the foyer was going to be a monumental task.

She turned to face everyone else in the room. "Stop what you're doing and come help me get this stone slab into the foyer. We're going to lay it on the floor directly in front of the doors. It can be on top of whatever you've already put there."

With a dozen people helping move the slab, it wasn't impossible.

Sliding it off where it had rested was a serious chore, but they finally had the thing off, revealing a dark pit below with steps leading down where the torchlight couldn't reach.

The fact that they could move it still didn't mean that it was easy. Everyone grunted and strained as they carried it toward the doors. Once they arrived, they discovered a problem. The opening in the stone wall was too narrow to get it in longways.

They settled for placing it at an angle, with one corner jammed into the door on the right-hand side, its adjacent corner right against the stone wall to that side, and the corner on the other end of the long side, braced against one of the massive stone blocks making up the left wall.

Jared grinned at her. "That's going to make it a *lot* harder for them to get those doors open. Let's see if the sides of that structure come off. A few more pieces like this, and we might just be able to keep them from getting in at all without demolishing the side of the building."

The stone slabs on the side of the covered structure above the stairs were attached to the floor, except for one of the shorter ones at what would be the foot of the structure. It was removable so that people could use the stairs revealed below the structure.

The steps leading down were wide and somewhat shallow. They wouldn't be easy to speed along. It was pitch-black below, but Kelsey could see that they went down a short distance and then began turning to the right.

That would be useful if they had to form a defense going downward. Frankly, that was probably why the turn had been designed into them. She'd seen something about this in a vid. Any archers going down the stairs would have their dominant hands obstructed by the wall to the right, so they'd have to expose themselves to fire. Any archers defending from below would have their dominant hands free and clear to fire up at their opponents and could use the inner stone wall as cover.

Of course, any lefties were going to get an advantage going down and be obstructed in defending. None of their archers were left-handed, so it wasn't going to inhibit them.

As several of the others carried the removable block of stone away and tossed it into the entryway, the remainder of them put their effort into pulling down the still-standing stone slabs that made up the sides.

While they *were* secured, they weren't that secure. Jared quickly ordered the slabs taken into the entryway and placed on top of the first slab, alternating the directions they were wedged. The smaller sections were placed on top of them.

"That was a great idea," he said as he wiped his brow. "Everyone not searching, take the castoffs into the entrance and throw them on top of everything else. I want to get that foyer packed so full of debris that nothing is going to be able to move, even with a ram smashing into the doors. Anything that gains us time is worth it.

"Julia and Talbot, head down the steps and see what we're dealing with. Get torches from the walls up here to light your way. Ralph, follow them down and be ready to be a courier to get us information or warning of what's down there."

Kelsey quickly returned to the pile she'd been working on. Even though her brother seemed to think they had plenty of time, she wasn't so sure. The sooner they could finish, the sooner they'd be out of there.

She only prayed that they could find the things that they needed and escape with their lives.

If the scepter wasn't here, then all of this was for nothing. If the spare medical kit Lily had left at the pinnaces wasn't here, they'd never get their implants back online. The same went for Carl finding the tools that he needed. Those items were absolutely critical to their success and survival.

With a sigh, she gave herself over to the task at hand. They were committed, and the next few minutes were going to show if the gamble had been worth it or not.

35

J ulia followed behind Talbot as he descended the spiral staircase. He had Kelsey's sword out and was being wary of anyone coming up from below, not that she thought they needed to be that concerned about that. After all, the entrance to the crypt—because that's just what this might be—had been sealed up tight and under guard. She doubted very seriously that anyone was down there.

Anyone alive, that was. This still might be a crypt. Hell, it might end up their crypt if things went badly.

She followed behind the large man with her bow out and an arrow nocked. She stayed as far to the left as she could so that she'd have as much range as possible, but with the relatively tight turnings of the stairs, that still wasn't very far. If enemies rushed up from below, she'd have time for one shot before they engaged her doppelgänger's husband.

As they were wielding their weapons, Ralph Halstead was holding three torches up high as he followed behind them. Their flickering flames cast more than enough light to see what was ahead, but the distortion in the illumination levels made her twitch every time she thought she'd seen something.

Julia tried to guess at how deep they'd come, but it wasn't easy. In fact, it was impossible. She'd started out counting steps but had lost track somewhere along the way and given up.

Then she'd started trying to estimate how many full revolutions they'd made, but that led to the same outcome because she wasn't sure what direction was what. In any case, whatever was below them was a long, long way down.

"I think I see something," Talbot said a few minutes later.

Julia could see that he was right. The stairs had terminated into a flat space that was void of steps. Perhaps it was the bottom or maybe only a landing. She couldn't tell.

As they reached the flat area, she saw that it did in fact lead out of an alcove into a much larger space. This was no landing. This was the bottom of the stairs and their destination.

The torchlight didn't extend very far, but it was more than enough to see that they were in the remains of one of the old tunnels that must've serviced the megacity. It had been greatly enlarged and the ancient flooring covered with paved stone that had been polished smooth, but the wall immediately next to them was made out of plascrete and still had a number of pipes and cables running along its length.

It also had a holder for a torch crudely mounted to it. A glance to the right showed a similar holder mounted to rough-hewn stone that had to have been added later. It looked much like the blocks that made up the building above, but these were much smaller.

If they'd needed to be brought in from the surface, they'd have had to come down the stairs, so that made sense. Stacked neatly next to the arch was a pile of unlit torches, a wedge of metal, and a rock. The last two things made no sense to her, but they had to serve some purpose, even if it was obscure.

"It looks like this started out as a tunnel," Talbot said, mirroring her guess, as he stepped into the large room. "Somebody went to a lot of trouble to dig it out, though."

The area closest them was empty, but out where the light was fading, she could see vague shapes in the darkness. Gray on black. That probably wasn't an accurate assessment of the colors involved, but in the low light at the edge of the torches' illumination, it was hard to tell. Nothing sparkly, so probably no gold, silver, or gems.

Whenever she thought of vaults, that's what she'd always imagined: a room stacked high with wealth in physical form. This didn't seem to be that stereotypical.

"Should I stay with you?" Halstead asked uncertainly.

"For a little bit, yes," she said. "I want to get at least a basic description of what we're seeing before you go back up to report. I'd also like to make sure there's not anything hiding down here before I put my bow away. Put one of the torches into the holder by the arch and light another one for yourself."

Once he'd done so, she and Talbot advanced side by side with Halstead right behind them until the shapes in front of them resolved into something that they could identify.

Wooden crates stood piled high enough that they rose at least four times Talbot's height. The wood was roughhewn, so she didn't think they were very old. At least not in the scheme of things on Terra.

Talbot stopped next to one stack and leaned over to examine the crates more closely. "I wonder what's in them."

"Something important enough to be this well protected," she said as she eyed the stack to make sure it looked stable. The last thing they needed was to be crushed by someone else's neglect. "There has to be some way of identifying what's in them. Are there any markings?"

He walked around the side of the stack in front of them and grunted slightly. "Yeah. There's a number carved into each crate. That must mean something to whoever put them here, but it's not going to help us determine anything about them. If we want to know what's inside, we'll have to open them up."

"We don't have any tools, and we certainly don't have the time," she said as she turned toward Halstead. "Give us two of the torches and head back up to report."

He handed them the torches as soon as they'd put their weapons away and retreated to the stairs, his bright torch dimming until it was just a glowing spot in the darkness, near the other torch positioned there. Then it vanished as he entered the stairwell, and they were alone deep under the surface of Terra.

"Should we split up?" she asked. "It looks like we've got a lot of ground to cover if we're going to discover what's down here, and probably very little time to do it. If there's an exit that we can force to get out into the tunnel itself, we need to know about it before they break down the doors upstairs."

The marine officer nodded. "Yes, but let's keep an eye out for each other's torches and make sure that we know where the other is. If one of us runs into trouble, we need to be sure that the other will come running when we shout."

She raised an eyebrow. "Do you really think we're going to run into trouble down here? I don't see how anything could live in the dark."

"Our entire stay on Terra has been filled with things that we never expected. Let's just be cautious and make sure we don't find another one."

The man had a point.

"I'll take the right, you take the left," she said. With that, she headed off to see what she could find.

If everything was in crates, it was going to be a pretty boring search, but if she found an exit into the tunnel itself, that would be worthwhile.

Her side of the cavern was the one that had the wall blocking off access to the megacity. If there was an exit leading to it, it would be here. She knew it faced the megacity because it had been blocked off here as soon as the people digging down had found the tunnel. That showed the horde's concern about the inhabitants of the megacity.

Talbot would be looking at the side of the cavern where the tunnel led away from the megacity. They couldn't discount there being a door on that side, too. Or no door on any side. They might have to make their own.

While a lot of the things she was seeing as she walked were stashed in crates, not everything was completely obscured from view. As she advanced into the darkness, her eyes searching all around her, she spotted an area with tables holding what looked like chests on top of them.

Curious, she made her way over and examined one. The was

made of polished wood that glowed yellow in the torchlight. It had a built-in lock, but she had the perfect lock pick for something like this.

She inserted the point of her marine knife between the lid and the body, using the palm of her hand to drive it in. Once it was wedged deep, she wiggled the blade through the locking mechanism itself. It took a little bit of strength to cut the metal, but not as much as it would have if her knife hadn't had an almost monomolecular edge.

When she lifted the lid, she was greeted with the pile of gold, silver, and jewels she'd been musing about earlier. Everything sparkled and gleamed. Too bad stuff like this had absolutely no value to them right now.

She did stuff a handful into her pocket. If they lived, they would make for memorable souvenirs.

Closing the chest, she moved on to explore more of the room. The chamber was ridiculously large for being just a treasure room. If the horde had wanted something like that, they could've just left the tunnel intact and blocked off both ends.

As she walked, the scope of the area became clearer, just based on the echoes from her footsteps. This place was massive. What all did they have in here?

That really wasn't something that she needed an answer to, she decided. Time was wasting.

She turned and made her way back to the area nearest the stairs. The stone blocks that filled in what had been the tunnel were perhaps as tall as her head and three times that wide. There was no telling how deep they were laid, but they had to weigh far more than even a pair of people could lift unassisted.

And they would be thick, of that she had no doubt. There was absolutely no way the horde would place a flimsy barrier between themselves and the megacity. Not if the people inside the damned place were as bloodthirsty as Beauchamp believed.

Walking up and down the length of the wall, she found no openings. That was exasperating and potentially deadly, but not really a surprise. They'd have to dig out the stones and make their own tunnel through whatever they found.

"Julia," Talbot's voice echoed from deeper inside the chamber. "I've found something interesting."

She turned and trotted deeper into the chamber toward where she thought his voice had come from. Spotting his torch in the darkness, she shifted course. He was at least a couple of hundred meters away. Her estimates of the size of this place kept growing.

The chamber was large enough to sit at least partially under the castle she'd seen in the way in. There didn't seem to be any stairs on that side of the chamber—because surely they'd have sent guards down by now—which was decidedly odd. Shouldn't the ruling class *want* handy access to their goodies?

Julia started to ask what he'd found as she approached but found herself jerking to a halt just before she reached him. Piled deeply on the floor beyond him were the remains of a number of suits of marine powered armor.

And by remains, she meant what was left over after the wearers had been killed with those damned antiarmor weapons. Everything was shredded and in pieces.

"Well, I guess the stories about them dealing with the Rebel Empire before were true," she said as she stepped up beside Talbot. "This is certainly gruesome. I hope they at least took the bodies out before they left the armor here."

"I'm not smelling anything," Talbot said as he turned toward her. "If they'd left any human remains inside this pile, it would stink to high heaven. Maybe not so much after a period of years, but who wants to smell up their treasure room? What did you find?"

"Oh, the usual. Gold, silver, precious stones, that kind of thing. I also examined the wall blocking off the original tunnel leading to the megacity. I can't tell how thick the blockage is, but there's no door and those stones are stout.

"Not as big as the ones in the building upstairs, but they're going to be a problem. I'm betting it's also packed full of dirt and debris from excavating this chamber, too. After all, why carry it up those stairs if you can just pack the tunnel in? There's probably two sets of stone barriers with fill between."

"Good fences make for good neighbors," the man said with a wry smile. "Yet another Kelsey saying that I don't really understand. I found the other tunnel exit, and it looks exactly like you described.

"I'd say the horde was paranoid about letting anybody into their treasure room, and by extension, into the city above. I looked on the far wall, but there are no stairs leading up. There's only one entrance, and it isn't leading to their castle.

"I also found an amazing number of crates. I'm not sure what they're storing down here, but it's like a huge warehouse. Why build something like this underground just to store your stuff?"

"It has to be something that they don't want anyone else to get their hands on. Obviously not something they access very often, either. This whole 'treasure room' vibe makes me suspect that we're looking at salvaged materials from the megacities.

"Old technology that maybe doesn't work anymore but was worth socking away. Hell, maybe some of it *does* work. There's no telling, unless we look inside every single crate."

The marine officer raised his torch a little higher and looked around. "This chamber has to be at least four hundred meters across. Probably a couple of hundred meters from the tunnel blockage on your end to the tunnel blockage on my end. Looking up, the ceiling is at least forty meters high. That's a *lot* of room to store salvaged material. Why keep it down here?"

"Probably because they're terrified to use most of it," she said grimly. "That also explains why it's buried so deeply. They don't want the AI to drop a kinetic strike on them for being naughty."

"This is like storing seeds for future use," Talbot said after a few moments. "This is what might grow Terra back into a technological world, if the AIs ever go away."

"You mean if we ever manage to defeat them," she corrected. "They're not going away on their own. We're going to have to stomp them and do it hard. And to do that, we've got to figure a way out of the trap we've gotten ourselves into.

"We're going to have to bust down the stone wall leading toward the megacity and dig out whatever is behind it before the horde forces their way into the building above and kills us all."

"No pressure," Talbot said dryly. "It's possible that somewhere in this pile of armor is a weapon that could breach the wall. That's not exactly going to help us dig it out, but it's a start. Somewhere in all these crates are probably a number of things that would help, if we only knew where anything was."

"The horde has an index somewhere," Julia said as she looked around. "We just have to find it. Let's start looking."

36

J ared was beginning to despair. They'd been searching the piles of captured gear for what felt like hours—but had to only have been twenty or thirty minutes—without success in finding the primary gear they needed, though they had found some useful items.

The guards had stopped beating on the outer door after about five minutes. At this point, he was certain they were busy searching for something sturdy enough to bash their way in and making sure the higher-ups knew what was happening. The question was, how long would it take them to build a ram or bring one here?

In the meantime, his people had piled a truly impressive amount of random gear into the foyer. It was almost full of stuff. Even if the horde managed to break the doors apart, it was going to take them precious time to dig everything out.

Unless they just decided to use a few of those antiarmor weapons. Those would be more than powerful enough to destroy the thick wooden doors and blow a good amount of the material they were blocking the foyer with back into his people like a giant shotgun.

He was going to have to hope that they weren't *that* desperate to get at them. After all, based on what Ralph had told him, they weren't going to be leaving the vault below anytime soon. With any luck, the horde would want to keep their building intact and use a less powerful means of gaining entry.

"I found it!" Kelsey said, triumphantly raising the Imperial Scepter above her head.

Jared had to be careful walking over to her because she was knee-deep in scattered supplies that might cause him to lose his footing or twist an ankle, which was something he desperately wanted to avoid.

"Do we have any way of knowing if it's operational?" he asked.

Kelsey turned toward Carl as the young man cautiously made his way to them. She handed it over without a word.

The scientist had found a few of his tools and was able to remove a hidden access plate and plug a cable into one of the ports thus revealed. The device he held showed something on its screen, and Carl frowned.

"I believe the main memory is intact, but the EMP must've shorted out something in the control circuits. I can *probably* fix it, if I can find the parts and tools I need somewhere in this mess."

"Then that's the priority," Jared said, raising his voice. "I want everyone looking for whatever tools and parts Carl tells you he needs, as well as any medical supplies or equipment for Commodore Stone."

Even though they'd already been searching quickly, his words spurred everyone to even more feverish action. They were going through what remained of their piles at a rapid pace and throwing whatever they didn't need or couldn't use toward the foyer. Most of it didn't make it, but at this point, that hardly mattered. The end was in sight.

Unfortunately for them, that was when someone chose to knock on the doors. Hard.

A loud, echoing boom seemed to shake the room as something massive slammed against the reinforced wooden doors. It sounded as though someone had finally found the ram they were looking for. Now it was only a matter of time until they broke the doors apart and the horde began tearing at the debris blocking them from getting in. His people needed to wrap this up as soon as possible.

"Lucy, I'm home," Kelsey muttered, to his momentary befuddlement. Sometimes, he figured that he'd never understand her.

Jared walked over to Lily, who was busy tearing open a pack that she'd taken off of one of the pack horses they'd brought with them as part of their cover. She dumped it out as he spoke.

"Do you have what you need to get at our implants?" he asked.

She shook her head and kept pawing through the pile. "I found some basic medical supplies, but not my spare kit. At this point, I'd have to crack your skull open with a rock to get to your implants."

"Hard pass. Is there anything that we've come across that you could use as a substitute surgical instrument?"

She paused long enough to shoot him a stare that told him that he was being an idiot. "Absolutely not. I *could* use a marine knife to cut open your scalp, but while it would cut through your skull quite easily, I'd be far too likely to cut into your brain and ruin your entire day. To get into your skull *safely*, I need the right tools.

"And even if I do manage to find them, I don't know if Carl has the necessary equipment to reboot the damned things. You know that old saying, that 'this isn't brain surgery'? Well this *is* brain surgery. I have to find my spare medical kit."

He understood. He really did. But that didn't change the fact that they were running out of time.

"If you can't find it in the next couple of minutes, we're going to have to leave without it," he said firmly. "As sturdy as those doors are, they won't last long. Once they're gone, the horde will have plenty of willing hands to pull out the junk that we've thrown in there. Find something that will do the job, or you *will* be using a marine knife."

That seen to, he made his way over to Carl, who was once again searching frantically through the scattered gear in the corner of the room. Like Lily, he barely glanced up as Jared stopped near him.

"No," the scientist said before being asked. "I haven't found my kit yet. I found a lot of other tools and equipment that *might* be useful, and I've tossed them into one of the packs, but I need to find a very specific kind of equipment to generate the correct pulse to reset our implants."

"Then I'm going to give you the same speech I gave Lily," Jared said. "You've got a couple of minutes, and then we've got to get down the stairs. Grab whatever you can and, if it might work, take it."

"Got it," his young friend said. "On the plus side, I did find both the FTL com and the small rings that Omega gave us. The com is burned out, but I can potentially rebuild it, if we can salvage the right kind of basic equipment. The quantum entanglement module isn't subject to being ruined by an EMP."

"What about the rings?" Jared asked.

Carl shrugged. "It's alien tech, so who knows? Until we have a power supply capable of feeding it, we can't test it. I packed both of them away for later examination, just in case."

Even as Carl finished speaking, Lily shouted behind him. "I found the spare medical kit!"

Jared turned toward Ralph. "Go carry her stuff. All noncombatants, it's time for you to head downstairs. Carl, find something that's going to work. Kelsey, Captain Beauchamp, Elise, and Olivia, meet me by the horses."

Once the four women had gathered, he made a gesture toward all the horses crowded into that side of the room. They were watching the humans who seemed to have gone nuts with wary expressions.

"I've got a crazy idea," Jared said, "but I don't know if it will work. Could we take the horses partway down the stairs with us? It would be a serious pain in the ass for the horde to have to get past them, either dead or alive."

Beauchamp looked skeptical. "Horses are intelligent creatures. They're not going to want to go into a dark hole."

Kelsey was rubbing her chin. "We might be able to make it work, if we can fashion hoods to put over their heads. Or anything that would cover their eyes. If they can't see where they're going, the odds are much better that they'll cooperate. I wouldn't count on the warhorses for this, though. We need to stick to the pack beasts. They're a bit more placid."

The local woman considered that for a moment and slowly nodded. "That might work. Let's see what we can get together in the next few minutes. If we can use some of the ropes to help take the horses down with us as a group, we can perhaps drive a few stakes of some kind into the wall to keep them from continuing down or backing up when we reach the midpoint in our descent."

"Make the magic happen," he told them and headed back over to Carl.

"Time's up. Tell me you've got something."

"Maybe," his young friend said, holding up an unidentifiable piece of equipment. "I *might* be able to tinker with this enough to produce the output we need, but it's going to be chancy. Our implants are embedded in our brains. If I screw this up, it could fry them and us. It wouldn't even take that much of a charge."

"We've run out of time, so we'll just have to hope for the best," Jared said, clapping the young man on the shoulder. "It's time to make our way down and hope the hole in the ground doesn't end up being our grave."

* * *

Talbot wiped the sweat off his face with one arm as he stared at the remains of the powered armor and what the troops had been carrying. The antiarmor weapons had done a real number on everything. No suit was intact or even close to operational.

Even if any had been, the Rebel Empire believed in locking their marines down, so none of the armor could've been activated without the appropriate codes, or the built-in self-destruct charges would've detonated.

Carl could've probably done something about that, if he'd had his implants active, but he didn't. Well, if wishes were horses, they'd all be neck deep in horse crap, as Kelsey liked to say.

What *had* survived intact was a plasma rifle suitable for powered armor. It would be locked, but Carl had gotten into the guts of similar weapons and overridden the codes before. These wouldn't be nearly as troublesome as the armor's self-destruct lockouts.

With his augmentation offline and no armor, this monster could very easily injure him if he fired it. That said, it definitely had the raw power to blow a hole in the obstruction. If, that is, they could find any of the pellets of tritium it needed for ammunition.

As he was considering his options, Julia walked up out of the darkness. In her free hand, she held a leather-bound book.

"What's that?" he asked.

"It seems to be an inventory book," she said as she sat on the floor and opened it. "It lists what each of the crates has in it, though unfortunately, since it's written by non-technological people, some of the descriptions are rather obtuse. They don't know what many of the things do, so they've made guesses at what the locations they were found in might have been for."

He squatted and added his torchlight to hers before examining the page she was looking at. It listed crate numbers with odd designations like "red metal room" and "dark mirror room." She was right, none of that was very helpful.

"Well, I suppose it beats a kick in the head," he admitted. "By any chance do you see anything that references invaders or marines or fighting?"

"Not so far, but let's flip through and see if anything looks interesting."

He watched as she flipped the pages and read the neat script as quickly as possible. They were out of time, and he really didn't hold out any hope that they'd find anything useful.

Then she stopped and poked a finger at a line on the page. "Look at this. 'Monster Invasion.' What do you think it means?"

Talbot felt his heart beat faster. "Maybe a lot. We have to find the crate listed here and get access to it to be sure. This isn't really an inventory. It seems like it's more of a map to take us to the areas in question, if you know what I mean. Let's go find this one."

"You're in luck," she said as she stood. "I think I've figured out how the numbers are patterned. If I'm right, this crate is somewhere over there." She pointed off into the darkness toward a distant pile of crates.

She hefted the book, he grabbed the massive plasma rifle, and they started toward the crates.

"Can you use that?" she asked as she eyed the huge weapon.

"Not without ammunition. That's what I'm hoping to find."

"Too bad I left the pellets Corporal Boske made me save back on the grassland with the dead plasma rifle," she said through gritted teeth. "It was exactly this model, and I'd really like to have it here to blow some of these horde asses up."

The cold rage in her tone reminded Talbot of some of Kelsey's worst moments. The times when she wanted to kill people that had hurt her or her friends.

He'd known Boske as well as a senior officer could, but Julia had worked with the woman. Learned from her. And, apparently befriended her before the woman had been murdered, along with so many others.

She wanted payback, just like he did, but this wasn't the time, so he said nothing to encourage or discourage her. She had to work through her own feelings on this in her own way.

They arrived at the stack of crates and began looking for the numbers at ground level. The crates above them would be out of view, so he hoped they got lucky.

He didn't, but he did find a number close to what he'd been looking for and called Julia over. "I think it might be further up this stack. Do you think you can climb it safely and look?"

Without answering, she jumped up on the crate and began pulling herself up.

"Found it," she said once she reached the top of the pile near the ceiling. "How do I get into it?"

Before he could answer, Talbot heard a shout off in the distance and turned to face the stairs. Their companions were pouring out, torches raised high, so that meant that they'd run out of time.

37

J ulia watched as her new friends and associates flooded into the treasure room. What the hell were they going to do now? They hadn't managed to find anything to break down the wall. This was going to end *very* badly if they didn't find ammunition for the plasma rifle.

She pushed against the crate, but it didn't even move. It was damned heavy, and she had no leverage. It was going to take some kind of assistance for her—for all of them—to get this crate to slide off the end of the stack.

"I need some help over here," she shouted to the main group. "If you have some rope, that would be awesome."

About two-thirds of their party rushed over to join them at the stack of crates, mostly looking around wide-eyed at everything around them.

Carl Owlet held up a coil of rope. "Got you covered."

His words made her smile. Of course he did. The man always seemed to have what they needed.

"Throw the end up to her," Talbot said. "Julia, run it around the crate and let the end of the rope fall down where we can get at it again. We'll center it as well as we can, and then you can hold it until we get a little tension on it. We'll spread ourselves out and pull until the crate slides off. What I'm looking for won't be damaged if the container smashes to pieces."

It took three tries for them to get the rope to her, but it was easy enough to run it down the other side of the stack until she had the middle of the rough hemp in her hands. She then held it near the top of the crate as the others spread out on either side and tugged it tight.

She was very careful not to get her fingers caught between the rope and the crate. Even with graphene-coated bones, that wouldn't end well.

They sounded off together and started tugging on the rope. The crate shifted a little, and that gave her more space to put her feet on top of the crate below it. She put her shoulder into the one they wanted to fall, and she gave it all she had.

Unfortunately for her, the next tug didn't move the crate at all. Instead, the stack began teetering forward, obviously unbalanced by their actions.

Not relishing the idea of a fall to the floor, Julia leapt for the stack directly behind her, even as the stack of crates she'd been standing on went over, eliciting shouts from everyone below.

She slammed into the side of the second crate from the top of the next stack and barely managed to get her fingers onto one of the boards long enough for her feet to find purchase. That was good. A fall from this height might have seriously injured or killed her.

From the continuing sounds behind her, the falling crates had struck another stack and sent it falling over as well. As the noises continued, Julia became convinced that this was not going to stop with just a few stacks.

A glance over her shoulder showed that she'd been right. Spreading out away from her, piles of crates were being struck by other falling piles and knocked over. She only prayed that nothing came back around to knock *her* stack down while she was still on it.

It took a full minute for the chaos to stop. In the darkness, she couldn't tell exactly how far the devastation had spread, but whoever was in charge of inventorying these boxes was going to be *seriously* pissed.

"Are you okay up there?" Talbot called from below.

"I think so," she said as she edged along the side of the stack until she had a better grip. "Is everybody okay?"

"We're good. Come down and help us look for the plasma rifle's ammunition."

By the time she'd carefully made her way to the stone floor, everyone was digging through the wreckage. There was all manner of salvaged materials scattered around, and it looked as if the crate they had been eyeing had broken apart, but at least its contents were on top of the rest. Mostly.

She threw herself into searching through the items along with everyone else. It looked like a lot of basic military equipment, but there were no weapons. Mostly it was what might be found at a campsite.

After digging for a couple of minutes, she found a single box labeled "tritium pellets, large." It was exactly the same size box as she'd had during the ambush for her plasma rifle.

She held it up over her head. "Talbot!"

He waded to her side and took the box from her, opening it quickly. Inside, three pellets just like she'd used were carefully set in cavities in the shock-absorbing foam. It looked as if there had once been half a dozen—just like in her original box—but the other three slots were empty.

"Jackpot!" Talbot said. "This is *exactly* what I needed. Everybody, break off your search and let's join the rest by the stairs."

Getting down off the huge pile of debris wasn't nearly as easy as she'd hoped, but they all managed it without injury. As a group, they quickly rejoined the rest of their party.

Everyone left at the stairs was crowded around the opening with their bows out. They obviously anticipated an attack from above. As they got there, Kelsey turned to face them and grinned at the sight of the huge plasma rifle.

"Now we're talking! You have any ammo for that thing?"

Talbot held up the box with the plasma rifle ammunition. "Three shots. I sure as hell hope it's enough. What's the situation upstairs?"

Kelsey grimaced. "Just as bad as you'd imagine. They were just breaking the door apart as we came down. It's going to take them a couple of minutes to clear the stone slabs and other junk we left in the foyer, but not that long. As soon as they get people through, I'm sure they'll send them right down.

"We brought the pack horses down about halfway and tethered them. Now they're sitting in the dark, and I'm sure they're not going to be very cooperative about moving anywhere without the hoods we used to calm them. Still, once the horde gets past them, we're going to be fighting down here."

"Then we should get the hell out of here," Julia said firmly. "Like right now."

Just how right she was. A terrible screaming began coming from up the stairs, followed by the shouts of men. The horde was in the stairs, and they were killing the horses. They'd be here in just a few minutes. It was crunch time.

"Carl, I sure hope you have the tools to remove the lockout on this weapon," Kelsey said grimly. "No pressure or anything, but I need this working right now."

* * *

THANKFULLY, Carl did have the tools he needed and quickly had the plasma rifle opened up and reenabled. He closed it back up and looked at Kelsey. "You're green."

Kelsey pulled the torch out of the holder beside the stairwell and dropped it in the center of the barrier that she needed to shoot. She then led the entire group back into the cavern until she had a clearance of about a hundred and fifty meters. Safe distance for the explosion of the plasma was going to be a relative thing, but she hoped that would be enough.

If things went badly, they'd bring the roof down. At least that would probably be quicker than the end the horde had planned for them.

She took the ammunition from Julia and gestured for her husband to hand over the weapon. "Give it up, sport. I've got a lot more experience firing that sort of thing than you do. We've got to get the placement of the blast absolutely right, or we're screwed."

He raised an eyebrow and shook his head slightly. "You *do* remember how much of a kick that thing has, don't you? Even with your augmentation online, firing that without a suit to back it up would knock you on your ass. If you fire it now, you might seriously injure yourself. Let me handle it."

"We're not going to get a second chance at this," she said firmly. "It doesn't matter if I get hurt so long as everyone gets away. Besides, I have a plan for that, and you're absolutely going to love it. Now, give."

With a sigh, Talbot handed her the plasma rifle, which she struggled to hold upright until she got it up onto her shoulder. She aimed it back in the direction of the wall she needed to blast.

"Somebody said we had two exits from this chamber," she said as she removed the magazine and handed it to Talbot to load with pellets. "How sure are we that the one next to the stairwell is the right one? We absolutely can't afford to waste ammunition opening up the wrong side of the chamber."

"It only makes sense," Julia said. "They dug the stairs down from the surface and broke into the tunnel right there. They'd want to seal it up as quickly as possible to keep any enemies from getting to them. That means they'd have sealed off the side leading toward the megacity before they dug much of the cavern out.

"They probably filled in after the first barrier with rubble they accumulated as they excavated and finally capped it off with more stone on this side, but they certainly didn't dig down to the tunnel and then expand the cavern before closing off the end nearest the megacity."

"I sure hope you're right," Kelsey said grimly. "If not, we're screwed."

She gestured for everyone to get behind her. The plasma weapon didn't have a back blast, so they weren't in danger of being incinerated. From their point of view, the danger was going to be purely kinetic. When Talbot said the weapon had a kick, he wasn't joking.

"I want everyone to get behind me and be prepared to help

absorb the recoil. For such a little bit of ammunition, this thing generates one hell of a kick. With everybody working together, we can minimize how much impact it has on me. Set your torches off to the side. We don't want to set ourselves on fire."

Everyone crowded close behind her and formed a kind of human barrier to try to hold her up and resist being thrown back when she triggered the weapon. At this range, she could see the torch she'd dropped clearly. Her aiming point became the spot just above it. She centered on that and waited.

After a few seconds, Talbot nudged her. "Are you going to shoot that thing? I thought you said we were out of time."

"Wait for it."

Time seemed to drag, and then she heard the sounds of men at the bottom of the stairs. The horde had arrived.

Kelsey smiled coldly as she saw the first of them come into sight with a sword drawn. Right next to the wall she was aiming at.

"Say hello to my little friend," she murmured as she triggered the plasma rifle.

The impact of the discharge sent her slamming back into everyone else. It hurt like hell and her shoulder felt bruised, but the speck of intense brightness flew straight and true into the wall where she'd aimed it before detonating.

The savage brightness overwhelmed her vision, leaving spots in her eyes that she had to blink away. Her low-light vision was gone, and she couldn't tell what had happened at the impact site.

What she could sense was the sound of falling stone and the lack of screams. She'd killed whoever had been stupid enough to come to the bottom of the stairs.

Hell, she'd probably collapsed the stairway at its base and killed most of the people that the horde had sent down.

"I need a scout," she said. "Somebody go make sure I hit the tunnel blockage squarely. Toss another torch down on this side of the cavity so that I can see it, and then come back. I need to know if I have to adjust my aim."

Chloe Laird ran in the direction of the blast and returned a minute later without her torch.

"You were spot-on," the marine officer said. "The plasma detonation took out the stone wall and a good bit of the debris on the other side. The tunnel is still clogged with melted junk, so I'm hoping this next shot will clear it out.

"The ceiling of the cavity seems to have been fused, so it *might* hold up under all of this. The second shot will be taking a chance, but it's not exactly like we have a lot of choice in the matter. On another positive note, it looks like you collapsed the stairway, so we won't be getting any more uninvited guests while we work."

Kelsey nodded. "Perfect. Everyone, brace me again."

The second shot hurt even worse than the first but cleared out even more of the tunnel and revealed stone blocks on the other side. The bottom of the cavity was now rough and deeper than she liked, and also *very* hot, but their boots would allow them a little bit of time to examine the final wall, if they'd cleared the debris all the way to it.

"I don't think we're going to need that third shot," Talbot said after he'd ventured in and returned. "Part of the far wall is ruptured, and I could see into the tunnel beyond. It's clear over there. Given a couple of minutes, we can clear enough space to get through."

"How long is it going to take for them to dig out the stairway and start after us?" Jared asked.

"They're not going to be chasing us this way," Kelsey said firmly. "As soon as we've got everybody inside the tunnel and safely away, I'm going to go use the last plasma charge to bring the ceiling of the cavern down."

"You have to be on *this* side to do that," Talbot argued. "You might bring it down on your head."

"That's a chance I'm willing to take," she said. "Let's get that wall broken out and get everyone on the other side. We'll want to set up a defensive perimeter, just in case all of this noise brings somebody from the megacity to investigate."

Over her husband's objections, Kelsey got him and the rest moving through the blown-out cavity her plasma rifle had created. The stone under their feet was hot enough to put the scent of burning leather into the air and to heat the soles of her feet to an uncomfortable degree. Still, it was bearable.

Even if it hadn't been, that wouldn't have changed anything. They *had* to get through there.

As Talbot had said, the far wall was partially breached, and she could see the original tunnel in the darkness beyond. The hole in the stacked stones wasn't that big, and that section of the wall around it looked dangerously unstable.

That didn't mean it was impossible to get through, though. The stones were large and wide, obviously meant to be hard to get through or move. On this side of the original blockage, they were stacked five deep. That meant it would take them hours of sweaty labor to clear enough space to walk through.

Thankfully, the part of the wall that had blown out was near the roof of the tunnel and was big enough for even Talbot to wiggle through. They took the time to push the more precarious of the stones over, where they fell on the ones that already littered the tunnel with a crash.

The rope Carl had found allowed them to lower their party down to the rock-strewn floor one at a time. Each person took care in the rubble not to twist an ankle.

Once they had everyone on the other side, they started clearing the floor nearest the breach. When Kelsey had to run through here in a few minutes, the last thing she'd have time for was dealing with unsteady footing after she cleared the wall.

When they'd finally cleared that section of the floor, Kelsey made a shooing gesture with her hands. "I want you to get as far down the tunnel as you can in the next few minutes. I'll use the floor in the cavern to brace the weapon and then haul ass after you as soon as I pull the trigger.

"We have no idea if the collapse of the cavern is even in the cards, but if it does come down, it might bring the tunnel with it, so I don't want anyone nearby. Understood?"

Talbot gave her a tight hug before hoisting her up to the hole in the wall. Once on the other side, she made her way back to the cavern and stared around at the huge cavern.

The best odds of bringing the ceiling down were to hit it in the center of the ceiling. There was no support at any point along the interior of the cavern, so that would be its weakest point.

With a final sigh, she tossed her final torch into the tunnel. It was going to have to provide her with light while she ran for her life.

She braced the weapon on the floor just outside the radius of the first impact crater, where the surface was smooth enough to provide steady resistance, and aimed the bore of the weapon at the ceiling in what she judged was the center of the cavern.

Kelsey took a deep breath and squeezed the trigger.

As soon as the plasma rifle recoiled against the stone and skidded past her into the cavity, she threw herself after it and raced after it toward the undamaged tunnel beyond the breach.

Kelsey didn't see the plasma hit, but the bright flash of the detonation lit her way forward like a strobe going off. Then she heard rumbling from behind her. The cavern ceiling was coming down.

Kelsey dug her feet in and dove through the breached section of the final wall, hitting the floor of the original tunnel hard, rolling, and coming to her feet, still running for her very life.

Even as she ran, she heard the sound of the tunnel behind her cracking and collapsing. She *might* have overdone it. The whole thing might come down on their heads.

Ahead of her, she saw that the others had come to the same conclusion as they turned to run farther up the corridor. Unencumbered as she was, she made up a little bit of the distance between them before the tunnel behind her finally gave way completely and collapsed.

Imminent death was an excellent motivator.

A wave of choking dust engulfed her, making her cover her face and slow down as she coughed. The ceiling above her seemed solid enough, so she hoped they'd gotten clear of the collapse zone.

Weary, she walked forward until she'd rejoined the others. Everyone was coated with dust, but they were all grinning at her.

"You did it!" Talbot said as he snatched her up in a hug. A hug that was soon joined by all the rest.

"*We* did it," she corrected. "That should keep the horde from following us. The danger behind us is over. We're probably going to have trouble when we try to leave the megacity, because I'm sure that I've just stirred the horde up like a nest of bees. They'll be looking for where we're going to come up for air."

"And we're going to have to be careful of running into anyone in the megacity," Jared said solemnly as they all broke apart. "With everything that Captain Beauchamp said, I think that they're just as unfriendly as the horde. In this case, the enemy of our enemy is *not* our friend."

"One life-threatening disaster at a time, please," Kelsey said as she tried to wipe her face with her hands, succeeding only in smearing dirt and grit all over her exposed skin. "Let's deal with tomorrow's problems tomorrow. Right now, we need to find a place to hide and recover. It's been a *long* day, and we've still got a lot to do.

"Once we get ourselves situated, we'll let Lily and Carl do their magic and see if we can get our implants back online. Then we have to figure out what we're going to do to get out of the megacity, while avoiding its inhabitants, and also dodging the horde once we do.

"Then we still got fifteen hundred kilometers to go before we get to the Imperial Palace and find out who or what might be living inside it. Piece of cake, right?"

All of them stared at her for a few seconds and then started laughing. She grinned and joined them. At this point, that's all they could do. This mission had gone bad early, and nothing had worked out the way they'd expected, but they'd made it this far.

Whatever it took for them to survive and get what they'd come all this way for, they'd do. The AIs would not win today or in the future. They'd overcome any obstacle in their path on the way to victory. They had to.

With the battle finally done, they turned as a group and began trudging down the old tunnel toward the megacity and their next challenge.

EPILOGUE

Leader Mordechai stood on the balcony and stared out from the top of the sacred tower toward the horde city. This structure was the tallest in Frankfort and had an excellent view of the primitive city that had been built next to it after the Fall.

He normally didn't walk up the stairs because the building towered over the megacity and five hundred flights of stairs were hard on a man his age, but he'd needed to see this for himself.

There seemed to be a lot of excitement in the horde city. Smoke rose from its center in a huge column, and it looked as if the palace had collapsed into a large hole in the ground. The savage warriors that ruled that place with an iron fist were milling around like ants disturbed in their mound.

At first, he'd thought that whatever had occurred had been an act of nature, but as soon as the horde started sending out armed patrols into the growing dusk, he knew that there was something more afoot.

Some of his people had reported loud noises deep underground at around the same time. He wasn't certain what was happening, but he needed to find out. The survival of his people might depend on it.

At the soft tread of boots behind him, he turned to see his son

Jebediah approaching. To his amusement, the young man seemed more winded by his climb than Mordechai himself had been.

"What news?" he asked his panting, sweating son.

"There are intruders below Frankfort," Jebediah said in a gravelly voice. "One of the blocked tunnels appears to have collapsed, but only after allowing a dozen or so people through. One of our scouts used an old lookout post to observe their passage. Shall I have our warriors trap and kill them?"

Mordechai considered that for a moment before shaking his head. "Not yet. I find my curiosity aroused. From the horde activity, I'm prepared to grant that they might not be friends of the barbarians. Their story might prove interesting."

He smiled at that last, but only for a brief moment. "If they were at that depth, it would take more than even lost weapons from the Empire to cause such a collapse. Who were these people, and how did they cause such devastation?

"Are they intruders sent by the computers above?" he asked rhetorically. "It's been many years since we've had such an incursion, but if this is the beginning of a new one, we need to know. Use all force necessary to subdue them but give them an opportunity to surrender first."

"And if they resist?"

"Kill as many of them as you need to break them," he said bluntly. "Take no undue risks. My curiosity does not require our blood to be spilled to satisfy it. Find a good ambush point and make certain that they have no chance to sense your presence before you strike."

After his son had departed, Mordechai stepped back out onto the balcony and looked over the ruined megacity that he ruled. The shadows of the approaching sunset were far below him, and the red light of the sun cast an almost bloody shade across his city.

He'd been born after the computers had crushed Terra under their heels, but he still remembered the stories his grandfather had told of the time before the Fall. The things he spoke of sounded magical, but impossible. If he hadn't had Frankfort itself as proof that such technology had once existed, he'd never have believed the tall tales.

Seeing the world from up here never failed to move his heart. Both from the beauty of nature, and the destruction and loss that he could see from this very spot. Also the sheer savagery that those beyond Frankfort exhibited on a daily basis.

Would the events of today send the cruel warriors into his city? Part of him hoped so. Their dead from any such excursion would remind them of their place in this world. Their fear of his people kept his charges safe.

Mordechai sighed and turned to start his long walk back down to the warrens underneath Frankfort. He needed to focus on the strangers and the danger that they brought to his people.

They would make the choice between survival and bloody death. One way or the other, he and his people would deal with them as tradition demanded. Even if they surrendered, they would never leave this place.

Whoever they were, their adventures were assuredly over.

* * *

WANT to get updates from Terry about new books and other general nonsense going on in his life? He promises there will be cats. Go to TerryMixon.com/Mailing-List and sign up.

DID YOU ENJOY THIS BOOK? Please leave a review on Amazon. It only takes a minute to dash off a few words and that kind of thing helps Terry make a living as a writer and gets you new books faster.

WANT the next book in this series? Grab *Victory on Terra* today or buy any of Terry's other books, which are listed on the next page.

WANT MORE BOOKS BY TERRY? Flip to the next page and grab one.

. . .

Visit Terry's Patreon page to find out how to get cool rewards and an early look at what he's working on at Patreon.com/TerryMixon.

ALSO BY TERRY MIXON

You can always find the most up to date listing of Terry's titles on his Amazon Author Page.

Storm Divers

The Scorched Earth Saga

Scorched Earth

Omnibus Volumes

The Empire of Bones Saga Volume 1

The Empire of Bones Saga Volume 2

The Empire of Bones Saga Volume 3

Humanity Unlimited Publisher's Pack 1

The Vigilante Series with Glynn Stewart

Heart of Vengeance

Oath of Vengeance

Bound By Law

Bound By Honor

Bound By Blood

ABOUT TERRY

#1 Bestselling Military Science Fiction author Terry Mixon served as a non-commissioned officer in the United States Army 101st Airborne Division. He later worked alongside the flight controllers in the Mission Control Center at the NASA Johnson Space Center supporting the Space Shuttle, the International Space Station, and other human spaceflight projects.

He now writes full time while living in Texas with his lovely wife and a pounce of cats.

www.TerryMixon.com
Terry@terrymixon.com

amazon.com/author/terrymixon
facebook.com/TerryLMixon
patreon.com/TerryMixon
bookbub.com/authors/terry-mixon
goodreads.com/TerryMixon

CPSIA information can be obtained
at www.ICGtesting.com
Printed in the USA
LVHW020903100122
708157LV00021B/242

9 781947 376298